THE SIREN PRINCESS

LITTLE MERMAID REIMAGINED

THE FORGOTTEN KINGDOM SERIES
FOUR GEMS, FOUR REALMS, ONE FORGOTTEN KINGDOM

USA TODAY BESTSELLING AUTHOR
LICHELLE SLATER

THE FORGOTTEN KINGDOM SERIES

The Four Stones of Tern Tovan
(Prequel to The Forgotten Kingdom Series)

The Dragon Princess
(Sleeping Beauty Reimagined)

The Siren Princess
(Little Mermaid Reimagined)

The Beast Princess—coming 2020
(Beauty and the Beast Reimagined)

Receive the prequel to *The Four Kingdom Series* for FREE by signing up for my newsletter at:
www.LichelleSlater.com

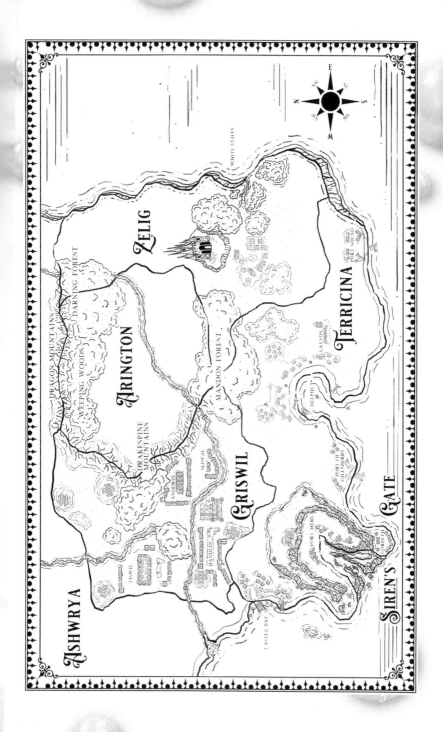

Edited by Maria Rosera of The Paisley Editor
editor.paisleypressbooks.com
Interior Design and Formatting by Melissa Stevens of The Illustrated Author Design Services

Cover Design by Melissa Stevens of The Illustrated Author Design Services

theillustratedauthor.net

To Maria Rosera
For always helping me to reach my greatest potential!

ONE

It wasn't the sound of the water slapping the hull of the ship that woke me.

It was the song.

The ethereal notes floated in the early morning silence, past snoring pirates, past the dull clink of the lantern rocking against the wall, and into my dreams. I didn't need to understand the words. In the fog of my waking mind, all I cared about was how lonely the voice sounded.

The ropes of my hammock groaned as I opened my eyes. I found one leg slung over the edge and my blanket somehow on the ground. My damp shirt clung my body, and I understood then why I could hear the siren's song. Either her magic had brought in the fog or the fog had lured the siren.

I shifted onto my side, snagged my boots, then sat up and tugged them on as fast as possible before jumping to my feet—adjusting my pants as I did. After a quick wiggle of the breasts to get them adjusted properly, and I ran to the stairs. I took three steps up before realizing I didn't have my hat and had to run back to the bent nail it hung on. With my hat and boots on, I darted up the salt-water worn steps to the main deck and grinned.

The thick fog suppressed the sound of the ocean as we glided across its surface. I could no longer hear the siren, and my heart sank like a stone tossed carelessly into the sea.

"Odette. Yer up early."

I turned so abruptly on the damp deck my foot slipped, but I managed to keep my balance and faced the first mate, a stout man with dark, graying hair, a wiry mustache, and a large belly. I smiled a bit too big. "Morning, Mr. Smee. I love when it's like this." I scampered up to his side on the quarterdeck and leaned heavily on the railing, trying to peer through the fog and see any sort of landmark . . . or siren. After all, she'd woken me.

He rose what would have been an eyebrow, had it not been burned off lighting a cannon last summer. "Nigh impossible to navigate in a fog like this." His blue eyes shifted back to the sea.

"Our crew isn't full of ordinary sailors." I pointed up past the barely fluttering Jolly Roger to the crow's nest. "Sammy can spot anything with his eagle eyes. That's why he's the lookout and not you."

Smee twitched his mustache. "Aye. Still. Fog makes me nervous. Bad things linger in the fog, mark my words."

"Like sirens?" I teased, knowing how many pirates were superstitious and that Smee was probably the most out of all of them.

Smee frowned and glanced at the water, clearly not appreciative my joke.

I chuckled and closed my eyes, then drew a deep breath of water and wet wood. There was something so eerie about the fog my skin tingled. Not to mention, the fog always brought back memories of that night.

It had been over seven months since the battle at Castle Bay.

Seven months since I lost my memory.

There were fragments I did remember. Something with a boathouse, running for my life, fighting a faceless figure with my sword, and waking on my mother's ship. I'd filled in the gaps to the best of my ability from overhearing pirates speak. Most of them covered their mouths with their hands and watched me as I passed now.

From what I'd gathered, I had been captured by the people in Castle Bay and locked up in a boathouse. Some kind of battle happened and my mother rescued me. There must have been some injury to my head, too, to account for the missing pieces.

Seven months, and I was no closer to restoring any of those memories.

Every time I replayed that night, something at the back of my mind nagged me that I was missing something imperative.

My eyes snapped open, and I looked to the right, having heard a woman's voice. "Did you hear that?" I whispered.

"Dunno what yer—"

"There it is again." I trotted back down to the main deck, toward the bow of the ship where I heard the song.

Smee shook his head. "I've been through the Siren's Gate many a time and ne'er seen one, miss. It's the fog playin' tricks on yer mind." He tapped the side of his head for emphasis. "Nothin' more." Still, Smee's eyes darted around, and his voice was tight with nervousness.

I'd always been able to hear things others couldn't, like the time a royal vessel tried to overtake us on a night with no stars. Or the night I overheard one of the pirates talk about Castle Bay and a boathouse. That's how I'd learned I'd been locked up.

The weighted feeling of the fog pressed on my shoulders, almost like being wrapped tightly in a blanket on too warm a night. I pulled off my hat to wipe my forehead when I heard the voice again, and I quickly shifted my gaze to the starboard side of the ship.

The voice was louder now, but the song had changed. It no longer pulled on my heart like sadness and wanting, instead sounding more like a lullaby.

Smee was muttering under his breath about something, so I—as casually as possible—walked to the side of the ship, placed my hands on the droplet-covered railing, and leaned over to peer into the dark

4

sea. The voice in the back of my mind warned me not to, but the song pulling on my heart begged me just to take a peek.

The song paused only to start again, this time much louder.

I scanned the water but couldn't see anything other than my own reflection on the waves.

"Odette, what are you doin'?" Smee called, his gruff voice growing more annoyed.

"I told you, I hear something." I dropped my hat on the deck, so the wind wouldn't swipe it, and licked my lips.

The mist from the fog caressed my face, like fingertips stroking my skin. Slowly, from the darkness of the water, the reflection of my face changed. At first, I thought it was just me needing to blink, or my own movement, but the dull colors began to take shape as it drew nearer to the surface.

The fins of the tail were much wider than a dolphin. Instead of one fin, there were two. Her body . . . *her* body . . . was covered in glittering red fish scales. Her blue hair flowed behind her in the water as though she were at the bow of the ship on a windy day, not a siren in the sea.

Her face silently broke the surface. Scales adorned the brow of her head, her jaw, shoulders, and arms. She wore a glorious silver necklace and white pearl earrings. Her lips moved with the song somehow thickened by the fog.

She was the most beautiful woman I had ever seen.

Her song was the most beautiful song I'd ever heard.

She was a friend, and when she locked her eyes on mine, I knew I'd known her forever.

I leaned my right arm down, holding tight to the railing with the other. I wanted to touch her fingers, to feel her and make sure she was there. I wanted to touch her scales and recall her name, remember how I knew her.

"Odette?" a voice somewhere in the distance called.

I couldn't answer.

I didn't want to.

The siren's deep green eyes pulled me in. Her song wrapped around me, begging me to come into the water.

All I wanted was a touch.

The siren reached her hand up, and our fingertips brushed. I smiled as a feeling of weightlessness and pure joy washed over me. My left hand relaxed its grip.

I felt the vibration of heavy footsteps running on the wooden planks.

I reached further down.

The siren's webbed fingers stretched up and touched my fingers again, this time locking our fingers together, and all the while, she smiled gently. The same feeling of elation encompassed me.

"The water, child . . ." her voice echoed in my mind, like a ripple on the surface of the water, different languages and tongues until I heard mine. "Come to me . . . come play." She tilted her head, still smiling.

"Yes," I breathed.

"Odette, no!"

I blinked stupidly and looked over my shoulder. Mr. Smee ran for me, but his movements were sluggish. I found him looking rather silly with his arms moving slowly at his sides, his right outstretching toward me.

I giggled.

The siren's webbed fingers wrapped around my wrist. "Come play with me."

I turned back to the siren.

And pushed off the railing.

The instant I hit the water was the same instant I knew I was in trouble. The icy water woke me from the siren's alluring stupor. I'd been a complete fool. In the water, the siren's true form revealed itself to me.

Her features twisted. Her teeth extended into long points like those of an angler fish, and her scales morphed to a mucky brownish red. They covered her entire body, including the fingers which moments ago had been human. She didn't have hair at all, but a single fin that ran down her head and spine, and it glowed blue.

Worse, she wasn't alone.

I pulled against her, fighting for the surface.

Growing up on the sea, one learns at a young age how to swim, and I prided myself in my speed and endurance. But neither helped me at that moment, fighting against a creature whose home *was* the sea. It was like a land-dweller stepping onto a deck and thinking they could stay balanced on a rocking ship well enough to fight a pirate.

The sirens dragged me deeper. I heard the muted movements of their tails as they swam circles around us. Their eyes reflected the little light still left, shining green like a cat's eyes, and they sneered through their fangs.

Sirens killed for sport, luring their victims into the water with their songs. No one who was dragged under by a siren ever survived, or at least the stories told. But they didn't only hunt for pirates, but any sailor—merchant or naval officer—foolish enough to fall for their tricks.

Had Smee been able to reach me, I would have been one of a handful of pirates to be lured and survive.

But he hadn't saved me.

I thought I was clever enough to outsmart their magic, but in a few minutes, I would be another victim of the siren's deadly game.

The familiar burning of holding my breath began in my lungs. But this was no game to see who could hold it the longest. Swimming against the siren wasn't working. I needed a different method. Instead, I stopped fighting her and swam *at* her, drawing her off guard. I used what little momentum I had gained and pulled the dagger from my boot.

Or would have had it been there.

I patted my leg in panic. I hadn't put it on when I'd woken that morning. It was likely hanging on the same nail my hat had been on. I did the only thing I could think of. I slammed my fist into her ribs, which was definitely *not* effective under water.

She snarled and dug her claws into my wrist.

I screamed. Air bubbles filled my vision, and I clamped my mouth shut, but it was too late. I had no air and no weapon.

I was going to die.

I was eighteen, one of the few female pirates, really only at the beginning of my story, and I was going to die because I fell for a siren's song. She smiled at me, victory in her stony fish eyes.

I gripped her fingers and twisted. Her bones popped in my hand. I kicked at her.

She screamed so loud my ears hurt.

My lungs wanted to explode, begging me to take a breath in.

The surface was lost to me. Darkness swallowed me.

And then I gasped a mouthful of water.

And then another.

And another . . .

I blinked, and my vision flickered from bursts of light to shapes in colors I'd never seen. The sirens had a sort of yellow hue to them, like when the moon lights up the outer edge of a form in the darkness. Slowly, I drew another breath.

Breathing. I am breathing. Underwater.

The siren gripping me suddenly recoiled, her eyes wide, her face no longer twisted in anger and hatred, but confusion.

I seized the opportunity and swam for it. But my legs didn't kick one at a time. They moved together. My hands moved easily as I clawed for the surface.

Slowly, the dim light ahead grew nearer, and as I reached the sunlight, I saw my own fingers webbed with translucent skin.

Frantically, I ran my fingers across my face and discovered gills at the edge of my jaw, three on each side of my neck.

I broke the surface.

"There she is!" someone shouted.

The pirates hauled me on board, but I couldn't quite comprehend how. My body was racked with intense pain, and when I reached the deck, I realized my clothes were shredded and torn.

Someone dropped a blanket on my shoulders.

Someone else hauled me over to a barrel, and everyone gathered round to demand what had happened.

I stared at my hands. My normal, web-less hands. Non-webbed? No skin stretched between them, and no gills resided in my neck. I wasn't a siren at all.

"Back off," Captain Avery said, pushing his way to the front. "What happened?" he asked, his tone much less demanding than everyone else.

"It was a siren . . ." I closed my eyes. "I was lured in by a siren."

"How did you get out?" someone called.

"I must have stabbed her with my dagger and escaped. I'm not hurt." I'd been careful to avoid telling them the part with me growing gills and webbed hands. Pirates are, after all, terribly superstitious. If they had heard I had become a siren, they may have tossed me overboard!

"That's good enough for me. Return to your duties!" Captain Avery ordered.

The crowd of pirates dispersed.

I got to my feet immediately, in spite of his hand motioning for me to stay seated. "*Please* don't tell my mother I fell for a siren's song and almost died. She'll never give me that new ship."

He gave me a wry smile. "Odette, you know I can't withhold anything, especially from her, of all people. Someone on board is bound to tell what happened. Even if they don't say you were pulled in by a siren, just mentioning you fell into the ocean in passing, she'll come to me furious I never told her." He lifted my bleeding arm. "I will, however, leave out the part where you ignored Mr. Smee's warnings." He raised his eyebrows and lowered his chin in a look of disappointment.

I gave him a relieved sigh. "Thank you."

Even though Avery wasn't my father, he was the closest thing I had to one. I sailed with Captain Avery more than anyone else, and I'd grown fond of the man. He was a fantastic leader, and I'd learned more about sailing and pirating from him than anyone, aside from my mother.

Of course, my mother had *assigned* me to sail with him whether I liked it or not. I only really complained because I had the right to. No other pirate complained about their crew or Athena would fine them and lock them in the brig for a week.

"Go on and change out of those wet clothes and take care of that wound. It's a good thing you fell in.

You were in need of a bath anyhow." He put his hands behind his back and smirked.

"Oy," I protested with a playful frown.

He gestured to the steps with a tilt of his head.

I wasn't in the mood to object or make a witty comment. My whole body ached from fighting, and my stomach growled loudly.

I made my way below deck and to the small trunk tied to the post with exactly two changes of clothing and boots inside.

"Don't forget your dagger."

I lifted my head and saw Smee standing with my dagger strap looped on his finger. I slowly straightened.

"Must have been some luck to get you out of the hands of that siren."

I snatched the dagger away with a glare. "I don't know how I got away, all right? So gut me."

Smee's gaze darted around. At first, I thought he'd come to let me know he didn't believe my story, but the way he searched to see if others were in the room, I wondered if he was trying to say something else.

"What are you getting at?" I pried.

He quickly shook his head. "Maybe it wasn't a coincidence. G'day."

I opened my mouth, but Smee turned and waddled away as fast as his round body could take him.

How could I explain to anyone what happened? Let alone Smee, the most superstitious of the pirates. No, I knew better. It was safer to stay quiet.

After dressing, I hurried back on deck, having slung my wet clothes over the vacant hammock at the back of the sleeping quarters. I went to the sun-warmed bucket of fresh water and washed the siren's bite carefully, then wrapped my wrist in strips of bandages.

"Aye there," Captain Avery greeted. "We're almost home." He motioned with his chin from the helm. He lazily turned the wooden wheel to avoid a familiar outcropping of stones.

"The sun's coming back out too," I noted, looking around us as the sun pierced through the fog until it had disappeared completely.

"You can report to your mother since you led this raid."

"Aye!" I saluted before I trotted up to the captain's side. "I can't wait to see what she says."

I pushed all thoughts of the situation with the siren aside and focused on what I should have been the whole time—my final victory. I had finally proved my worth. My mother would forget my weakness at Castle Bay and give the newest ship for her new fleet to me. I just knew it.

Within a few minutes, the *Naiad* entered Port Mere.

My home.

TWO

The high cliffs leading to Port Mere bottlenecked into a treacherous pass any normal sailor would avoid. No pirate captain in my mother's fleet was afraid, however. They'd come to know every dangerous edge of every stone, especially when the tide ran low and deeper fragments rose to carve into the hull of any ship, no matter the skill level of her crew.

Yet, when the pass widened and revealed our thriving town, I always got a homesick ache at the bottom of my belly. Returning home was always bittersweet. Being out at sea was fun. Every day was something different—except those particularly long voyages.

The tall cliffs remained at the same height around Port Mere, hiding every docked ship. To the left of the docks, a zig-zagging trail had been carved against the cliff's face leading up to a cluster of wooden homes and a stone building that once acted as one of the naval forts for the country of Terricina. Thanks to my mother's ingenuity, Terricina lost the fort, and now we lived in its shadow. The king must not have cared, because no one bothered us.

The rest of the city—stone buildings pressed snuggly against each other—lay at the base of the cliffs and stretched up the hill beyond to the right. Some were shops, a few taverns, a doctor, smithy, jeweler, and so on. The architecture was hardly the work of pirates.

We could build a solid ship, but buildings on land? Let's just say my mother, Athena, had ensured the city wouldn't collapse during the first rainstorm by hiring men from nearby towns to build everything. A few even stayed after.

Captain Avery drew a loud breath, drawing my attention to him. "Feel good to be home?" His dark eyes focused on me from under the brim of his wide hat. The purple feather plume in his hat needed to be replaced.

"I'm excited to tell my mother of our good fortune," I answered simply.

The *Naiad* drew close to the dock, and Captain Avery began barking orders. Some of the crew tossed two thick ropes down to the dockhands, who secured them around the wooden piling.

I jumped from the deck of the ship to the wooden dock below, landing easily.

"Oy! You're responsible for helpin' us unload everything," Smee called from the deck. "Your responsibilities aren't over yet!"

I waved my hand. "I don't see you or Captain Avery rolling barrels down the gangplank." I smirked over my shoulder and blew him a kiss.

His face went red before I returned my attention forward.

The market bustled with pirates of smaller ships trading their wares: fine clothes, hats, fabric, rare foods, and whatever else they brought in. I carefully dodged the row of tables for the fishermen to clean and sell their fish but couldn't avoid the stench of scales and entrails. The farther down the path I got, the smells were blotted out by pipe smoke, body odor, smoked meat, and hot dust.

I knew Port Mere like I knew any ship.

Mother had settled in a stone villa on a ledge overlooking the town, port, and bay. I took my time glancing at the tables of trinkets before I stopped at the cobbler to see about a new pair of boots.

I peered through the window and bit my bottom lip softly as I stared at the black leather boots I'd had my eyes on for weeks. They'd been designed with brass accents with a brass toe, a skull on the side of each boot, and brass eyelets. I'd finally saved up enough money to purchase them, and if I had finally proven myself to my mother, I needed to look the best I ever had at the captaining ceremony the next day.

Athena rarely added a new pirate to her fleet. Typically, a pirate gave away control of his ship to a loyal and trustworthy crewmate. To have a new ship, a new pirate captain . . . I could remember once in my life when that had happened.

My gaze drifted to my right. Down in the shipyard, a glorious oak ship had been under construction for months. I just knew in my bones that it was meant for me because I'd finally proven myself worthy enough to captain it.

I rounded my shoulders and entered the small shop. The old man with a crooked shoulder was at work replacing the sole on the bottom of a boot as I approached. "I'd like those boots in the window."

He raised his eyes to gaze at me over his spectacles. He blinked twice as if his eyes were adjusting to the sunlight behind me. "Boots?" He straightened so slowly I imagined his bones falling back into place after being hunched over all day.

I pointed over my shoulder with my thumb. "The ones with the brass skulls."

"Aye. Those." He set down his tools, and his chair scraped inside two familiar divots worn in the wooden floor as he rose to his feet. "Those are sixteen reales."

I guffawed. "Sixteen? Are you crazy? No. I'll give you eight. That's how much they were when I was last in port a few weeks ago, and that's how much I'm paying. You can't swindle a pirate, old man."

"I said sixteen. I'm stickin' with it. You don't have to buy 'em." He pushed his wrinkled lips to the side of his face, and I couldn't help but compare him to the shrunken ogre heads I'd seen from the pirates who came from the island provinces to the southwest.

I narrowed my eyes and reached into my coin pouch. I dug through the coins, counted out eight, and set them down on the counter. "Eight. It's all I've got. I need them for tomorrow."

"Odette . . ." His lips tugged, his brows shifted, and I thought he would once again refuse. Instead, he heaved a sigh, his shoulders lifting and dropping, and then he rubbed his hand over his scruffy cheek. "All right. Eight reales."

I grinned and rushed to the window and picked them up. The black leather was beautifully polished and they looked like they would fit perfectly. I looked back over at the old man. "What made you change your mind?"

"You was right. And I got other things to worry about than gettin' another eight reales from you."

I grinned. "Thank you."

"Luck tomorrow!" he called as I dashed from his shop and up to my mother's house.

The salty breeze was much stronger without the shield of the cliffs or buildings, and I sucked in another deep breath of it as I reached the top of the pathway, only to stop in my tracks.

A familiar young man sat on the edge of the porch in a sweat-stained tan shirt with an unbuttoned brown vest. He fiddled with a prosthetic clamp before placing it on top of his hand-less left wrist.

James "Hook" Barrie.

Sensing my presence, he looked up at me with his deep brown eyes. Lighter brown flecked around the pupil, and they had a way of always drawing me in. His dark skin only emphasized his stunning eyes. He had his black hair pulled back in a ponytail. I had no idea how he managed that with only one hand, but I wasn't going to ask. He wasn't built like a typical sailor either. He didn't have a large beer belly or lean muscles from starvation. His muscles were thick from continual use, as were all of the men on his father's ship—which possibly said something about the labor on that ship.

James had always intrigued me. Since Castle Bay— whatever had happened—I'd catch him staring at me while keeping a safe distance. I didn't know whether to be flattered or more on guard. Instinctively, I leaned toward the latter.

"My father is in a meeting with your mother," James explained, returning his attention to his makeshift hand—a clamp that opened and shut, though it was clearly giving him trouble because he kept adjusting the screw's tightness. "This is futile," he muttered to himself.

I rolled my eyes. "Oh great. How long have they been at it?"

James lifted his shoulder in a shrug. The silver hoop hanging from his ear swayed with the motion. An ivory skull sat in the middle of the hoop and a set of beads dangled from its teeth.

"And you've been out here listening?"

He lifted his eyes again, face unamused. "I was given instructions to stay here. And here I stay. Besides, I can't get this to work." He raised his left arm.

I eyed him. "How *did* you lose it anyway?"

James ran his tongue over his teeth before suddenly looking away. "I'm certain you've heard one story or another. Why does the real one matter?"

I rolled my eyes. "Because I don't think you lost it to a saltwater crocodile. Those aren't native to our shores, *and* you had to of been doing something really stupid if you got close enough to have one chomp off your hand."

"Hm. I suppose." He tilted his head and stabbed the screwdriver into the soft wood of the front deck of the house, making it stand straight up. "Maybe I got it rescuing a damsel in distress." He yanked off the clamp and replaced it with his normal silver hook. The hook looked much better anyway.

I scoffed. "Right. You do that sort of thing all the time, don't you?" I put my hand on his shoulder. "James Hook! Hero of weak women!" I flourished my hand across the horizon as though presenting him to an unseen crowd.

He shrugged me off.

"Touchy." I walked to the paint-chipped front door and pushed it open. "Athena!" I yelled. "I'm back!"

The floorboards overhead creaked.

I looked over my shoulder at James, who wasn't looking at me anymore. "What deal was your father making today?"

That comment made him snap a glare at me. "Your mother is the one who arranged this meeting."

"Please. I know your father. What is his bargain today? A new hat for her? Necklace? Perhaps sheets for the bed?"

He rolled his eyes. "She isn't worth his time for those worthless trinkets."

I drew my sword.

"What are you going to do? Poke me?" he asked in an unamused voice.

"I could kill you for insulting a captain, our leader, and no one would think otherwise."

James rose to his feet, towering above me. "All right, then. Go ahead. Show me how much of a pirate you truly are, Odette."

"Your father is—"

"Doing whatever he wants," James cut in. "He's a pirate captain. What he does is his own prerogative, not mine."

I tried to stare him down, but James had called my bluff and won. No matter how tough I acted, I knew I was no match for him. "Fine. *Hook*." I sheathed my sword.

"It's Pan now."

I blurted a long laugh to show him how stupid I thought the name was. "Why would you change out 'hook' for 'pan?' I mean . . . c'mon. A frying pan? Over a hook?"

"It's not that kind of pan," James glared.

"Oh, you must mean a bedpan."

James's dark cheeks began to take on a red hue, and I gave a victorious smirk. "It's Pan, like the goat that plays the flute." He demonstrated moving the flute across his lips with his one hand.

I feigned ignorance by raising my eyebrow. "You're like a goat now?"

James's face shaded an even darker red, but I couldn't decide if it was out of embarrassment or anger.

"One for me." I winked and strode inside, swinging my new boots from my fingers.

I skipped steps as I ran up the grand staircase and reached the top just in time for Mother's bedroom door to swing open. Captain Barrie walked out, fully clothed but adjusting his belt.

James looked like the younger version of his father, only Captain Barrie had a beard down to his ribs, which he kept braided in several strands, and James was always cleanshaven whenever I saw him. Captain Barrie's skin was weatherworn, like his leather boots and grand black hat, and he had a permanently cruel glint in his dark eyes. Again, unlike James—whose eyes still held light and joy.

I folded my arms, my boots still dangling from my fingers. "You're shameless, aren't you?" There was no question in my voice.

He greeted me with a smirk. "You made it back in one piece, huh? I thought for sure—"

"Yeah, yeah. You're not the only one. You should have seen the stares I got walking up here. People thought I was a ghost. I almost shouted 'boo' in their faces just to see what they'd do." I rested my elbows on the railing at my back.

Barrie chuckled and placed his hat on his head. I knew what my mother saw in him. He was one of the six pirates I knew who still had all their teeth. What I didn't understand, however, was why she would waste her time with men like him when Captain Avery at least had some dignity.

The bedroom door swung open again and Athena exited. She wore her typical brown trousers, white tunic, and sea-green vest.

"Odette! I'm thrilled you made it home." She pushed past James and gave me an awkward hug. She'd never been much of a hugger. Physical affection wasn't really her thing.

But I gave her a little pat with my hand. "And I've returned with a hull full of riches." I grinned proudly.

Athena let go as quickly as she'd hugged me.

She eyed me with a skeptical glint, but I didn't miss the pride in the corners of her smile. "What are we doing up here, then? Let's see what riches you've brought back." She glanced at Captain Barrie. "I trust you know your way out?"

He snorted. "It's not exactly difficult."

"And it's not like he hasn't been here before," I chided, trotting down the stairs. I opened the door to the bedroom I claimed while on shore and set my precious new boots on the chest at the foot of the bed before joining my mother at the entrance of the house.

Together, we walked back down the stone pathway and to the harbor, followed by James and his father. Athena's red hair was much more manageable than my own. At least, she made it look that way. She kept the sides braided back in three wide braids, then gathered at the back into one massive braid.

She wore two rings in her left eyebrow and one in the middle of her nose, not to mention those that dangled the entire outer edge of her right ear. I always envied the colorful tattoo of scales on her chest. The scales started under her jawline and spread down between her breasts, disappearing beneath her shirt. The green-blue tone had been so well done I'd often caught myself staring to see if they were real. They weren't, of course, but they looked it.

The final piece that always drew my attention was the curled seashell with a shimmering pink-pearl hue on the inside. A band of gold nuzzled deeply in the spiral. I didn't know how she'd found it, but I'd always found it positively stunning.

"Tell me how you pulled this off," Athena said, her boots clapping on the cobblestone road with authority.

Aware of James and his father behind us, I knew I had a captive audience. I knew they'd be just as impressed as she was, whether they would admit it aloud or not.

"Remember a few months ago when I got that tip?" I looked over my shoulder. "I managed to seduce a sailor into giving me information."

Captain Barrie raised his eyebrow and exchanged a look of disbelief with James. Not the kind of *impressed* disbelief, but the kind that said he didn't believe *I* could seduce someone.

"She put a dagger through his hand and broke his nose," Mother explained.

That made the pirate captain smirk. "That's more like it."

"Technicalities." I shrugged. "As I was saying, I got information that this merchant ship would be coming from the Tyrrenhia Isles laden with goods, gold, and precious stones. It was supposed to have a fleet of three ships protecting it. Apparently, it was on its way to Delphi, the capital. The sailor said it was a payment for some sort of trade route opening or whatnot." I waved my hand dismissively.

We turned down the main road as the sun began its descent over the cliffs.

"How did you find this particular ship?" James asked.

"I got the name from him, took Captain Avery, and we headed to the southern isles." I walked with a proud strut. "She was massive, and with three other ships, it wasn't exactly easy. The three smaller ships were frigates."

I carried on with the story of how we had to separate the frigates from the large merchant ship by drawing them away one at a time. I told how we stayed just in their view for a few days, near enough to threaten, but not close enough to cause harm. When we peeled off and went to the other side, we somehow managed to annoy the first frigate crew. Unfortunately, it was open sea without anywhere to run and hide, and the smaller frigate was faster than the *Naiad*.

I built up suspense with battle and ended with us raiding the merchant vessel for their goods, just in time before the ship reached the naval guard at Delphi's harbors.

At some point, Captain Barrie and James disappeared. I hadn't noticed when, though I was offended they didn't see my plunder.

Captain Avery stood on the docks, overseeing the cargo as it was carefully stacked. He removed his hat and bowed to my mother the instant we came into view. "Captain Athena."

"Captain Avery. I heard you had quite the adventure getting this bounty."

"Indeed. We captured a lot of food, materials for trade, and some things I know you'd like to see." He motioned for her to follow him up the gangplank to the main deck.

Smee jumped to his feet, having been sitting atop the largest chest we'd pulled from the merchant ship. Behind him were stacks of crates. He ran his hand over his greasy hair and cleared his throat. "Captain."

My mother nodded in response. "Let's see what you got."

He pulled the key from the rope around his neck. We'd replaced the broken lock with one of our own, just in case any of our crew decided to get sticky fingers. Since we didn't typically count our earnings before getting back to port, some pirates could steal gold coins or gems without anyone knowing. Sometimes the laws of the land didn't make it to the sea.

Smee swiftly unlocked it and lifted the lid.

I kept my attention focused on my mother.

Her eyes lit up at the mound of gold piled inside. "There's more than this?" She looked at me.

"Yes. That crate behind has expensive fabric. Captain Avery also has two—"

"Three," he corrected and removed the pouches from an inner pocket of his jacket.

"*Three* bags of gemstones." I rested my hands on my hips, beaming.

Athena ran her fingertips over the coins, then turned to investigate the gemstones. "You truly had an incredible raid. I am extremely impressed." She faced me. "Take ten gold coins for yourself, Odette. You earned it."

A grin split my face, and I counted out ten gold coins in front of them. I slid the coins into my pocket and kept my hand wrapped around them. "Thank you, Athena."

She nodded. "You'll get your cut too, Captain Avery. I trust you to count out everything so it is correctly distributed?" She arched her brow. There were taxes for being part of her fleet, for running the port, and basically for staying on her good side, but she was generally fair or pirates wouldn't stay.

Avery handed her his ledger. "Already added up, Captain. We had a long journey back."

I really wasn't in the mood to watch my mother scan the pages, but if I were to be the captain of the newest ship in the fleet, I needed to show my mother I was no longer a child. So I stood there on the deck for thirty agonizingly boring minutes before my mother finally concluded her assessment.

She slapped the ledger closed and she handed it back. "Very good. Bring my share to the house when you're ready."

I trailed behind my mother as she headed back down the gangplank to the docks, then skipped up to her side. "Do you need anything else from me?"

"I want you to go have some fun. You earned it." Athena stopped and faced me. "I mean it, Odette. You made me very proud today. Everyone will look at you and see the pirate queen's daughter. And soon you'll be just as well-known as I am." She smiled.

"And tomorrow, when you announce the newest captain of your fleet, I'll be at your side." I grinned.

"Then I'll see you in the morning. Say hello to Sky for me."

I pursed my lips, resisting the smile tugging at the edge. I was only mildly embarrassed she knew where I was going.

Mother winked before carrying on her way.

I turned and headed for the Flounder Tavern.

THREE

The boisterous drinking song echoed down the street long before I pushed the Flounder's door open. It was sticky hot and smelled of lamp oil, men, alcohol, and the best food in Port Mere. Sky stood on one of the tables, leading the drinking song and keeping beat by stomping his foot. He called out the first line and the crowd of men shouted back the next.

Listen to this tale of woe.
A tale of woe, aye yo-ho!
A maiden fair whose hair does glow.
Glows in the water, hey yo-ho!
To your heart, she'll strike a blow.
The blow will kill you, aye yo-ho!
She'll come take your blackened soul.
Take it to the depths below!
Yo-ho! Yo-ho!

Take it to the depths below!

Although I stood out of the way of the rowdy clientele, their faces flushed from drink and food clinging to their beards, I couldn't resist joining in the chorus at the end of the shanty.

The pirates roared with laughter as Sky jumped down. Men patted him on the back as he passed. One man pushed a mug into Sky's hand. Sky turned and slammed that mug against the other the man was holding, then took a long swig.

"Sky!" I called, trying to pick my way to his side. "Sky!" Either he couldn't hear me or he wasn't acknowledging me. I played a little dirty and shouted, "Scuttle!" knowing he hated it.

The men nearest me halted their conversations, and Sky's bright-blue eyes scanned the crowd until they settled on me.

The anger dissipated, and he grinned. "Odette! I told ye not to call me that."

Sky, or Scuttle as I liked to call him, was dashingly handsome, with fair, sun-bleached hair so blond it was nearly white. He had a scar on the left side of his face from his nose across his cheek to his jaw.

He got the scar when he was a cabin boy aboard my mother's vessel, *The Pirate Queen*. We'd been boarded by a crew of the Royal Navy, and one of the men had come at me. Sky had stepped between us, and the man didn't hesitate to strike Sky with his sword. I thought Sky had been killed that day.

I vowed that day that I would never hesitate to act ever again.

Reaching Sky, he pulled me into a bear hug with one arm, holding on to his mug with the other so it wouldn't spill. "You're not supposed to call me Scuttle," he repeated with a playful scowl.

"I can't help it. It's not my fault you earned yourself an unfortunate nickname."

He pouted. "It's hardly my fault we scuttled at the port of . . . wherever. The goblin ship took us by surprise, *during* a storm."

"But ya still did it. You were the man behind the helm. Therefore . . . your fault." I poked him on the nose.

He rolled his eyes and pressed his forehead to mine. "It's a good thing I missed you or I wouldn't let you get away with that."

"Well, I'm positively famished," I said in my haughtiest voice.

"We need to rectify that, your most belovedness," he replied and tipped his drink to his lips, keeping the pinky up.

I laughed and pushed my way through the crowd to a back table, dragging him with me. "What did you do while I was out at sea?"

"Waited like a puppy dog, loyal as ever."

"And how do I know you weren't making your way around the women of Mere?" I blinked innocently.

He gestured with wide arms. "There aren't any women here!"

I pointed with both arms to the group of harlots hanging on the necks of men just inside the door.

Sky sighed. "They hardly count."

"Still women. Not to mention the blacksmith's daughter, the seamstress and her daughters, or your own sisters."

"Eew." He reached across the table and grabbed my chin. "I haven't been messing around. Promise." He crushed my lips in a drunken, desperate kiss.

Sky and I had known each other our entire lives, as well as James and almost every other pirate. Sky was a good year older than me. He was always my right-hand whenever we had to practice our sword fighting, and he'd always taken time to explain ship things to me when I was younger. The last few months had drawn us rather close.

The prickly hairs of his two days' worth of stubble scraped against my skin, and I had to pull back to rub under my nose. "That's got to be shaved," I protested.

He grinned. "I'm rather proud of it." He smoothed his hand over his scruff. "If I'm going to be a captain, I should look like one, yes?"

"If you're going to be captain, you need more than a beard." I looked him up and down. "Besides, who says you're going to be a captain?"

Sky tilted his head. "What else could I possibly need to be a captain?"

I pursed my lips. "A new tattoo? I got some new boots with skulls on the side, and after my incredible success on my voyage, I would like to get another tattoo next to my Jolly Roger. I'm thinking a ship or siren." I patted my left arm.

Sky frowned. "Truly? You just get into port and the first thing you want to do is get a tattoo?" He let out a disappointed snort and got up to get me some food.

"I didn't say it was the *first* thing I wanted to do!" I hollered after him.

Sky returned moments later and set a plate of food and mug of ale in front of me. "Here you are, your majesty."

"Did you eat yet? Or did all of that alcohol just fill your belly?" I picked up the fork and knife.

"I'm not a cold fish." He pursed his lips when he realized it didn't come out right. He took another gulp from his mug. "I'm not new to drinking. A mug is hardly enough to cause anything."

"Uh-huh," I deliberately looked him over, long enough for him to get the hint he was, in fact, a little tipsy.

I told him all about my voyage—including the embellishments. He told me how he took a short voyage to pick up the sails for the new ship.

We finished eating and walked out of the tavern. The night was humid, and the light from the lamps left a hazy glow on the streets.

"Who do you think will be assigned captain of the new ship?" I asked as casually as possible.

Sky gave me a confused look. "Your mom already chose."

"Yeah, but she doesn't make the official announcement until tomorrow." I stopped walking. "Do you know?"

He opened his mouth, but there was a pause before words came out. "I think you and I should go to my place." He slid his arms around me, a teasing smile on his face.

"Sky," I let my voice trail off. We'd never done anything other than kiss, and I knew where his drunk mind wanted to go.

"You don't like that idea. How about the beach?" he asked.

"I could go for a walk," I said, trying to tell him we weren't going to do *that* act.

Sky's blue eyes glinted in the lamplight. He took my hand and ambled through the still noisy town, past the docks, and down the path that ran along the west side of the bay, under the cliffs, and out to the caves that were dangerous in high tides. We walked through the caves to the small, private beach beyond.

I didn't know how many pirates knew about it, but no had ever been there when Sky and I had gone. I'd considered telling my mother about the vulnerable location, but any invader would be a fool to try and infiltrate our hideout through that direction. They would have to disembark their ships, carry their artillery through the caves, and hope they had enough men to fight us on *our* terms in *our* port.

We'd barely set foot on that hidden beach when Sky turned, grabbed my face, and kissed me passionately. When he pressed his lips to mine, I saw James and instantly got a splitting headache and had to pull away.

"You okay?" Sky asked as he pulled away.

I rubbed my temple. "Just a headache. I thought I remembered kissing James."

"Hook?" he blanched.

"Did I ever kiss him? Before Castle Bay?" I asked.

Sky blinked. "I . . . don't know. Look, it's not my place to be nosy."

"Since when?" I frowned.

"Want to sleep under the stars?" Sky's dashing smile melted away my anger.

I was grateful for Sky not pressuring me. He obviously saw my headache, or maybe it was the discussion of James that turned him off. He sat on the sun-warmed sand and patted the spot at his side.

I took the position at his side and leaned my head on his shoulder. "Thank you, Sky. You're a good friend."

"Yeah, I know." He chuckled.

I smiled and closed my eyes, letting the lapping of the waves wrap around me like a blanket. When Sky began to hum, that was it.

I hadn't expected to fall asleep.

I was rather surprised when Sky shook me awake the next morning at the kraken of dawn. I thought maybe he wanted to beat the incoming tide so we could get through the caves dry, but we were a good two hours early.

"Why are you in such a rush?" I asked, stumbling through the sand. I dusted it from my hair and clothes as I chased after him.

He was tying his faded red scarf around his neck. "I just want to get there early for when Athena makes the big announcement."

I narrowed my eyes in a glare. Catching up with him, I grabbed his arm and yanked him around. "You know something!"

Sky pulled away from my grasp. "I have a hunch I might be part of the new crew. That's all."

"You're not the captain?"

He tilted his head and ran his fingers through his hair, sending particles of sand everywhere. "Do you really think your mother would choose me to captain her new rig? Me? Scuttle?"

"Well, if you aren't the captain, who is?"

"You'll just have to wait and see." I hated how easily his perfect smile slid onto his handsome face.

As we walked through the caves, I spotted a rock with a big lip on it. Normally, I didn't care about the oysters that clung under those rock lips, but one big white oyster caught my eye. I carefully stepped on the slimy rocks and crouched to pry the oyster from its grip on the stone.

"Odette, we don't have time to hunt for pearls," Sky said, his tone annoyed.

"I know. I'm just taking this one." I pried it off rather easily, careful of the sharp edges, and hurried as fast as I could back to Sky. "I've never seen a white one." I held it up for him.

"Huh." He shook his head. "Come on. I want to bathe before the announcement."

"Well, it must be a very special announcement for you."

"You should probably take a bath too." He looked over his shoulder at me, the curl of his grin taking the edge off his snarky response.

"Are you implying something?"

"Oh, I'm not implying anything. I'm being blunt. You stink."

"Oy!"

He laughed and easily dodged a punch I aimed at his shoulder. "I'll see you back down here in an hour." He leaned down, pecked me on the cheek, then carried on to his house.

He lived with his parents and younger brother at the top of the cliff to the west. Funnily enough, they were farmers. Sky's dad had never been much of a sailor, nor his mother, but for some reason, they settled right in with the pirates and didn't mind one bit that Sky loved to sail.

I made it to the top of the ridge where Athena's house sat.

Seeing the sea at sunrise was stunning enough, but to see the sun stretching its rays through the clouds of night . . . it was nearly indescribable. The sea reflected the purples and oranges cast by the sun. The cliffs kept the bay in darkness for now, but the light climbed over the top and warmed my face. There was peace. There was calmness.

If I was ever stranded on land, I hoped I could grow old and die in Port Mere.

A deep ache settled into my chest, and I found myself blinking at the water. Like the siren's song, the ocean called to me. I rubbed at my headache before walking through the front door. I set the oyster on the table and headed into my bedroom for a much-needed bath.

FOUR

I walked out of my room, fully clothed in my brand-new black leather boots with the brass skulls. I wore my brown pants, sleeveless white shirt, and black vest with bronze buttons to match my boots. My wild red hair took an extra-long time to get right that day. I settled on braiding the sides of my hair back in two braids on each side and puffed the top before I pulled it all back in a ponytail.

When I exited my room, I found my mother leaning against the table, the oyster shell open on the surface behind her.

"Is something wrong?" I asked.

She straightened immediately, as though I'd startled her, even though I hadn't exactly been quiet. "Not at all. I hope you don't mind I took the liberty of opening your shell. A white oyster is rather rare."

I shrugged. "I don't care. Was it empty?"

"No. But I had hoped the summer stone had been reclaimed by the sea and that it would have found its way . . ." Her voice trailed, eyes taking on a distant look. Then she seemed to suddenly remember my presence, put a smile on, and held out her hand.

In her palm sat the most stunning black pearl I'd ever seen. It had a translucent purple sheen and was about the size of my pinky nail. It was positively perfect.

"It's beautiful. Why does it upset you?" I asked, lifting it into the sunlight.

"Because the summer stone holds magic. It is said whoever possesses this stone, possesses the power of the sea." Athena wiped her hands on her pants. "Take that down to Timbony, the jeweler. Do with it as you please, then meet me down at the docks for the announcement of our newest captain. "Don't take too long," she warned, but her smile was bright.

I dumped the oyster shell in a crate for garbage and ran from the house as fast as possible. I thought about having the pearl embedded in the hilt of my sword, put on an earring, or ring, but none of those felt right.

Timbony affirmed those ideas were bad after I spoke with him. "Nah, a pearl this rare and you don't want to hide it. I got just the thing." He grunted when he bent over and rummaged under the counter. I could have sworn I heard he let one rip as he straightened. He set something on the counter in front of me.

I looked down, and my breath caught. The golden charm was a siren with her hands spread. Her wavy hair flowed over her left shoulder, and her face was simple, with only the curved shape of eyes and a nose. Her scaled fin extended downward.

"May I?" He held out his hand.

I handed over the pearl, and he placed it in the hands of the siren. With a tool and a delicate touch, he pinched the siren's arms closed around it.

The pearl fit perfectly.

Timbony grinned and scratched at his sweaty blue bandana. "I made her to hold a diamond but haven't found the right one. I think a black pearl's perfect for her."

"How much will this cost me?"

The pirate tilted his head. "I know." He crouched again and set a skull charm in front of me. "I need two gemstones for the eyes. Preferably rubies."

I frowned. "How do you think I'm going to obtain two rubies?"

Timbony smirked. "I heard about yer plunder."

I placed my hands on my hips. "Add in a sturdy chain for this mermaid, and I'll see what I can do. I'll have to take this, of course, to find the perfect size." I pressed my finger to the skull's face and dragged the pendant toward me.

"Then I'll hold onto this until yer done." He picked up my pearl and mermaid charm before I could snatch it.

"Fine. I need that for the announcement of the new captain today." I pushed the skull back to him, and he gave the siren charm back to me.

Timbony pulled a box off a shelf and picked through it until he found the perfect chain. He strung the charm on it and held it out to me.

When I put it on, the pendant rested perfectly on my chest. I found myself fingering it as I walked from the jeweler and down to the bay, which was already crowded. Almost everyone in Port Mere had gathered in front of the stage. Athena had it built for special occasions, such as musical celebrations, announcements, or auctions. Today, she would announce her newest pirate captain.

Sky stood near the stage wearing clean blue pants, a pale-blue shirt with a faint white design, and his typical red scarf tucked around his neck. He had even polished the hilt of his sword.

My throat tightened, nerves starting to take over.

I trotted up the wooden steps and took my place at my mother's side.

Athena leaned toward me. "You're late."

"Pirates are never late," I said with a proud sniffle.

Athena held what would soon be the new captain's hat. It was black with a gold ribbon around the edges and had a beautiful, new, red feather plume even larger than Captain Avery's hat.

"I would like to take a moment and explain how I chose this new captain. As tradition details, the honor of a captain is typically handed from captain to first mate. However, I felt it was time to add a new ship, especially to replace one recently damaged."

I glanced unintentionally at Sky, who averted his gaze from everyone knowingly.

Athena continued. "I chose this captain based on their ability to take charge of a crew, high success rate of missions, and the amount of income they've provided for us. Isn't the new ship beautiful?"

Everyone applauded.

I wiped my hands on my pantlegs with nervous anticipation.

"It is also fit that I announce the new captain and first mate." She turned to her right, away from me, and held her hand out. "Meet the newest captain of our fleet. Captain James 'Pan' Barrie."

My jaw dropped.

I stared as a wave of shock, horror, and disbelief washed over me and ended in an explosion of pure anger. I balled my hands into fists. *That* was the real reason Captain Barrie had gone to my mother the day before. Earning the honor of captain in such a way wasn't something I imagined James doing.

To have his *father* sleep with my mother to secure his role?

Disgust tingled on my tongue, and I suddenly wished I had rammed my sword through his chest when I had the chance the day before.

James appeared at my mother's side as the crowd of pirates cheered. He waved, flashed his stunning smile, and when he met my gaze, winked.

The audacity!

Athena held up the new captain hat and placed it on top of James's head. I didn't care that he looked like he'd bathed or that he wore a new, crisp white shirt with a red vest and black and red coat, or that he looked stupidly handsome with the whole matching outfit. I also didn't care that the wink he gave me was sexy.

He'd taken *my* ship!

"Captain, tell everyone the name of your ship and introduce your first mate." My mother stepped back, allowing James to bask in his stolen glory.

James bowed to her. "Thank you, Captain Athena. I have chosen to call my ship "The Sea Devil." And my first mate will be Sky O'Beron."

"What?" I blurted. I threw Sky a glare, but he'd moved from where he'd been standing and was soon at James's side. I wheeled toward my mother and lowered my voice. "You gave the new ship to Hook and Scuttle?" I made sure she felt the animosity in my voice.

And my mother, Athena, the pirate queen, eyed me. "Why . . . of course. Did you think I was giving it to you?" Her tone was condescending as if I should have known all along she would never give the ship to me.

I squeezed my lips together so tightly they tingled. I marched off the wooden stage, my new heels pounding loudly on the wood and then stone roadway as I headed for home.

I heard quick footsteps on pebbles behind me before Sky yelled, "Odette! Aren't you going to congratulate me?"

I spun around so quickly, I stumbled on the uneven ground. "No! Because you knew! I asked you, and you knew, and you didn't tell me!"

Sky's grin froze, and his face folded into confusion. "Knew what?"

"That you were going to be *Hook's* first mate! And that *Hook* is the captain!" I shouted.

"It's Pan now, remember?" Sky corrected.

James approached behind him with a bemused smirk.

I gripped the hilt of my sword tightly. "What would everyone do if they knew your father slept with my mother so you could be captain?" I kept my voice as calm as I could.

"I don't think anyone would care." He frowned. "But that isn't how I got the ship."

"Oh, I'm sure it's not." I spun on my heel.

"Don't go after her," James said. "Let her have some time alone to accept this."

I raised my finger in a crude gesture.

The instant I made it back to the house, I stalked to the old oak tree behind the house. I threw my worn hat onto the ground, then ripped my sword from its sheath. I didn't waste a single moment more before smashing my sword against the trunk with all the force I had. The vibration stung my hands, but I didn't care.

I had done *everything* my mother asked of me. I had gone on voyages, fought in battles, and *this* was how she thanked me? By giving *my* ship away? And to Hook of all people!

I pried my sword out of the thick bark with a few wiggles and hit the tree again.

And again.

I'd brought back a bounty bigger than anyone had, aside from Athena herself. I'd proven my worth over and over. I'd proven I could lead a crew on a mission, keep them safe, and return home!

Chipped wood flew this way and that, and after several minutes I had successfully managed to dull the blade until the blade could no longer bite the tree.

Drenched in sweat, my hands stinging and arms aching, I finally lowered the tip of my ruined sword to the thick grass.

From the corner of my eye, something moved, and my attention darted to it. My mother stood with her shoulder against the house, and the movement I'd caught was her adjusting her stance.

"Why are you so angry?" she asked innocently.

"That was supposed to be *my* ship!" I spat.

She laughed. She actually laughed. "Odette, darling, you're a wonderful pirate." She shrugged off the side of the house. "And you're going to make a fantastic captain someday."

"*Someday*?"

"You're only eighteen. Why in the deep blue sea would you think I'd give you control of a crew of your own?" She inclined her head.

I lifted my chin defiantly, my hand squeezing the hilt of my sword so tight my hand went white. "Because I deserve it, and you know it. My age has nothing to do with it. James is barely two years older than I am. Yet look at everything I've done for you. Look at what I just brought back!"

"I know, Odette. You did bring back something impressive."

"Impressive? That's all you've got to say?" I yelled. "What will it take for me to prove to you I'm ready to be a captain?"

Athena put her hands on my shoulders. "You're still young. You still have a lot to learn."

I pulled away from her. "That was supposed to be *my* ship. Did you truly *never* consider me for it?"

She sighed. "I can't put you on a ship with a crew of men who don't respect you, Odette."

Her words struck me like a dagger. "Why not? Because *you* claim I'm too young? The men listen to you. If *you* showed them you respect me and think highly of me, maybe they would too," I snapped back.

Her eyes narrowed. "If I showed *you* respect?"

"Yes! How many sailors have you bragged to that I returned home successfully? That *I* am the one who found and executed this better than any other sailor could have?" Tears stung my eyes, but I wouldn't give her yet another reason to look down on me. "Is it because of whatever I did at Castle Bay?"

Athena stood silently watching me for several tense moments. My stomach dropped and my hands went clammy. I didn't know what she was going to say or do. Whatever happened that night, she didn't want to tell me.

"No," she answered plainly.

I tossed my blade at her feet. She'd given it to me as a gift the year before. I wasn't even sure it could be repaired, and I didn't care. I swallowed my welling heart and walked past her.

"Odette, how dare you turn your back on me! Get back here."

"Or what? You'll ground me?" I glared over my shoulder before rounding the corner of the house.

I would prove to her once and for all that I was forced to be reckoned with. I would prove to her that I was a much better captain than Captain James Hook.

FIVE

I knew I was being impulsive.

I knew better than to yell at my mother.

But what eighteen-year-old hadn't run away from home? Of course, my situation was a little different than others. Most girls my age were working on their parent's farms, sewing dresses, knitting blankets, flirting with men to find a husband, swimming in the sea, or whatever else people who weren't pirates did.

I grabbed my pack and shoved in a set of clothing, then stormed into the kitchen to find some pieces of food that weren't spoiled—like dried meat and berries.

"Odette, stop being so dramatic." Athena stopped beside the table.

"I'm not being dramatic," I said, flatly and shouldered my pack. "The last few months, you've done nothing but restrict everything I do. I sail with Captain Avery and him only."

"Because you are part of his crew," she cut in.

"Yes, but ever since whatever happened at Castle Bay, you treat me like I'm made of glass." I faced her. "The pirates lower their eyes and hurry on like I'm a leper. A few brave souls will actually nod before they walk away. I still can't remember exactly what happened, but whatever it was it must have been terrible for you and the pirates to treat me that way."

"Odette, I nearly lost you." Athena walked to me and put her hands on my shoulders. "You almost died that day. I know I have been a little more protective lately, but the thought of losing you . . ." She reached up and stroked my hair. "I simply can't bear it."

I didn't respond right away. Anger still burned in my veins.

She reached down and held the mermaid pendant on my neck. She ran her thumb and then index finger over the pearl. "I want to keep you safe. You're all the family I have."

"At some point, you'll remember I'm not a child." I grabbed the chain and lifted the pendant from her fingers.

With that, I left the only home I'd known behind.

I couldn't afford to sit and wait any longer for my mother to see me for the woman I was. I had to prove it once and for all.

I reached the Flounder Tavern and spotted Captain Avery sitting alone, his hat on the table across from him.

I marched over, pulled out a chair, and sat.

He paused his chewing and looked me up and down. He tucked his food in his cheek. "And to what do I owe the pleasure?"

"I need you to get the crew so we can leave immediately."

Avery resumed chewing on his food as he leaned back in his seat. "And why?"

"Because there's something I need to do!" I tried to keep my voice low while showing him how important it was to me that we leave. "We need to leave tonight before my mother can stop me."

He swallowed. "What is so important that we leave after having just returned from a three-week voyage, without telling Athena?"

I didn't want to tell him my plan because I didn't want it to get back to my mother, but I needed him on my side. I finally leaned forward, arms resting on the table, and grabbed his mug of rum as soon as Stoon, the owner of the Flounder Tavern, put it down.

Stoon raised a brow and glanced at Avery, who waved him off.

I dragged my arm over my mouth and set down Avery's mug. "I want to go after something almost impossible to find. But I think with your expertise and my talent combined, we can bring it back. *Then* my mother will see I'm worth becoming a captain."

He gave me an unamused frown. "Oh, of course. Especially considering how we took on *three* frigates?"

I rolled my eyes. "No one needs to know the truth. Everyone embellishes their voyages. But *this* will be even better than our last victory!"

"Odette, I appreciate your tenacity." He grabbed his mug and pulled it away from me. "But, no. I'm not taking you on a voyage I know nothing about with a crew that just barely made it to land. It will take us at least a week to even stock up the necessary supplies. You know this. If you can give us a week, allow me to clear it with your mother—"

"The point is *not* letting my mother know."

Avery ran his hand over his bearded face. "Then I'm afraid the answer, for now, is no."

I tightened my lips and tapped my fingers across the surface of the table. I trusted Captain Avery with my life, but it was imperative I left immediately. I *had* to find the summer stone, no matter what it took.

"Thank you," I said, lifting my gaze to him. "You've taught me a lot about being a pirate. Including going after what I want." I got back to my feet.

"Odette, if yer mother comes askin' . . ."

"Tell her when I get back that she will finally recognize I'm worth something to her." I snatched my pack from beside the table and turned sharply on my heel.

"She's just tryin' to keep you safe!"

I didn't look over my shoulder. I made it out to the street only to stop in the middle of the road. I looked down into the calm waters of the night. *The Sea Devil* sat with the lights on in the captain's quarters and lanterns on deck were lit. I imagined Hook was having quite a fun time celebrating his new responsibilities as captain, showing off his captain's bed to the girls, and drinking with his new crew.

It made me sick.

And then my eyes settled on a smaller ship. A barge, really, and I didn't even hesitate to head down to the waters. Its crew was loading the last of supplies, which meant they would be leaving soon.

When I drew nearer, I recognized the slanted sails of *The Black Cape*. I knew Captain Josiah only by name. He didn't exactly have a good reputation. There was a story that floated around the summer before that he had sacrificed a crew member to the sirens for safe passage.

The sound of my boots clomping on the wood announced my presence to the crew, and I was greeted by a shirtless, overweight pirate leaning on the railing of the ship.

His smirk shifted to confusion when he eyed me. "Who're you?"

"My name is Odette. I need to talk to Captain Josiah."

He rubbed his plump finger over his bushy eyebrow. "What're ye needing him for?"

"It's not your business."

He grinned, but one side of his face didn't move. "Well then, I'm afraid I can't help." He pushed off the railing and turned.

I took a step. "I need to speak with him about joining his crew temporarily and about a possible bounty."

Slowly, the man turned back. "Bounty? What kind?"

"Something more precious than anything he could ever get from a raid or plunder." I stood my ground, watching the man intensely. I didn't know if this was the best idea. The captain already had a reputation, but I didn't want to waste time waiting for another crew to prep their ship over the next week.

He ran his tongue over his teeth. "A'right. Come up." He motioned for me to climb the gangplank.

I pinched my shoulders to my neck for a few seconds, drew a deep breath, and straightened my spine as I relaxed before walking up the gangplank and onto the deck.

The man was now lounging on a barrel, opening a small burlap sack. "Tell me about the voyage and my payment."

I inclined my head. "*You* are Captain Josiah?"

"Aye."

"Where is your proof?" I glanced at the few crew members on board.

One was a cabin boy, tying back some sail rope, and another man stood up at the front of the ship looking over the edge. It appeared as if he were checking the cannon doors.

"Aye, boy!"

The cabin boy, a lad probably ten years of age, lifted his head. "Cap'n?" he asked.

Josiah gestured a beefy hand. "Proof enough?"

I folded my arms. If I weren't so desperate, I would have said no.

Josiah picked out a large date and popped it in his mouth.

I finally conceded. "I want to go after the summer stone."

He blinked.

I didn't budge.

He shifted his gaze beyond me, likely taking in the reactions of the other two on deck. He frowned. "Ye can't just go find it. Don't the rumors say somethin' about King Eric havin' it?"

"I know where to look."

"And where is that?"

"I'm not telling you until your crew is on board and we are on the open ocean." I knew I was gambling because Josiah was right. According to my mother, the king of Terricina was in possession, and Josiah didn't need to help me.

"Ye drive a hard bargain." He picked another date. "My payment?"

"We will discuss that later. You likely heard of the plunder I brought back with me only yesterday?" I raised my eyebrow. "I shall pay you when we return."

He wagged his finger at me. "Not so fast, dearie. I want yer pearl as payment."

I reached up and wrapped my fingers around my newly obtained treasure. I shouldn't have felt so possessive of it, it wasn't as though it held any significance. I'd merely gotten lucky enough to find the right oyster.

"No," I said with finality. "I'll pay you in gemstones or coins."

"Then no deal." He shoved another date in his mouth. His fingers looked like dates. Fat and wrinkled. They barely even had nails on them. He was starting to annoy me.

I let out a soft scoff. "I suppose you don't get to share in the glory when my mother receives the only piece of treasure she's ever searched for. I bet Captain *Pan* would be willing to share in the glory. Could you imagine how famous he would become? A new pirate captain returning from his first voyage with the most precious gemstone in the sea . . ." As I spoke, I headed slowly back toward the gangplank.

"Now, you wait here." Josiah got to his feet quickly. "Yer gonna go to Barrie's kid?"

I gestured my arm toward the fantastic vessel. "He's got a full belly of supplies, his crew is eager, and it appears everyone is already on board. If I made this deal with him, do you think he would turn it down?"

"Why did ye come to me, then?"

"Because I hate him, and I didn't want to have to use him, but . . . here we are." I sighed. I set my foot on the ramp.

"You promise the pirate queen truly wants this gemstone?"

"Well, *I* certainly have no need for it."

"All right." He inhaled through his nose, sucking in a wad of snot, then turned his head and spat it over the railing into the ocean below. "We might have an extra hammock below. We leave at dawn."

"No!" I blurted, then plastered a smile on my face to cover my nearly yelling at him. "I mean, we should go now. Before anyone else has time to catch wind of where we are headed. We don't want them getting there first."

"Aye, good idea." He tapped the side of his nose. "Solomon. Go fetch the crew. Wake 'em up and tell 'em we're leaving immediately."

The cabin boy didn't hesitate to scamper below deck.

The pirates weren't happy to be woken and spat curses at the boy, but realized he was serious when they noticed me putting my pack in an available hammock. I heard a few of them mumble about me being on board, but they headed above deck, and we set to work preparing the ship for sail as ordered.

Sails were lowered, the gangplank dragged up, anchor retrieved from the waters, and ropes tied off. However, every time I attempted to grab a rope and do my share, a pirate stepped up and took it from me.

I found myself standing to the side, glowering at the pirates as they finished their responsibilities.

Gradually, we made our way through the bay. As we drew nearer to James's ship, I saw people on the deck. Someone played music and a small group of men sang loudly. I leaned on the railing, trying to spot Sky. I finally did, and my heart ached a little to be leaving him when I'd just barely returned. But I was still mad at him.

He stood on the quarterdeck, dancing. He'd always thought he was a great dancer, and he always managed to make me laugh. In fact, I was smiling as I watched him. Until Lilly, the smithy's daughter, approached. He swooped her up in his arms and danced around the deck.

My jaw clenched.

I tore my gaze away and spotted James leaning his backside against a crate with a pan flute in his hand. He turned his face toward me so slowly, I wondered if he'd sensed me staring at him. Time seemed to slow with the movement.

I blinked and saw the side of his face bleeding, his face twisted in a grimace.

I blinked again, and he was completely normal.

James watched me with his stunning brown eyes. He lowered the flute, shifted his gaze from me to the ship, then over to the captain and back before he climbed to his feet and walked to the edge of the deck. "Where're you headed?"

"You'd like to know, but I'm not going to tell," I called back with a satisfied smirk.

"You do know what ship you're on?" He glanced away from me again.

I shrugged. "Some of us weren't gifted a shiny new boat." I pressed fingers to my lips and blew him a kiss. "We'll see if you get to keep that ship of yours when I get back."

He arched his brow.

A young man I didn't recognize approached James. "You must be Captain Pan?" He wore light trousers, a vest buckled to the neck, and a brown overcoat. The crevasse on his neck made him look like he was trying too hard to fit into our pirate culture. It was too crisp. New.

"Aye." James turned to address him.

"I'm Gerard." He extended his hand and they shook hands.

My ship drifted too far away for me to hear the rest of the exchange, but I shrugged and returned my attention to the sea ahead. My heart leapt with excitement at the thought that I would soon return victorious.

When we got out to sea, Captain Josiah turned to me. "All right. Where we heading, lass?"

"Head east along the coast."

"That's not much to go on." He frowned.

None of them would be too happy if I said we were heading to Terricina's capital city, Delphi, miles down the coast. I couldn't reveal my hand too soon. Pirates were completely illegal.

"I'll tell you when we're further out to sea. Good evening." I trotted down the steps and wound my way through the hammocks to the one I'd chosen a few minutes earlier.

The ship was filthy. By nature, most ships were, but at least Captain Avery made his crew clean everything once a month. Even the hammocks got washed to prevent them from rotting. I hadn't considered other captains wouldn't keep their ships in tip-top shape. I'd always been taught it was an honor to be on a vessel and every captain should treat their ship likewise. I frowned at "my" hammock, understanding very well why it wasn't occupied.

I climbed onto the brown fabric, praying the frayed strip by my knee wouldn't give in the middle of the night. I did my best to fall asleep.

In a few days, I would be a captain. If I didn't get lice first.

SIX

Delaying information was going to get me killed.

At breakfast, Captain Josiah asked me where we were headed.

We'd made it past the tip of Corinth and were headed up its eastern edge toward the Port of Gillsberry. It would still be a few days before we reached Delphi.

I was able to satisfy the question by saying, "If I tell you in front of your men . . ." and let it hang. But as soon as we were away from the men after eating our afternoon meal, he took my arm and pulled me aside.

"As the captain, *your* captain, you need to tell me where, exactly, we be going."

I shrugged off his sweaty grip. "I need to go to the capital of Terricina. To Delphi."

"Delphi?" he squeaked. "Are ye crazy?"

"I have to get there because the king knows where the stone is."

"And what's yer plan? Walk in and ask if he's got it?" He threw his arms up in the air. "Yer a *pirate*, lass. Pirates are outlawed. We set foot in that city, they'll lock us up. None of my crew are riskin' their freedom on this quest." He started away. "We're goin' back."

"No!" I ran after him. "Captain Josiah, you don't have to disembark. I'll go alone."

"We can't even get close to that port! Think about it. We pull up flyin' a skull and crossbones, and we're good as dead."

"Then we take down the Jolly Rodger."

He wasn't convinced.

"Then we go to Gillsberry, and I'll walk there! Please. This is the only way I can prove to my mother that I'm skilled enough to be a captain."

Josiah stopped and looked at me. "Part of bein' a captain is knowin' yer limits. Knowin' laws. This is a law, little miss. We ain't riskin' it." He turned to his first mate. "Turn the ship around," he called.

"If you turn around, I'm jumping overboard."

He looked over his shoulder at me, then at the expanse of ocean surrounding us. "That would be suicide."

My mind raced. "James saw me on your ship. If you return without me, he'll tell my mother you murdered me, and you'll be hanged."

"And ye'll be dead too."

He had an unfortunate point. My jumping overboard wouldn't help my situation at all. "Put me in the rowboat, then!" I gestured to the one sitting on the starboard side of the ship. "I'll row to shore and go from there."

He shook his head. "Yer crazy."

"Desperate," I corrected.

He stared and then rolled his eyes. "Then take the rowboat. Joshua, go get her pack. Storm and Row, lower the rowboat. The faster yer off this ship, the better."

Two men stopped what they were doing and walked to the rowboat. They must have overheard our conversation because neither questioned the captain as they lowered the boat into the ocean.

I didn't know what to do. My lifelong vow of not hesitating had put me in a sticky position.

Captain Josiah was turning the ship around. I didn't know exactly where in the ocean we were, and trying to get to shore in a rowboat was as foolish an idea as it sounded. I doubted Josiah would give me provisions either.

I *had* to get the summer stone. If I stayed on board and returned back in Port Mere, I would be returned to my mother like a foolish child, and she would never allow me to own a captain's hat until I was at least forty! It wasn't like I could just jump on the next ship and hope that crew would risk their lives.

It was up to me.

A rowboat it was.

I dropped my pack onto the tiny boat, which banged and bumped against the side of the ship in the rolling waves.

"Yer sure ye want to do this?" Josiah asked as I lowered myself down.

"You won't take me, so yes. I have no other choice." I grabbed the oars.

"Head that direction." He pointed. "That's north. Ye know how to navigate?"

"Of course I do." I heaved the oars through the water, pulling away from the boat, only to be forced back to it, then another wave came and pulled me away. I used the momentum to gain some ground but realized just how difficult it would be.

Captain Josiah shook his head at me. "I hope to see you again, miss."

With effort, and luckily some help from the ocean current, I was able to pull away from the ship. I watched it sail away, the movement so subtle that it appeared as if it weren't moving at all until it was far enough away and there was no turning back.

I had made a very foolish decision.

Within the hour, my shoulders burned with the effort of rowing to shore, and I still had hours to go. No matter how many times I looked over my shoulder, it didn't bring the horizon any closer.

The sun beat down.

The waves seemed to fight me.

And my hands blistered.

I kept my head down as I rowed, focused on keeping my breathing level. Even with my hat shielding me, the sun burned. This was probably the most foolish thing I'd done in my entire life. All I could hear was the wind in my ears and the waves splashing against my small, poor excuse of a boat.

My mother might not have wanted me to captain my own ship, and I might have felt like she was wrong, but I was certainly a fool to be *rowing* to shore. If I wasn't careful, my anger and desire to prove my worth to my mother was going to get me killed.

Something about the water changed at the same time a gust of wind blew my hat off my head. I reached up and snatched it before it disappeared into the ocean.

My eyes locked on the black sky in the distance. It wasn't darkness from the setting sun but an incoming storm.

My stomach sank with dread.

I glanced over my shoulder and thought I could see a mountain peak on the edge of the horizon. I was still several hours from shore, and the storm was moving fast.

I was in trouble.

I tried to tap into the small reservoir of strength I had left and rowed with all my might. Lightning flashed, and I slowly counted. *One. Two. Three . . .* until I got to eleven when I heard the thunder.

The storm was eleven miles away.

I couldn't gauge how far away I was from shore. The same distance? Who knew?

But I didn't have a chance of outrunning it.

I gritted my teeth against the pain in my hands and ache in my shoulders. It didn't feel as though I'd moved a foot, let alone miles, when the storm's waves reached me. I pulled on my pack and placed the oars inside the boat, knowing it was pointless to fight the sea. The rough waves tossed, and I lay down on my side.

As a child, I remembered storms never scared me on land, but being on the sea was completely different. And being in a rowboat, I was completely terrified.

My heart pounded, and goosebumps rose on my body. I covered my ears, feeling very small and insignificant being heaved about in the enormous swells.

I suddenly found myself feeling something I'd felt a few months earlier, at Castle Bay.

Hopelessness.

As the waves attacked my tiny boat, I recalled being in the ocean, beneath the waves, being dragged by a current I couldn't fight.

Had that been what my mother meant when she said I almost died?

No, it was something beyond that. And like so many times before, I saw a flash of memory of myself standing in front of an abandoned shed in the middle of the night. Another flash of lightning and the memory snapped away.

Rain pelted my exposed body. My small boat was at the mercy of the sea. I was completely useless against it. My stomach lurched as my boat dived down one wave and was dragged up another. Water started to pour in, and then the rain increased, striking me with such force it stung. Soaked to the bone already, I curled up and held onto myself, praying to the ocean that it would allow me to survive.

I wondered if anyone would miss me when I was gone. Would they even know I had drowned? Or would they assume I made it to land? How long would it take for them to realize I wouldn't be returning home? With the way the pirates had avoided me, I doubted it.

A wave lifted the boat, and I cried out before plunging into the waters. Tossing and turning as I rolled with the waves, I couldn't find any sense of direction until I surfaced just as unexpectedly as I'd been flipped.

I gasped for breath.

Another wave came toward me, and I swam for it, hoping to ride it instead of getting buried by it. I'd heard that the sea could be calm under the waves, but I would need to be a whale!

Or a siren . . .

The thought hit me at the same time as the wave.

It carried me while my mind raced. I tried to look through the storm to gain some bearing, but it was impossible through the curtain of rain and the sky the same color as the angry waters.

If my hallucination from a few days ago was real . . . I might actually be able to survive the storm.

I couldn't decide whether to risk it, to plunge under the waves and try to summon the transformation. I didn't have enough time to recall all the siren lore or to weigh the dangers and advantages of me becoming a siren.

The sea chose for me, sinking me again as two waves collided. Only, this time, I focused on my body. If I was going to survive this storm, I had no choice. I had to transform.

But one thing was certain—if I became a siren, I wasn't losing my new boots.

I tugged them off as quickly as I could manage and hugged them to my chest, and wiggled my boot dagger holster off and shoved it inside of one of my boots. My toes felt the cold water for the first time as I kicked forward. I tried to summon whatever it had been that caused me to start to change last time.

I recalled panic as I was about to drown. Fear from seeing the sirens. And determination to survive.

It was that determination I clung to.

Come on, fins! Appear or whatever I have to say! I thought.

Almost instantly, I gulped in a breath. And I smiled to myself in relief. I reached up with one hand and felt the frilled gills on the sides of my neck. I looked down at my body and saw the glittering scales of a fish-like fin. I couldn't see the colors in the dark water, but I didn't care. I needed to get to shore, or at least near it enough to be safe.

Being under water, I had to take a gamble on which direction to go. The waves had hurled me about, and I'd lost sight of the horizon. I hoped the ocean was on my side.

It wasn't so easy to figure out swimming either. Moving my legs up and down together at the same time—in the form of a fin—felt clumsy and unnatural, and I wasn't certain I was swimming at all. I had to get past my instinct to try and kick one leg and then the other and started moving them together until I finally swam forward.

There was also something frighteningly exciting about being under the waves, able to feel the current without the pain or pressure or the waves crashing against me. I also chose to ignore the deep pit of fear in my stomach while trying not to look at the deep blackness below.

Without warning, a current dragged me forward. It was stronger than anything I'd felt before, and I knew I must be caught in a riptide. I tried not to panic, taking deep breaths and swimming with it until I was able to swim out. Only, I couldn't swim out.

A dark shape appeared in my path, wide and dangerous looking. And I realized it was a huge stone too late. I tried to swim away, but the current was too strong. I held tightly to my boots with one arm and tried feverishly with the other to grab on to something, anything.

As I struck the stone, rough barnacles tore my flesh.

I cried out as I was dragged, pulled back, and thrust against the stone once more.

I whipped my tail and got away from the dangerous place. The ground below became shallower until the waves beat faster, signaling I was near shore.

Finally, clawing my hand through the sand, I heaved myself out of the water and onto shore.

Breathing in air hurt the gills in my neck, and the sand felt like acid under my body. Like a sunburn, only worse. The rain offered no comfort. I found myself wanting to crawl back into the water, but the scales on my legs began to shed like a snake, and I cried out in agony when I tried to move.

The gills on my neck finally closed, and I looked around the small beach to try and distract my mind from the pain. The rock I'd been beaten against was a huge boulder that should have belonged to a mountain. Instead, the opposite side ended at a tree line.

I wasn't on the shore of Terricina.

I was on an island in the middle of nowhere.

SEVEN

Being stuck on an island without food or water was a *fantastic* experience.

I remained curled up under a nearby tree I had somehow managed to drag myself to and fought for sleep that night.

When the sun rose, I didn't want to move. I stared at the sea, tears welled up in my eyes, and wanted nothing more than to pinch myself awake from this nightmare and have a hot bowl of grits for breakfast. But there was no waking from this because it wasn't a nightmare.

I considered returning to the water and transforming to a siren to swim to shore. But I didn't know what sort of stamina I had, if I could swim that distance in one go, or what dangers lurked between me and my destination. Any manner of monsters could have been between me and the opposite shore.

It was one thing to discover I was a siren, and another to realize it had been hidden inside of me. To transform once was a hallucination. To transform twice meant it was real. I wondered if my mother knew, and my mind circled back to the thought that she very well could have known all along and kept me under the watchful eye of captains who would prevent me from discovering it.

Perhaps my being a siren was some sort of curse and she didn't want me to be a captain because she didn't want to risk someone else finding out? Or maybe my being cursed had to do with Castle Bay? Or maybe I'd been cursed *at* Castle Bay?

My head hurt.

I sat my back against one of the damp palm trees, naked save my slightly shredded shirt, and tried to comprehend what it meant to be a siren. I had discovered one thing about becoming a siren—my clothes did *not* transform with me. By some miracle, my pack had made it through the storm, though the clothes inside were completely soaked. I'd also somehow kept hold of my boots, though they were useless on the sandy beach. My pearl necklace had also survived. I fished out my wet clothes and laid them out on a rock.

Luckily I was alone and didn't need to worry about anyone seeing me walk around the island without anything on. It was bigger than I initially thought, with a small hill in the middle covered with trees. There were even small pools of water from the rain, I just hoped they wouldn't dry up before I could get off or saved.

However, the only source of life were birds and bugs. I couldn't find anything to eat, save grass and a few fruitless berry plants.

By noon, I had walked the entire width of the island, ending at my clothing. My shirt was dry and my pants mostly dry, so I put them on, then leaned against the warm boulder and looked down at the scratches on my arms from the barnacles. I'd scrubbed them out in one of the pools of fresh water, but they were still red and angry.

I thought being stuck on a ship with no wind was boring.

Here, I was completely alone!

I managed to keep myself relatively busy by searching for dried reeds—there were none. I ended up picking up whatever pieces of wood and palm leaves I could find and laid them out in the sand to dry.

If I could create a fire, I might be able to get off this island.

Finding a way to start a fire proved more difficult than I'd hoped. I sat on the still-warm sand as the cool night gathered. I struck rocks together I'd found on my walk around the island. I had been hoping the stones would spark and be able to start a fire.

When I was finally too exhausted, and my fingers ached too much, I lay down and tried to get some sleep. But I struggled between shivering from the cold and my stomach growling.

The next morning, I sat on the beach, exhausted, starving, and frustrated.

On the horizon, I saw the tip of a mast now and then. Ships sailed just out of reach. If my little island wasn't in the path of a ship, no one would find me. And by the looks of the ships going east and west on the very edge of my vision, I was in the wrong location to be found and rescued.

My stomach growled louder than ever.

I got up, dusting off my legs, too desperate to sit any longer.

Captain Josiah should be arriving back in Port Mere right now, I thought glumly. *Which means Mother knows I was foolish enough to attempt this on my own. I only hope she doesn't come after me.*

The waves licked at my toes like an excited puppy, and a tingling sensation tickled up my feet and legs, giving me the urge to go in the water.

I tugged off my only pair of pants, tossing them to the sand, then stepped into the shallows and walked until I was in up to my waist. I tried lowering my hands in the water and letting them rest, hoping the fish would be curious enough to get closer. Apparently, fish aren't as brainless as they appear, and they wouldn't get near me. I tried snatching them but only managed to splash around and expend more energy.

I stood with my back toward the sea and scanned the shoreline for a stick I could sharpen and make a spear.

"Now, *that's* what I call a pirate booty!"

I spun around, and to my complete and utter shock, *The Sea Devil* floated in the distance with a small boat rowing toward me. Sky sat in the boat with a handful of men.

I gasped and darted for my pants to cover myself. "You could have shouted a warning!" I yelled at him. But I'd never been so relieved to see him. "How did you find me?" I tugged on my pants hastily.

"We passed Captain Josiah. He told us you sailed out in a rowboat to make it to shore." His voice drew nearer, and then I heard him splash as he jumped out of the boat into the water. "Of course, Captain Pan didn't believe him, and we started sailing the coast for any sign of you."

I grabbed my pack. "Pretty amazing you found me, to be honest." I gave him a relieved smile as I hurried over.

"Yeah." Sky gave me that adorable grin of his, his scar tugging, and he opened his arms to give me a hug.

I waded into the water and wrapped my arms around him. "I'm so relieved you found me."

"Of course you are. I'm happy to see you too." He gave me a warm squeeze.

I didn't realize how exhausted I felt until Sky had to help me into the boat. Any other time, I would have objected and told him I could manage on my own, but I hadn't eaten for two days, had been stuck in the sun, and hadn't recovered from swimming through the storm.

I leaned against Sky while the men rowed back to the ship.

"How did you survive?" he asked, stroking my cheek.

"I was thrown into the water," I mumbled. "I didn't know what else to do, so I turned into a siren and swam for it. I had to hope that I would arrive on shore because I couldn't see anything under the water." Sky's body went rigid, and I looked up at him. "Sky? What's wrong?"

"It's nothing." He flashed a quick smile. "Seems like you had quite the adventure."

I closed my eyes and rested my head on his shoulder again. "I could sleep for a week."

"Captain Pan won't allow that, but he'll probably let you sleep the rest of the day."

"James can shove it where the sun don't shine," I muttered.

"Just don't let him hear you say that. Don't roll your eyes, I mean it. He's the captain now."

Sky knew me too well to not be able to see my face and know I'd rolled my eyes. I didn't bother answering because he was right. As much as I hated that James was now the captain of the ship I'd fought for, he was still a captain and still deserved respect.

But I was going to make him earn it even if he had just plucked me off an island in the middle of nowhere.

We reached the ship, and Sky grabbed the ladder swinging over the side. He held it steady while I started to climb.

"Are you certain you can—"

"Shove a fish in it!" I made it to the deck, without any help, and set my feet on the other side.

James stood there in his gaudy captain attire, the same he'd worn when he'd been presented the ship, with his hands tucked behind his back.

He nodded his head at me. "You're alive, I see."

"Sorry to disappoint you."

He arched an eyebrow. "You're welcome."

Sky landed on the deck beside me and cleared his throat loudly before ramming his elbow into my side. He hinted at me with his head.

I rolled my eyes again. "Thank you for rescuing me."

Sky coughed in his hand.

I gritted my teeth. "Captain."

James's lips curled in a little smirk. "That was difficult for you. While you're on board the ship, I'd like you to help the cook with his tasks. His name is Louis."

The hair on the back of my neck bristled. "You know I was raised on ships. I'm just as valuable as any other crew member on board. You have no need to banish me to the galley."

"This is our maiden voyage. All positions are currently filled, and I'd rather put you to work somewhere." He shrugged. "So the galley is where you are assigned." But his smirk didn't leave his face.

I found it rather insulting to be put on kitchen duty, but at least James didn't make me the cabin boy. "I suppose I should thank you again," I said and gave a flourishing bow. I adjusted the strap of my pack as

I passed him, and I went to slam my shoulder against James's side, but he anticipated the movement and stepped aside.

"Captain, a word," Sky said.

My ears perked, and I overheard him whisper, "She said she turned into a siren and swam to the island."

"A siren?" James looked back at me.

I stopped walking, intentionally meeting his gaze. If they were going to talk about me, I deserved the opportunity to listen.

But James put his hand on Sky's back and guided him away.

So I stormed down to the lower deck and climbed into a hammock for some rest before I would be forced to interact with anyone else.

Luckily it didn't take long for me to fall into a solid rest, but when I woke, it was to someone shaking me. I peeled my eyes open and found a short, round man with a mustache staring at me. He grinned. Several of his teeth were missing. I rubbed my eyes to make sure he was really there.

"You are Odette. I am Louis. You vill come 'elp, yes?" I couldn't pick out his accent.

"What if I say no?" I grumbled.

The man's smile dipped to a frown. "I vill tell Captain and 'e will not be 'appy. I vould rather not. You seem a smart girl."

I groaned and made my way out of the hammock, nearly falling in the process. "Do you have any food ready for me to eat? I haven't had anything in a few days."

"Of course! This vay." He limped between the rows of hammocks to another set of stairs that led to the kitchen and beyond. One leg was gone below the knee, and he had a wooden leg in its place.

"How do you get your boot to stay on your leg?" I asked once we made it down to the galley.

"Same as you." He bent down and tugged at the boot on his good foot.

"Not that one."

"I know." He chuckled. "Food for you." He quickly put together a chunk of bread, some cheese, and even fresh grapes.

I was so hungry and thirsty I barely even enjoyed the delicious food. I also ate nasty hardtack and an apple, then drank a good three or four mugs of water.

"'Ow long are you knowing of Captain Pan and Sky?"

"My entire life. Sky and I have always been inseparable. James . . ." I sighed. "I guess I've known him as long, but he's not exactly the type who takes a liking to girls like me. I don't know if it's because my mother is the head pirate, or if he's just intimidated because I don't fawn over his muscles like the other girls in town. We just don't seem to get along much."

"Ah yes. He is 'aving lots of attention from girls. You are jealous, no?"

"What? No!" I got up and set my bowl back on the counter so he could use it again. "I have nothing to be jealous of. I'm with Sky. He is more important to me than Hook will ever be."

"Hook? Ah. Vhy did 'e change his name?" Louis set potatoes on the counter in front of me.

"I don't know to be honest. I heard he got tired of people calling him that. I suppose it's because the way he lost his hand is a little sensitive to him."

"How was that?" He handed me a small, thin knife.

I shrugged. "I don't know. I've heard different stories. Some say it got eaten by a saltwater crocodile, others say it was a shark, and I've also heard he cut it off himself to sacrifice it to the sirens." I glanced at the man. "How long have you been a cook on the ships?"

"I used to sail vith your mother, vhen you vere a vee lass." He smiled. "I vas younger den too, of course. And thinner." He patted his belly and let out a laugh.

I don't know why, but Louis made me comfortable. I relaxed. "I suppose it's good we have you on board?"

"No vun complains, but no vun else can cook."

I joined his laughter that time.

After he taught me to peel with the paring knife, I set to work cleaning the potatoes and prepping them for our dinner. Louis showed me which seasonings and other vegetables to put in the stew. He explained that stews were good for ships because they were easy to make and satisfying.

I personally rang the bell, signaling the crew dinner was ready.

Sky walked over and kissed my cheek as soon as he entered the room. "You're looking a little better."

"What did you tell James?"

"About what?"

I leaned my chin down and cocked a brow.

Sky glanced around. "He wants to talk to you after dinner. Just wait until then."

I tried to remain as patient as possible but also made sure to make myself known. I got my dinner and sat beside Sky. James sat across from us. The young man I'd seen a couple of days ago on James's ship, the one who had introduced himself as Gerard, sat beside James.

"What brings you to a pirate ship?" I asked, locking my attention on the stranger.

"Captain Pan is helping me with something," he answered cryptically, his green eyes staring at me intensely.

"What is that?"

"My business is my own," he replied flatly. He scratched the stubble on his jaw with the back of his fork.

I rolled my eyes to Hook. "He takes after you."

James ignored me.

I looked back at Gerard. "My name is Odette."

"I heard." He nudged his head in James's direction. "Captain Pan told me when he saved you."

"You never *did* tell me why you changed your name." I dipped my bread in my stew.

Sky leaned to me. "Odette, back off."

"Back off? I only asked a question!"

"Yeah, with the intent of getting information to use as ammunition later. I know you." Sky smiled and kissed me on the cheek.

I didn't miss the hesitation in James's chewing as he glanced from me to Sky and back. I drew in a long breath.

Was James jealous?

The thought made me both panic and feel giddy at the same time. Because *that* was the best ammunition I could ever ask for. Something about that thought made me extra giddy.

"If you won't tell me about your hand, perhaps you'll tell me about who you are interested in?" I quirked a grin. I took Sky's hand and draped it over my shoulders.

"Not a chance," he said flatly.

"So there is someone!" I knew it.

James locked his gaze on mine. "Yes, there is."

"And? Who is she?"

"Why don't we talk about how you survived on the island?" Sky asked.

James nodded. "What was the worst part for you?"

"I think the worst part of being stuck on an island was being alone."

"For you, I imagine that was extremely difficult," James threw in.

I narrowed my eyes. "Why do you say that?"

"Because you never stop talking." James's lips spread into a big grin.

I gasped.

Sky laughed, and even Gerard broke a smile.

I scowled at Sky and jabbed my finger in his ribs. "Don't be rude."

"He's right." Sky shrugged. "Don't take it personal. You know it too."

"No more kisses for you." I pulled out from under his arm and pushed him away when he tried again. "Where are we headed?" I asked James.

James's lips teased a smile. "We're heading to Delphi."

"I'd like to go on shore with you when we arrive." I spooned the last of my stew into my mouth.

"We will see," he replied. He got to his feet. "Odette, I need a word with you." He motioned for me to follow.

I cleaned up my bowl before I followed James to the upper deck.

James went to the helm and relieved the sailor so he could get his dinner.

"What did you want to talk about?" I asked.

James kept his eyes on the stairs where the sailor disappeared, then lifted his gaze to the sea. "Sky told me you believe you changed into a siren."

I flexed my jaw, my hands fiddled with the bottom of my shirt.

"What makes you believe you became a siren?" James looked sideways at me.

"I don't *believe* it. It really happened. But I'm not telling you unless you tell me how you lost your hand." I folded my arms to stop myself from picking.

He inhaled through his nose and looked over at me. "All right."

I nodded. "I was in the rowboat, got hit by a storm, and the waves threw me into the sea. I had no choice than to transform or I was going to drown."

"You act as if this isn't the first time it's happened."

"Because it's not," I blurted before I could stop myself. Of course I had to let slip to *James* of all people. I turned away.

But my outburst *really* got his attention.

James glanced around again, and I realized it wasn't only to make sure we were alone. It was as if he were afraid someone else could overhear us in spite of the drinking song being bellowed from the belly of the ship.

"I thought it was a hallucination the first time," I muttered.

"Tell me more," James urged, his voice low.

"I got . . ." I sighed and folded my arms. "Why does it matter?"

"Because it's very important." His brown eyes locked on me, intense with sincere earnestness.

"I got pulled into the sea by a siren a few days ago. When I sailed with Captain Avery and we were returning to port. I thought the siren was going to kill me. And then, when I ran out of breath . . . The siren let go." I bit my lip and closed the gap between myself and James. "You *can't* tell my mother. Because if you do and she finds out I'm a freak . . ."

He shook his head. "How do you know you transformed?"

"Because I could breathe."

James's eyes took on a glint, one I knew to be joyous, though his smile only lingered on the edges of his lips. "Go on."

"There's not much else to tell. When I looked down, my fingers were webbed, just like the siren, and I had gills. To top it off, I swam to the surface so fast, I couldn't believe it." I shook my head. "I know it sounds crazy."

"And what happened in the storm? When you did it again?"

I shrugged a shoulder. "I knew I was going to drown. But I wasn't going to let that happen, and . . . sort of just did it."

This time, James's smile spread. "I'll be damned."

"What does it mean?"

"It means you're crazy." He straightened and returned his attention forward.

EIGHT

hat's rude." I frowned. "And uncalled for."

"I was teasing," he replied, and his grin showed it.

I put my hands on my hips. "How did you lose your hand?"

James's teasing smile faltered, and he looked at me. It was almost as if it hurt him that I'd asked. He cleared his throat and faced forward. "I'll tell you another time."

"James—"

"It's Captain."

I flexed my jaw. "Well then." I glared. "You had your father sleep with my mother to arrange this. You only became captain because your father can't keep it in his pants."

"That's disrespectful, Odette," he snapped.

"But true! You don't even deny it. And you agreed to tell me. What sort of captain are you if you go against an arrangement as easy as that?"

"That's enough."

Anger started to boil in my chest. "You didn't earn this ship. You didn't earn the title of captain." I glowered. "You're just as despicable as your father." I turned on my heel.

"Odette!" he yelled.

I stopped dead in my tracks and looked over my shoulder at him. On the inside, his shout had startled me. I'd always pushed his buttons without him reacting much, but there he stood, anger and hurt in his gaze.

"You will learn to call me captain and show me respect while you are on board *my* ship. You clearly don't know what I've done to earn this ship, and yes, I have earned the right to be called *captain*. It is not my fault you don't remember. Get a mop and swab the deck."

"Pardon me?" I blinked.

"You heard me. You won't be allowed to sleep tonight until every inch is spotless."

"It's a new ship, and I've barely slept in—"

"Do it. Now." His voice was calm but had the sharp edge of a sword and the burn of anger.

This was the lightest punishment he probably could have given me.

As I got the bucket and lowered it into the water, I understood I had crossed a line. Had he been Captain Avery, I never would have spoken to him in such a way. It was completely within his right to do what he was doing. I was a crew member who had stepped out of line.

I didn't say another word of objection. I didn't even slap the mop around or risk doing a crappy job. My aching muscles protested as I moved the mop back and forth. The drinking song below grated on my nerves. Within a few minutes, my legs began to tremble from weakness, but I wasn't about to stop.

I heard footsteps before James said, "Odette, you can be done."

"I haven't finished," I replied, bitterness in my voice.

He exhaled through his nose. "You need rest."

"I haven't finished," I repeated, putting an emphasis on each consonant.

James reached out and put his hand over mine, stopping the mop. "Odette."

I finally lifted my eyes.

His expression was soft. His brown eyes looked like an apologetic puppy. "Go get some sleep. You can barely stand."

"You gave me an order, *Captain*."

James stared at me, then let go and straightened. "Why must you be so stubborn?"

"I wouldn't want you to think I'm disrespecting you by not finishing your command."

"Blimey, Odette!"

I flinched.

He ran his hand through his black hair. "I'm trying to apologize," he said through gritted teeth. "Go below deck and get some rest. You can finish in the morning if you're so set on following orders."

I dug my thumbnail into the wood of the mop and nodded softly.

James lingered.

I thought he wanted to add something, but he turned and walked away, muttering a curse under his breath. I knew I was stubborn. My mother had raised me to be such. One of my biggest flaws was never knowing when to stop. I knew it. But it still hurt that he hated me so much. What did I ever do to him?

"Jame . . . Captain, wait." I dropped the mop and walked after him, reaching him quickly.

He turned and faced me.

"I'm sorry. You're right. You are the captain, and I should respect that."

He nodded to me.

"I . . . didn't thank you for saving me either. Not properly. If you hadn't come, I would have been forced to try and swim for the land. Or would have died." I wrung my hands. I needed to stay on his good side.

"You're welcome."

"I um . . . I guess I'll see you in the morning," I added awkwardly. When he stayed silent, I turned away and headed for the stairs.

"You know, Sky isn't loyal to you."

I turned.

James held his hat in his hands and picked at dust that didn't exist.

"What do you mean?" I pressed.

He lifted his gaze to me. "You're attached to him. But he's using you, mate." He flashed a half-grin, I dared say it was apologetic. "You're better off as friends, not lovers."

My lips tightened. "Oh? And why do you say that?"

"Think about it. You saw him on my ship, didn't you? When you left with Captain Josiah?"

"I know he's friendly. A bit of a flirt," I admitted.

"A bit?" He hinted with his brows.

"I believe you are jealous, Captain Hook. Because he has someone who cares about him, and you don't."

James laughed. "He does, does he? Someone loyal in spite of it all? You grew up with him, the same as me, and you know what he's like." He stepped forward and took my hand. "Just like you know what I'm like." His brows softened.

My heart raced at his touch. Heat crept up my face.

He turned away.

I tightened my grip on his hand before he could leave. "Who is it that you like?"

"My ship, of course." He winked.

"James."

He shrugged and pulled his hand from mine.

I was suddenly overwhelmed by a rush of emotions. Embarrassment, desire, and suspicion. Before thinking, I impulsively snatched his hat. "Tell me who."

James stared at me, brows pinched in confusion. "What are you doing?"

"Tell me who!"

"Odette." He relaxed his stance and held his hands out to his sides. "What do you want from me?"

"To know. Come on." I grinned. "You can tell me. We're alone up here!"

"Give me my hat." He reached for it.

"Nah uh." I ran from him, to the edge of the ship. "Is it Sarah Beth?"

He blanched. "Sarah? No."

"Lucy?"

He rolled his eyes. "Give me my hat." He stepped close to me, close enough I could smell him, and he reached around me for his hat.

I yanked it away, but my arm struck the railing, and I accidentally dropped the hat. The wind caught it, and is spiraled over the edge.

That had *not* been my intention.

I gasped in horror and clamped a hand on my mouth.

James stared at me in shock. "You little . . . sea urchin! That's my captain's hat!"

I knew I would be furious if someone threw *my* captain's hat overboard. In honesty, I hadn't expected the wind to catch it. I just wanted to tease him by tossing it to the deck.

"I didn't mean to!" I exclaimed.

James pointed with his hook and it caught a glint of the moonlight. "You're going in after it."

"No, I'm not! It's night! The ocean is treacherous at night! And the waves have already carried it too far away. I'll buy you a new one when we dock."

He seized my arm and pointed toward the water.

"Hey!" I protested, trying to dig my heels in. "I'm not going in! James, ah!"

He shoved me against the railing. "One."

"You're being ridiculous! It's only a hat!"

"Two!" He wasn't going to let me get away with this, and he wasn't letting go. "Three."

That was my last warning. With all his strength, he dragged me over the edge. My weight did the rest of the work for him. Caught off-balance and with nothing to hold on to, I plummeted into the waves.

I gasped when I surfaced.

"Better swim fast so you can make it back to the ship!" James called from above.

I wished I hadn't been so impulsive. "You bilge rat! What if I die?" I yelled back as I treaded water and tried to keep my head above the waves.

He raised his hands up to his sides in an innocent gesture. "Turn into a siren."

"Stupid yellow-bellied codfish!" I shouted at him. "Is this your stupid ploy to see if I turn?"

James only waved back.

"Well I'm not going to!" I grumbled curses under my breath and looked around the dark sea for "Hook's" hat. I swam with the waves, hoping to find it still floating nearby. Even more, I hoped I could find it in the darkness.

And if James left me behind, so help me, I would make sure to haunt him!

I felt a deep-seated fear—and excitement—that there was an entire world in the ocean below to me.

Panic began to speed up my heartbeat.

Get the hat. Get back to the ship.

I spotted James's hat floating just a stroke away and my heart jumped. "There you are!"

I finally reached it, grabbed the soft fabric, then put it on my head before turning to head back to the ship.

But the current had carried me much further away than I thought possible, and the ship floated a good distance off. On the open sea, things always appeared much closer than possible, and my stomach dropped like a stone.

"I hope you send someone to help, you ungrateful swine," I muttered.

I kept my eyes focused on the lamplight aglow in the captain's quarters, rhythmically moved my arms, gulped in breaths, and yet my arms grew heavy, my lungs burned, and I didn't feel any closer than when I'd started swimming. I was *not* going to turn into a siren to satisfy James's idea to prove myself to him.

But I didn't look to be getting any nearer to the ship.

That same anguishing fear I felt when the sirens dragged me under settled into my bones. My heart raced like I'd never felt it before. I'd felt the adrenaline of a good swordfight, had my share of injuries, but to be left behind like this . . . thrown overboard for a mistake that was supposed to be flirting, left for dead, left behind to be dragged into the ocean . . .

Something brushed my foot, and I recoiled.

My breath came in quick gasps and I searched the pitch-black water of night for the source of what had touched me. The thought of sharks flashed in my mind, and I plunged my hand into the water and drew my dagger. I took slow, stretched strokes, keeping my eyes on the water.

It had to be my imagination.

We were too far out into the ocean for sirens. Perhaps even sharks.

But the ocean was full of sea monsters.

I tried to swallow, but my mouth felt like I'd just eaten hardtack. Fear was beginning to override my sanity. My clothes were beginning to feel heavy. My body was becoming exhausted. No sailor, no matter how experienced, could swim against the waves of the ocean for a long period of time.

I tore my gaze away from the black water to glance at the ship again. To my relief, it was headed back toward me.

Apparently, James had *some* loyalty.

Then again, he likely knew my mother would hang him if he returned without me.

I tried to pick up my pace, but this time, there was a stroke from my thigh to my foot.

It wasn't a shark.

Sharks can't stroke your leg.

"You better hurry!" I shouted, trying not to move and not sink at the same time.

I adjusted my grip on the dagger, no longer caring if I returned James's hat to him or not. I just wanted to get out of the water.

I would have believed the light touch wrapping around my right leg to be seaweed had I been in shallow water.

When the grip tightened and squeezed, I sliced my dagger through the water, cutting at whatever grabbed me. Instantly, pain exploded into my right thigh, and I screamed in pain. I'd not only cut through whatever held on to me, I'd slashed my own leg. As whatever had held me began to fall away, a ripple of glowing purple dots spiraled down my leg and through the water, igniting tentacles and then a long florescent head with a triangle fin at the top.

A kraken.

A living, breathing, kraken.

NINE

All dignity left me. I screamed as loud as possible and turned to swim, but the tentacle re-gripped my leg, this time squeezing so tightly I thought it would tear my leg right off. I hadn't looked to see how far or near the ship was. I couldn't look away from the monster about to eat me.

The kraken dragged me under.

Another slice of the dagger and the tentacle dropped. I broke the surface and screamed again. The light on its body flashed and rippled white and pink, and more tentacles reached for me. One seized my waist, another gripped my wrist, and a third pinned my legs tightly together.

Helpless, I screamed a third time, now breathless with panic.

A cannon exploded and struck the water just feet away. Splashing water blinded me, the shockwave took my breath, and before I could gasp, the squid yanked me under again.

All went silent, save the muted sound of another cannon and another. Beyond the light of the squid, the cannonballs whizzed through the water.

If I transformed now, I would lose my boots. If I didn't, I would die.

There was only one choice. I didn't waste a moment before I transformed into my siren form so I could breathe. I couldn't, however, escape.

The nearer the kraken pulled me, the bigger I realized the creature was. It was probably as long as the ship. Maybe even longer.

I wondered what it would feel like to be eaten.

A cannonball followed by another slammed into the squid. A surge of color burst across the squid's body, a silent explosion before its tentacles released me. Unconscious or dead, I didn't wait to see. I fought for the surface and gasped for breath the instant I broke through the waves.

James swam for me, one arm and then the other pulling him swiftly through the water.

"What are you doing?" I shouted at him. "Do you want to get eaten too?" I kicked my fin to swim toward him, only to feel an explosion of pain through my right side so intense I cried out.

"What happened?" he called, drawing nearer.

"I cut myself with my dagger. It's not a big deal."

James finally got close and reached out with his left arm, remembered he didn't have a hand, and extended his opposite. "Come on, I'll get you back to the ship."

"Oh, *now* you want to be a hero?" I laughed at him. "No, thank you." I pushed his hand away and started swimming past him.

"Odette, I'm sorry. Look, I didn't mean—"

"To throw me overboard or have me get attacked by a kraken?" I glared over my shoulder at him. "Because you sure meant to throw me overboard."

He flinched. "I shouldn't have reacted like that."

"But you did. And here I am." I continued toward the boat.

A group of men had lowered one of the rowboats into the water and were working on separating it from the ropes when ripples of red and white light ignited beneath me.

"James!" I shouted.

Tentacles shot up all around me, provoking the waves into a fury of movement that sent me crashing into one of the tentacles. It gripped on to me and dragged me back down into the darkness yet again.

This time, however, the initial panic and terror were gone, and I wasn't going down without a fight. I held fast to the dagger in my hand and transformed into a siren before it could get the better of me. I kicked my tail and slashed the thick tentacle.

It reacted by slapping me with the tip of a smaller tentacle. I saw a burst of white and shook my head. But the slap had stunned me, and I'd dropped my dagger. I watched it disappear into the inky blackness.

I had no weapon. No way to fight.

I pushed against the tentacle, managed to wiggle my slippery fin out of its grip, but only for a moment before it moved and regripped me before I could escape. Frustrated, I screamed with all my might.

The tentacles tremored with a yellow flash of light, and I had a thought.

If a siren could use her song to lure a sailor to their death, was it possible my voice could have another effect in a different way? Could I use my voice to stun the kraken?

From the corner of my eye, I spotted James swimming toward the kraken at full-speed. The kraken's gaze was locked on me, distracted by my attempts to escape. It never shifted its murky, disgusting eyes toward James.

I sucked water in my mouth and let out another scream.

Once again, the body trembled with yellow light and the tentacles curled. This, of course, caused the kraken to draw me uncomfortably close to its body, only feet away from its beak-like mouth.

Through the dim light radiating from the kraken, I saw James's body.

Not a human body, oh no.

The body of a siren.

He had a shocking red tail with a black fin along the back, thin and wispy in the water. His black hair moved in the water with the same rippling movement. In his hand, he had his long, deadly, captain's sword. And he led with it toward the monster's head.

Its beak opened.

I gasped three more times to get enough air to scream one final time, then squeezed my eyes shut, anticipating the feeling of being crushed by the powerful creature's mouth.

Pain didn't come.

I thought it had put me in its mouth and swallowed me whole. But the tentacle's squeezing slowly ebbed, and I felt something much smaller grasp my arm. My eyes shot open, and James put his wrist nub on my cheek.

"It's just me! It's me," he soothed. His voice sounded odd in the water—muted, yet crisp.

I looked down.

The kraken's body began to sink. The colors that had once glowed in the dark were gone, and it wasn't long before the form disappeared completely, sunken into its grave.

"You're a siren!" I shouted, moving my eyes back to James's face.

"Back to the ship." James swam for the surface, dragging me along with him.

"James, I demand an answer!"

"We need to get you back on board and take care of your wound. You're getting blood in the water, and now with the kraken's body, we're extremely vulnerable to other creatures."

My heart rate began to slow down as we made it to the surface. The adrenaline was gone, and pain in my right leg radiated up into my hip and down to my toes.

"You can return to your human form by thinking about it," James explained.

"I know."

I didn't mean to rely on him so heavily to get me to the surface. I didn't *want* to rely on him for anything, but I could barely move my fin independently. "It hurts when I change back," I complained.

Stars appeared in my vision.

My tongue felt fuzzy.

We made it to the surface, and James used his left arm under my arms to keep me above the water. I didn't know if it was working, transforming back.

James's head tilted. No . . . it was my vision.

"Odette, you're pale." He looked down as if he could look through the water. "Is it your leg? How deep did you cut?"

A wave crashed against me, and something pumped into my back. I jerked, thinking it would be the squid again, but it was James's wretched hat.

"There they are!" Sky called. "James, we're almost to you!"

I had no strength left. I couldn't even move my legs.

"Odette," Sky gasped. He grabbed under my arms and hauled me onto the floor of the small boat.

I coughed and closed my eyes, trying to keep my breathing even.

"Why in Poseidon's ocean did you jump overboard at this time of night?" Sky scolded.

"Oh. You know. Perfect night for a swim," I replied sleepily.

James grabbed on to the edge of the boat. "I think she's lost a lot of blood."

"From what?"

He shook his head. "I heard her scream."

I felt Sky lay something over me and peeled my eyes open enough to see his sea-worn blue jacket over me. I broke into a coughing fit.

"She's bleeding," Sky announced. "Badly."

My head lolled to the side when I tried to get a look.

James grunted as Sky pulled him into the boat and he winced as he climbed in. He was naked, and another sailor handed him a jacket too.

The lamplight shone enough to expose the red hue to the wet spot beneath me and a nasty-looking cut to my right thigh.

Absently, I reached down and touched my leg. "I cut myself with the dagger . . ." I pulled my hand away and my fingers shone red.

"Don't think about it." James grabbed a handkerchief from one of the men and pressed it against my cut. It looked so tiny compared to the wound.

I winced.

"You got her?" someone called from the ship.

"Aye!" Sky shouted back. "She's hurt. Fetch medicine and supplies!"

"I'm just fine. It's only a scratch," I protested.

"You might've cut something inside," James muttered, squeezing so hard, I cried out. "I know. Shh. I'm sorry. We've got to stop the bleeding."

I pushed feebly against him, not realizing he was trying to help me to my feet. We'd somehow already made it to the ship. Had I blacked out a moment? Sky and James grabbed me under the arms and pulled me to my feet.

"I can do it myself," I mumbled.

"Oy, you can't stand," Sky protested.

"I'll get her up. Help me get her over my shoulder," James said. "Keep the jacket wrapped around her."

"James, this is unnecessary." I put my left leg up on the wooden rung.

"You sure you got her, sir? How are you going to get you both up the ladder with one hand?" Sky said, meaning no disrespect by it.

"I can manage, Scuttle."

Hands grabbed my hips, and Sky adjusted his jacket on my waist before putting me over James's shoulder. I tried to protest but couldn't open my eyes. I felt James rise to the ladder.

Sky patted my cheek and tried to move my damp hair from my face.

"Pull the ladder up," James directed.

The ladder suddenly jolted and began to rise. Pirates worked together to pull the ladder, dragging us up the side of the ship until we finally reached the top.

Gerard lifted me from James's shoulder carefully. "She's pale. Lost a lot of blood." He lifted the jacket and hissed. "That cut is nasty. We'll need to stitch it. She'll need ointment to prevent infection. Do you have anything like that in your stores?"

James landed on the deck and shook his head. "I don't know. Let's get her to my room. Put her on my bed. We need to get her dry, so she doesn't catch a cold. See about the wound." He swooped his left arm under my knees and his other arm around my shoulders, taking me from Gerard. "Stay awake."

"I got your hat." I motioned. "In the boat."

James didn't even look at me. His brows pinched and his eyes were tight with worry. Worry? He was worried about me? "Get rum, bandages, and a needle with whatever medicine we've got," he repeated. He carried me directly to his cabin.

"Just put me down." I tried to wiggle free while he carried me to the left side of the bed. "I'll be okay."

"Will you stop squirming?"

My legs slid off his left arm, and he nearly dropped me but somehow managed to set me on the edge of his bed. I wiggled to try and get up, but he grabbed my shoulder firmly.

"Odette. Stop. Now."

I blinked away the pressing darkness. "Would you treat any other sailor like this?"

"You aren't any other sailor."

"Yeah. Because my mom is the pirate queen," I mumbled.

"No." He kept his dark eyes on mine. "Because you're not like anyone else."

In my fuzzy mind, I saw a genuine look to him. He cared.

"You need to get out of your wet shirt, and we have to wash out your wound. Every sailor knows those two things," he insisted.

"You didn't need to throw me overboard to get my clothes off."

His neck grew pink, and a smile tugged at his lips.

I gave him a weak grin in return and gave up fighting him.

Gerard walked through the open doorway, his arms laden with blankets, rum, and a small box of medical supplies.

"Odette," James said gently. "Let me take care of you."

I didn't like it. But I also decided I wasn't stupid enough to try and make it below deck on my own, let alone try and change into dry clothing, or even take care of my cut alone. I'd seen men die of infections from a small cut on their hand. Even if I didn't want to admit it aloud, I knew the cut on my leg was in great danger of infection. And I was completely fine letting James help me.

"Gerard, fetch me her clothes, please? You can leave the things here. Close the door so we can give her some privacy. I may need another bottle of rum."

Gerard set the pile of supplies on the bed at my side, then left, closing the door behind him.

James helped peel my shirt from my body. Through a half-lidded gaze, I watched him avert his gaze while he held a blanket out toward me. "Can you manage your undergarments?"

"Yes." My fingers had no sensation, my arms felt like logs, and I knew I couldn't get anything off without help, but I still tried. Until I couldn't. "Would you mind?" I glanced at James.

His eyes darted to me. Pink crept into his dark cheeks, and he deliberately took the bottom of my shirt. His fingers were warm as they brushed my exposed skin. I hadn't realized until that moment how cold I was.

"I'm sorry."

I blinked at him.

He was apologizing. Actually apologizing.

James wrapped a blanket around me. "Now, I'm going to empty this bottle on your leg. It will hurt."

I licked my lips. "I didn't mean . . . the hat . . . it was an—"

"No," he cut in. "It was my fault. I never should have . . . done that. Thrown you overboard."

"I was trying to flirt," I replied, sighing.

James met my gaze and touched my cheek. "It was still foolish of me."

"It's not like I helped," I admitted. "I mean I *did* throw your hat overboard. That's very important to you."

He looked down at his hand. "I swore I wouldn't be a captain like my father."

"Why not? He's greatly respected."

"I think you mean feared. It is very different."

"What do you mean?"

He shook his head. "You look down on me because of my father's relationship with your mother. He will do anything to maintain his reputation. I mean anything."

There was a knock on the door, saving him from further explanation. "It's Gerard. I'm back with her clothing."

"Come in." James grabbed the cork and yanked it out of the bottle of rum, then held my leg carefully over the side of the bed.

The gash started at the front middle of my thigh and moved down and out toward my knee. It was definitely bigger than a scratch.

"You missed the kraken," James pointed out, giving me a smile that made my heart skip.

"I cut *through* the kraken," I corrected. I grabbed the rum from him and, before James could pull it from my lips, managed to get three big, burning gulps down my throat.

"That is for your leg." James plucked it from my fingers. "Gerard, help her with a shirt, will you?" He didn't warn me before tilting the bottle and pouring the burning liquid into the wound.

I couldn't suppress my scream. I gripped my thigh above the gash with both hands and squeezed in an attempt to prevent the pain from continuing up my leg and into my body.

Gerard put his hand on my back, keeping me upright.

It didn't work, and I gasped for breath.

"Sorry," James said for the second time that night.

There was a knock, and the door opened a crack. "It's Sky. Can I help?"

James's jaw flexed before he pressed a towel against my gash. I thought for certain he wouldn't want to deal with me on my own. He pressed hard enough to bring tears to my eyes, and I looked away while trying not to bite through my bottom lip.

"It's better if he helps," Gerard pointed out.

"He's just going to stitch me up, and then I'm going to pass out," I grumbled.

Sky climbed onto the bed. I knew he was being kind, but I found myself wishing he were James. I'd always sort of known my relationship with Sky was more out of convenience. We'd grown up together, so moving forward into a relationship had been expected. But to have me suddenly longing for James . . . I had definitely lost too much blood.

"I'll leave you to it," Gerard said, looking only too happy to leave.

"Get me another bottle of rum?" I called to him.

"Sure thing." He turned and left.

"Okay, I think her wound is pretty clean now. Thread that needle and I'll get it stitched up," James directed.

"That's really bad," Sky observed.

James shifted his attention from my leg. "Don't you faint on me! Odette is going into shock and probably going to pass out soon. I don't need you passing out too."

"Yeah," Sky said weakly.

"Since I only have one hand, I'll need you to push the wound together as long as you can while I stitch. Can you manage that?" His brows furrowed with worry.

Sky nodded but paled.

James looked at me with those big chocolate eyes of his. When our eyes met, I felt my whole body tremble. "You're going to be okay. Ready, Sky?"

Sky wrapped his hands on my thigh and pushed the wound together.

Tears stung my eyes, and a wave of nausea washed over me the moment of the first needle prick. My eyesight blurred, and I swayed. At the same time, the pressure from Sky's grip disappeared.

James spat a curse and yelled for Gerard.

The last thing I saw before caving into the darkness was James's handsome eyes and their intense worry. "Hang on!"

TEN

Metal groaned on metal with the motion of the ship rocking side-to-side. The familiar grating whine of a swinging lantern dragged me from my nightmare, out of the darkness of the ocean and away from the tentacles of the kraken.

When I opened my eyes, I found I was lying on a bed, and as my eyes blinked into focus, I discovered I faced someone's back.

The stuffy air stunk of stale cologne, infection, and sweat.

In the orange-pink hue of the sunlit room, I watched the shape beside me rise and fall in deep, soundless breaths. The sunlight spread across the bed through the warped windows, discoloring everything in the room with the same orange hue.

Dawn.

My gaze traveled the shape of James's bare broad shoulders, and I couldn't help myself but to reach out and trace the shape of a siren's tattoo on his shoulder blade. My gaze continued to the scar on his ribs and on down to the exposed hip bone barely covered with a sheet.

His black hair spilled across his pillow, and I moved my hand to the side of his face to smooth that hair. He wasn't awake to know what I was doing. I could actually admire him without hiding it behind anger or bitterness.

I licked my lips. They tasted of bile and had a thin film over them as though my breath had layered them with poisoned skin. Each blink brought a flash of memory—my leg burning as though it were on fire, the sound of my sobs and screams filling the air, and distant voices.

I rubbed my eye with the back of my hand and pulled the cover away. Where the stitches pulled through my skin, the flesh was red and swollen, and I didn't need to touch it to feel the heat of infection lingering, though it appeared I was on the mend.

James suddenly groaned as he stretched, drawing my attention to him. He rolled to his back, his black hair sticking up on one side as though he hadn't moved all night. He saw me and his stretch halted. "You're awake." Sleep clung to his voice, making it husky, which stole my breath.

There was something oddly . . . romantic about the room. The light streaming in behind him, the relieved grin on his full lips, and even the joy in his weary gaze.

As if his face wasn't handsome enough, I now had a full view of the body he always kept hidden beneath his shirt, and it was beautiful.

I got a proper look over his pecs, chiseled abs, and a tattoo on the front of his hip bone I didn't know he had. He had a couple of light scars on his back that carried across to his left side and disappeared against the bed, almost like claws of a beast, and a wide scar on his right shoulder. His right arm was also adorned with pirate tattoos—a ship, a cat sitting on top of a skull wearing a cute little pirate hat, and a compass. There were a few more details I'd like to get a better look at later.

A fevered memory flashed before me of me curled up and crying on James's lap. He had rubbed my back and rested his cheek on my head. He had been there through the entire fever from what I could recall.

I should have said something to thank him, but instead, I said, "My leg?" like a buffoon.

James propped himself up on his elbow and looked over my body to check the wound. "You're healing from an infection. You've been in and out for a few days, mate." He reached his left arm over and brushed my hair with the stump of his wrist. "Your fever's finally broke! That's good." He grinned.

My heart jumped.

I tore my gaze away.

I could *not* be attracted to James! Throwing the hat in the sea had just been a game. I tried not to look at his scruffy face, the way his chin dimpled in the middle, or the broken curve to the bridge of his nose.

James Hook was off-limits. Because I was *supposed* to be with Sky.

"You were quite ill," James continued. "Think you feel well enough to eat?" He climbed out of the bed, wearing only trousers, which did nothing to help my attempt at not staring at him. James opened his door. "Scuttle! Get some food, she's up!" He turned and caught me staring at the way his muscles shifted against his ribs. He flashed a grin.

I cleared my throat and ran my fingers through my scraggly hair. "If I've been out for that long, we should be at the capital of Terricina. What's it called again? Delta?" I asked through the lingering haze.

"Delphi," he corrected. "And uh, yes. But there's a little problem." He walked around the bed to my side and crouched to assess my leg.

"Care to elaborate?" I asked in a flat voice when the silence lingered too long.

He lifted his attention. "It's gone."

I blinked. "My infection?"

He shook his head "The city."

"What?" My eyes widened. "How can an *entire* city be gone?" I swung my legs over the edge, but the force of my right foot hitting the hard wood sent a wave of pain up my leg and radiated through my wound. I gasped so hard it hurt my chest.

"Oy, stop," he said, trying to push me down. "Gerard said there was a rumor the city had been dragged into the ocean."

"Gerard?" I asked.

At the mention of his name, I recalled Gerard had helped stitch up my wound while James held me on his lap. Gerard asked something about magic to heal and said his magic wouldn't work the same way on the open sea. And then he'd left and returned with an ointment, which he rubbed into the cut.

We pirates were normal people, not like the strange fae, trolls, goblins, or whatever magical creatures plagued this land. Normal humans. But Gerard had magic.

"Are you all right?" James asked, pulling me out of the memory.

"Yes." I cleared my throat again. My voice was exhausted. "I don't understand how a city can sink or how Gerard would know about it." I put my hands on James's chest to push him away, but as soon as I felt his exposed muscles under my hands, I didn't want to put them down.

I vividly recalled James had been the one to soothe me through the fever. He had stayed with me night after night, stroked my hair, dabbed my face with a wet cloth.

Not Sky. Why not Sky?

James moved his hand from my shoulder and brushed his knuckles against my cheek.

I lifted my gaze, my heart fluttering. I tried to argue it away as being lightheaded because I still hadn't recovered from the fever, that I trembled because I hadn't eaten for days. But the flutter and trembling meant so much more—I really did like him.

James lingered close. He touched my jaw with his thumb and traced it until he stopped at my chin.

My brain didn't connect with my mouth, and for that I was grateful.

For the first time, he'd caught me truly speechless, something he pointed out.

"Cat got your tongue?" he whispered. His breath washed over my face like the sea's breeze. He pressed his warm lips to my forehead, then brushed them against my cheek.

My heart beat against my ribs as though it wanted to hold on to James just as tightly as I did. I turned my face and met his lips.

His touch felt familiar. So familiar I didn't want him to ever part from me. We could lock ourselves in this room for the rest of our days, and I would be content. I didn't believe in destiny, but if I did . . . I might have dared let myself believe he and I were meant to be.

The door swung open, giving James just enough time to flinch, drop my chin, and straighten before Sky walked in. I didn't want James to pull away, but I couldn't bring myself to stop him either. He'd moved too quickly for me to grab and hold on to.

My head swam.

I wanted to yell at Sky for interrupting us.

James crossed to the chest and lifted the lid to grab a clean shirt, acting completely casual while Sky entered, carrying a bowl over to me, then sat at my side.

Sky smiled in relief. "I thought you were as good as dead! If Gerard hadn't been here with that ointment, or whatever, you would have died!" He handed me the bowl of food. "How are you feeling?" He touched my cheek, but I didn't get the same zing I did with James.

I looked down at the oatmeal. Or was it grits? Some sort of breakfast I wasn't in the mood for but knew I needed to eat.

"She should keep her leg up," James said. He'd already tucked in his shirt and was buttoning a blood-red vest over it.

"Oh, right." Sky stood and picked up both of my legs and placed them back up on the bed. "There we go." He winked.

My heart skipped. Between Sky's dashing looks and the heat of James's kiss, I didn't know what to think!

"Is the royal family safe?" I asked James, scooping up a glob and putting the tasteless stuff into my mouth.

"I am going now with a few men to see what we can learn." James shrugged on his black coat. "Scuttle will stay here with you and the remaining men."

"Oh no he won't." I got to my feet, shoved the bowl into Sky's hands, and took the thin sheet with me to at least cover my lower half. "Sky, get my pants. I'm not staying here."

James tilted his chin down and shook his head. "Odette, I don't think you can walk enough to keep up with us. I don't even think you could get pants on with that cut."

"I need to get that stone, James," I insisted.

His brows shifted and his lips tightened in a way that made me wonder if he knew something I didn't. "What stone?"

I tightened my lips. I hadn't meant to let slip that I was looking for it. "Nothing. It's just good for me to get fresh air, right? You need to look like you aren't a scallywag," I added. "You should brush your hair and shave. Look halfway decent."

James leaned to his looking glass on the wall and absently touched the bottom of his hair. He opened the drawer and quickly brushed through it, getting out all the knots. "Thank you."

"James, please. I should move my leg. It's stiff." I bunched the sheet and limped toward my captain.

James sighed and studied me. Finally, he rolled his eyes and took his metal hook from the foot of the bed. "There's a dress in the chest. Put it on and you can come."

"A dress?" I nearly shrieked.

"That or the sheet. You'll need this to help keep it on." He tossed me a length of rope, smiled, and strolled out the door.

I had half a thought to tie the rope around me and use the sheet as a makeshift dress, but I would look a fool. I pointed to Sky and then the chest. "Get it for me."

"You don't get to boss me around. I'm the first mate," he pouted. He set the bowl of barely eaten food on the desk and rummaged through the chest until he pulled out a beautiful blue dress. "I'm not even going to ask him why he has a dress." Sky held it up to him. "It's too small for him to wear."

"Oh, shut up and hand it over."

ELEVEN

I made it out onto the deck before anyone could leave me behind, although a handful of men already sat in the long rowboat.

James climbed down the ladder and sat toward the middle beside Gerard.

Sky remained on the deck, a glum expression on his face as he stopped at my side.

"What's wrong with you?" I asked, preparing to climb over.

"I didn't realize being first mate meant I wouldn't be joining on the excursions," he muttered, careful I was the only one who could hear.

I patted his shoulder. "There, there." I grinned, and he rolled his eyes at me.

After gathering my skirts—an obnoxious maneuver—I carefully lowered myself down to the boat. As long as I didn't put *all* of my weight on my injured leg, or bend my knee, my pain was tolerable.

A hand suddenly rested on my right hip.

I glanced down to see James steadying me.

"May I help you the last bit?" he asked. "The waves make it a bit difficult."

Indeed, the waves were causing the rowboat to rise and fall, and if I didn't time it just right, I would drop and likely injure myself again. Besides, if James was in the mood to be polite, who was I to refuse?

"That would be best," I replied.

Cool metal touched my other hip, and I reluctantly let my foot down from the last rung, holding my weight with my hands until James said, "Let go."

I obeyed, and he caught me with a gentle grunt. "I'm sorry."

He made no acknowledgement of my apology as he set me on my feet.

Peering up at his face, my breath caught, and I wanted nothing more than to touch the curve of his strong jaw and feel his lips once more.

"Just don't keep us delayed," he replied, but his voice held no edge, and his lips had a gentle curl to them.

All of a sudden, the sun felt too hot and the dress, stifling.

He pulled away too soon and took his seat. I sat opposite him, aware of the small group of men staring at us, most with knowing smirks.

"There are some questions I didn't get to ask you," I pointed out, hinting with my head toward the sea. "About that night you pulled me away from the kraken."

The men waited with bated breath, all trying to avoid my gaze while listening for James's response.

"We will speak when we get back," James answered cryptically.

I didn't say anything else while they rowed us to shore, though I had a million questions about that night.

"If the capital disappeared into the sea, are the king and queen even alive?" I started.

"We don't know," James answered.

"What happens if we get there and don't know who to talk to?"

"I'm sure we'll figure it out."

"What if they identify us as pirates and arrest us on the spot?"

James gestured to himself and then the ship. "They won't."

I quickly looked back at *The Sea Devil* and saw it had no skull and crossbones flag posted, and James didn't wear his typical regal pirate captain uniform. Instead, he had chosen to wear common blue trousers, mid-calf black boots, a white tunic, golden vest, and a matching short navy jacket in place of the long tailcoat. He also didn't wear his captain's hat, or any hat for that matter, and had replaced his big hoop earring for a small diamond stud.

"Are you nervous, miss?" Gerard asked with a smug look.

I shifted my attention to him, almost having forgotten he was there. "Not at all."

He shrugged. "You sure? You're injured. And you seem anxious about being a pirate in a city where being one is illegal."

James elbowed him in the side, but the unapologetic smirk remained on Gerard's face.

"I can handle myself, thank you very much," I said sharply.

"With a wounded leg?"

"Yes," I answered, and before James could intervene, I raised my good leg and kicked Gerard where I knew it would hurt the most.

He grunted and doubled over.

James snorted a laugh but put his fist to his mouth and tried to mask it—rather unsuccessfully—with a cough. "Odette," he scolded, but the grin plastered on his face showed he wasn't really upset at all.

Even the others chuckled with laughter.

I followed James's gaze to the shoreline.

Some sections had evident fissures as if the land had broken clean off. I looked down through the clear waters to the seafloor. As I predicted, I saw the edge of darkness revealing the drop-off only a few meters away.

"What would cause a city to sink into the ocean?" I asked.

"Likely the sea witch," Gerard suggested.

I frowned. "Those are only legends."

James looked at me with raised eyebrows. "Do you truly believe that after . . . everything?"

I understood then what he was hinting at. If we could turn into sirens, why couldn't the sea witch be real? After all, there had to be a reason why we were both humans and mythical creatures at the same time.

"Speaking of which," I started.

"When we get back," James insisted.

"How long are you going to keep it a secret from her?" Gerard said unexpectedly.

James's gaze snapped to him.

"What secret?" I looked at James, who refused to meet my gaze and looked like he might fling Gerard overboard. "Tell me *what*?" I put my hand on James's knee. "You mean to tell me *Gerard*, a stranger to our land, a man I've never met, knows more about me than I do?"

James tilted his head and grimaced. "When you put it that way . . ."

Something bumped against the side of the boat, making us rock to the right.

The face of the man behind Gerard paled. "Row faster!" he shouted.

It didn't take long for me to process what was going on. Faces of sirens peeked out of the water, sneering at us with fanged mouths. Together, they pushed against the port side of the boat, heaving with everything they had.

We leaned into it, keeping the balance. I was one of the three who'd put a hand on the opposite side to try and help, and my wrist was immediately seized by the webbed fingers of a siren and given a hearty yank.

James grabbed on to me, preventing me from going overboard, but one of the other sailors wasn't so lucky.

"We're not avoiding this," James muttered, looking around at his men.

One who had been rowing tried to use the oar to bludgeon a siren, but it was no fool. It grabbed on and let out a terrifying guttural cry that made me think of the bottom of a boat being torn apart on a reef.

"I can try and scare them off," I offered quickly.

"Odette, you don't understand," James objected.

I tried to get to my feet as the sirens pushed again. Unfortunately I sat on James's left side, and it was his hook that reached out to grab me. It snagged on the skirts of my dress, throwing me further off-balance. I ended up on his lap, rather ungraciously, with his hook still snared in my skirts.

"Will you listen for once?" James snapped. "I'm trying to tell you something important! I think these sirens want you."

I looked up at him, confused. "Why would they want me?"

"Because . . ." He sucked air between his teeth and shook his head. "Because there's things you don't know about pirates and sirens, Odette."

"The things you can tell Gerard and not me? The things clearly the other pirates know too? Something no one will tell me in spite of us being in this current predicament?"

James nodded his head. "We're all sirens."

"All?" I looked at all the pirates, and not one objected. "But how is that even possible? How could I not remember something that significant?"

"Because your memories weren't lost," James said. "They were t—"

The sirens heaved the boat suddenly in the opposite direction, throwing the boat off balance. Before James could pull me back by his hook, I went weightless and then plunged into the water.

"Odette!"

I expected it to be easy. Transform, talk to the sirens, get them to leave us alone, help the pirates back to the ship.

But as soon as I hit the water, two of the sirens grabbed on to me—one on each wrist. They both looked like me, not serpent-like sirens, with golden fish tails, patches of blue on their shoulders like armor, and the same blue scales on their foreheads like helmets.

"I only wish to speak with you!" I tried to remain calm but was completely helpless as they dragged two of the pirates deeper into the waiting darkness beneath me.

"Prince Ulrich will be anxious to speak with you, witch," the one on my left snarled.

I tried to look over my shoulder and back at the boat, hoping to catch a glimpse of James, but it was surrounded by sirens. The men dragged me toward the drop-off.

"Ow! You don't need to be so rough!" I protested.

"You didn't show us any kindness."

From the edge of the precipice, I could see mysterious lights at the bottom. The men didn't pause before they carried me down into the suddenly cooler waters.

Debris littered the ground—pieces of stone and broken buildings. There were few corals or natural underwater features.

"Is that Delphi?" I asked hesitantly.

"Yes."

"How long ago was she sunk?"

"We were taken into the sea before the winter ball," the man on my left answered.

"And no one has come to save us." The other glared at me.

As we drew nearer, the shapes in the darkness revealed their true form as the remnants of Delphi. Mighty marble pillars lay toppled in the streets or resting against crumbled walls or the side of a building. What should have been a road lined with small homes was a broken pathway lined with gaping holes. Those had once been the homes of politicians, tradesmen, maybe even fishermen.

I could only imagine how grand this city had been on the land with the white stones glistening under the afternoon sun, reflecting and igniting the land. I imagined the king and queen of Terricina had been very proud of their home.

Now, the buildings appeared ancient and forgotten. Glowing algae had been smeared on the walls of the buildings to offer some light and décor, though it was a poor excuse for paint. Small sea anemones were beginning to set up their homes in the crevices of the broken pillars and between the stones of the buildings. Small schools of fish darted about.

At the edge of the light, I caught the reflections of eyes, much like a wild animal's. Beyond the light, I saw a parent draw their child to safety. Neither was a siren like those I'd met at the Siren's Gate.

I tried to round my shoulders, appear braver than I felt, for as I neared the palace, my stomach lurched as if I'd been caught in a storm again.

The palace was shaped like an *I* with longer wings out in front. It was rather boxy but had two floors on the main and back section, while the front wings were one level. The top floor was crumbled on one side, and the sea-worn copper roof was missing on the front right wing. Other than that, the palace appeared well intact.

"Get Prince Ulrich," the man to my right called out as we neared the entrance.

Someone had been smart enough to use wood debris or seaweed to make small cages in which floated glowing jellyfish. I had to hand it to these people, they were resourceful.

A young man appeared. He had dark hair and striking green eyes, full of anger. He had a long iridescent blue and black tail. By the intensity of the glare on his face, I knew immediately he must have been Prince Ulrich.

"You," he hissed at me, hands balled into fists. "Are you satisfied?" He stopped mere inches from my face. "Was this your plan all along?"

I stared at him in stunned silence several seconds before I convinced myself to blink. "Do I know you?"

He laughed. "You . . . you're clever enough to have deceived my father, but you won't deceive me." He turned and faced me again. He eyed me up and down. "Hiding yourself as a pirate. I never would have imagined. Not until one of the scouts reported to me that an ancient siren pulled a girl into the sea and she became one of us."

"I'm sorry, I don't mean to interrupt your monologue, but I truly have no idea what you're talking about. I've never seen you before."

"Maybe some time alone will help you remember." Prince Ulrich pointed with his right hand. "Take her to the cave."

The men pulled me away from the front of the palace.

"You don't need to be so harsh!"

They took me to a mountain of stone with a gaping cave mouth. They shoved me in, and Ulrich stopped in the doorway with his men flanking him.

"Where is the contract?" he demanded.

I threw my arms up in frustration. "What contract?"

He folded his arms over his chest. "You truly don't remember?" He gave a little snort. "How convenient."

I sighed. "Not really. About seven months ago, I got injured and can't remember," I explained.

His face fell, and his eyes narrowed. "You mean you honestly don't remember? That means you don't remember how to undo the spell?"

"What spell?" I almost shouted in exasperation.

"The one that dragged us into the ocean, you fool!" He lurched forward, hands balled into fists.

My first instinct was to punch him, and my blow landed square on his cheek. Apparently, hitting as a siren was different than hitting as a human, and Prince Ulrich's head actually snapped to the side. I seized a rock and threw it at him. It turns out, stones don't really throw well under water, siren or not.

Ulrich blinked at me, stunned, and held his hand up quickly toward his men, who lunged forward to defend him. "If you were the sea witch, you would have used your magic, not your fist."

I blanched. "What? The sea witch? First, I'm not old enough to be the sea witch. Second, I don't have any magic. Third . . . what in the deep blue sea made you believe I'm a witch?"

His shoulders slumped. "I was told you turned into a siren," he repeated. "A pirate who is also a siren? I thought . . ."

"That automatically makes me the sea witch?" I rolled my eyes. "You're that desperate for help, aren't you?"

He slowly let his breath out, looking rather defeated. He reached up and grabbed a pendant hanging from his neck. "Yes. Because if I don't break this by the summer solstice, Delphi will be stuck here forever, as will my people." He gestured behind him. "Not to mention, my kingdom on land will have no ruler."

"That's foreboding," I said.

Ulrich made a very human gesture by running his fingers through his hair. "You have no idea. I need that contract. I need to break it."

"What's in the contract?"

"If I knew how to break it, do you think I would be demanding answers from you?"

I tilted my head. "I can understand why you might be upset. But I barely learned—or remembered—that I'm even a siren at all. I don't know how to help you."

"Perhaps you are too low on the rung of leadership to know," he pondered aloud.

"Unless, maybe, you have the summer stone."

He looked me up and down. "How do you know about that?"

"Everyone does. Just like they know about the witch," I shrugged.

"Well, it was lost when the witch sunk us. I recommend you get some rest."

I gasped. "You're leaving me here?"

Ulrich pointed to a hole at the top of the cave. "You'll get sunlight for the next few hours. I'll bring you dinner when the sea grows dark. If you won't answer my questions, perhaps your friends will."

I swam to the doorway and watched Ulrich's hand glow white. A gigantic boulder grated on rocks as it rolled and blocked my only escape route. I pressed my hands against it, then heaved with my shoulder.

And I was alone again.

Alone in a cave beside a city I supposedly helped sink.

TWELVE

I wished Ulrich had taken me with him so I could have at least overheard their discussion. After what seemed like ages, I wondered if they'd forgotten about me. I had no sense of time in the ocean, though I kept glancing at the opening in the cave above to try and gauge the passage of time. Slowly, the light overhead began to fade.

The sound of the rock grinding open actually made me excited.

Ulrich entered. "Your dinner. He held a dead fish in his hand.

I stared at the fish, then looked at him. "*That* is my dinner?"

"Yes."

"It's raw!"

There was a long pause between us while Ulrich let me process the stupidity of my statement.

"Of course it's raw," I finally muttered. "We're fish too." Still, I looked down at the fish carcass held out to me and couldn't imagine how it would taste. "Distract me with conversation. You mentioned old sirens. What did you mean?" I took the fish and turned it over, trying to figure out the best way to eat it. Ulrich hadn't brought any utensils, so I assumed he wanted me to just tear into it, but that thought was disgusting.

"When my people were pulled into the sea, we were all transformed into this." He gestured to himself. "We discovered some are more fish-like. Few can speak anymore, but one explained they have always been part of the sea. The longer we stay, the more like them we will become. At least, that is what they said. I wouldn't be surprised if they eventually lost their humanity completely. Flotsam and Jetsam, the two you met, say the sirens further down the coast have already resorted to nothing but singing and shrieking." He paused, watching me still examining the fish. "If you keep thinking about how to eat it, it's only going to be worse for you." He reached out, grabbed on to the fish in my hands, then tore the fin off and peeled it open, exposing the meat. "Aren't you a pirate?"

"Yes, I'm a pirate, but I've never had to eat raw fish like this!" I gagged.

"It was hard for all of us at first, but you will get used to it if you want to survive." Ulrich studied me with handsome green eyes, not so different from my own.

I bit into the fish and it tasted . . . just like fish. There wasn't anything exciting about it, just the strange squishy texture. It wasn't half as bad as I thought it would be until I realized on my third bite that I had to have eaten some of the entrails because the fish hadn't been gutted prior to me eating it, and therefore each bite I'd managed to get that stuff in my mouth too.

That was enough to make me shove the fish back at Ulrich and grip my stomach to stop myself from vomiting. I didn't want to experience vomit under water in a small cave with no escape.

"It happens to the best of us," was all Ulrich had to say. "I must admit I'm surprised you have no powers."

"I told you I didn't," I growled.

"We couldn't believe that until your inability to escape proved it." He gestured to the open entrance. "Would you like to come stay in the castle? I'm afraid the accommodations aren't what they would be on the land."

"I want to know what happened," I said firmly, not moving toward him. "I want to know about this sea witch and whatever spell she put on your people to make you sink. Why did she feel your people were such a threat? And what did you talk to the other pirates about?"

Ulrich shook his head. "You ask a lot of questions. I don't believe we *were* a threat. My father hasn't allowed men to murder sirens in years, and the shipping lanes don't cross in sirens' waters. As for your men, they confirmed you are not the sea witch and you've lost your memories fairly recently."

"What is next for us then? What do you want?"

Ulrich rubbed his chin. He was about a year or two younger than me but definitely seemed older. "If I show you what happened that day, perhaps you can see something I don't? Since I can't find the physical contract, this may be the best way to try and find a hint."

"How do you plan on doing that?"

He reached out a hand toward me.

I refused to take it.

"I don't bite." Ulrich gave me a sweet half-grin.

"I don't know that."

"Do you want to know or not?" One hand wrapped around the circular pendant I'd noticed earlier. It reminded me of my own pearl necklace.

I didn't know what he had planned, but I decided I had to trust this boy in order to find out or remain locked in a cold cave in a world I knew nothing of. I took his hand, and then to my complete and utter shock, Ulrich's hand began to glow green. I looked up and saw the same green aura surrounding his entire body, and in the hand that had clutched the necklace, he now held a beautiful green stone.

"The summer stone?" I muttered aloud.

He smiled coyly.

"You've had it all along?"

"I had to make sure you weren't the witch."

I gasped as I was suddenly pulled out of the sea and into a hazy memory.

I stood in a bedroom, buttoning up a green vest with golden buttons, but quickly realized I was seeing through Ulrich's eyes. I'd imagined, being a prince, he didn't get out of the castle much, but his skin was tanned, and the light shade of his chestnut hair told me he spent a lot of time in the sun.

He tucked in his shirt and pulled on an expensive silk vest but didn't button it. Instead, he leaned over his desk, studying a parchment with neat writing. His voice echoed in my head as he read the text.

Ulrich stopped to check himself in the mirror, remembered he needed to button his vest, and did so.

From what I could see in the reflection of the mirror, the room was elegant yet simple. The walls were the same white limestone as the pillars in the city and only had one tapestry above the four-post bed, which had been built out of a rich dark wood. The bedding was askew, telling me the servants hadn't been in yet to fix it.

Ulrich tugged at the bottom of the vest, and I realized just how muscled he was. He was built more like a younger James, with broad shoulders and a thick chest, but not nearly as tall.

He ran his fingers through his hair a few times to fix it, then returned to the desk. One paper had notes scribbled about it in a way I couldn't follow, like a jumble of thoughts that take place as you wake.

"There's got to be something I'm not seeing," he muttered.

Ulrich's gaze suddenly locked on a phrase toward the bottom of the contract, and I felt my face—his face—spread into a grin. "That's it. That right there."

He snatched a quill from his desk and circled part of a sentence, then ran from the bedroom.

He ran down a hallway lined with paintings, so familiar he didn't take time to stop at any of them. One painting, however, caught my attention. It was a family—husband with dark hair, wife sitting in a chair with an infant in her arms. A daughter stood at her side, and the king's hand was on her small shoulder.

Ulrich slid around the corner and burst into the throne room. His father sat upon a white throne with emerald-green cushions. The king's head with a simple silver and gold crown with white diamonds, his neatly trimmed hair and beard were starting to show graying patches, and age lines pinched the corners of his eyes and mouth.

"I figured it out," Ulrich blurted, rushing to his father's side.

"Ulrich," his father said in a low tone.

"Please listen. I've been trying to tell you all week something is wrong with this contract. I've figured it out."

"Ulrich, the advisors picked through every line."

"I know but look here." He stuck the contract out to his father. "The beginning letter of each line makes the phrase, *A curse to break*. The end of each line says *Summer Solstice*. See?" He beamed with excitement. "It's a curse!"

The king, however, tilted his chin down. His eyes softened. Captain Avery had given me that look before. The look that told me I wasn't right or that my idea wasn't good.

Ulrich felt the same gut-sinking feeling at the look I felt every time it was given to me. "You don't believe me."

"The advisors saw nothing wrong with it. I see nothing wrong with it." He motioned, and for the first time, Ulrich turned to see the advisors standing at the foot of the throne. Feet away stood a woman in a flowing purple dress, but her face was hidden behind a black veil.

"I . . . I don't understand," Ulrich said. "You've taught me my entire life to pick through contracts. It's the one thing I excel at. I've caught numerous errors that saved our country money and maintained safety, and this one time you are going to trust your advisors over me?"

His father didn't reply.

"Please think about this further," Ulrich urged.

"Think of the trade!" his father whispered back, excitement sparking in his eyes. "A new route is just what we need, especially with the siren pass causing delays."

Ulrich took a step back. "I never thought I would see the day where you would risk the safety of your own people to obtain more money."

"Then you truly don't know your own father, boy," a woman's voice said.

Ulrich turned and looked at the faceless woman. He wanted to say something. He returned his attention to his father and, one last time, pleaded with him not to make a foolish decision.

But the advisors handed over the contract, and his father took the quill.

"The land of Terricina will accept your trade offer." He signed the document and handed the quill back to his advisor. He himself stood and approached the woman, contract in hand. "I look forward to our partnership."

The woman's hands closed on the parchment, and she let out a deep, dark chuckle. "You foolish man. Now you will suffer for what you did to me."

The king's body went rigid. "You?" he breathed. "Impossible!"

"Not so, dear king. And now, you shall get what you deserve." She took a step back, and the ground trembled violently. "You should have listened to your son. As the contract states, if someone doesn't find a way to raise you from the depths of the sea by the summer solstice, you and your people will be mine forever!"

There was a mighty crack.

The ceiling broke, large stones dropping.

Ulrich ran forward, shouting for his father. But a stone slammed into Ulrich's back, and he slumped to the ground.

THIRTEEN

I looked at Ulrich in shock. "What did your father know about her?"

Ulrich shook his head. "I assume he knew she was the sea witch. When I woke, I was under a pile of rubble, and my men pulled me out. I saw the extent of the damage, but . . . my father was never recovered. Either he perished that day or the sea witch took him." He closed the pearl around the stone.

I didn't know why, but my heart ached for him. "How old are you?" I asked.

"Nearly seventeen."

I looked around at—what should have been— the capital city of Delphi. His father hadn't listened, hadn't believed Ulrich had found that error. Ulrich was in charge of an entire kingdom, most of which he couldn't access, while trying to figure out how to get the people-turned-siren back home.

While I had thrown a fit because I wasn't a captain.

In a way, I understood where he was coming from.

"Do you think you can help?" Ulrich asked, eyes pleading.

"How?" I held my hands out. "What can I possibly do?"

He licked his lips. "Maybe you can't directly. But, perhaps, you could take me to Zelig and I could get help from Queen Grimhilde. They're our ally."

I looked at the chain around his neck. "Maybe we can help each other. I can help you, in exchange for something."

Ulrich's eyes narrowed. "Of course you would want something," he muttered. "You're a pirate after all."

I nodded. "I want the summer stone."

Ulrich's hand grasped it. "This is the power of my kingdom. What need have you of the summer stone?"

I wanted to tell him about my mother, but I wasn't certain yet if I could trust him. Instead, I said, "It lets me know that you're serious about needing our help."

"You mean desperate enough," he said sharply.

I shrugged. "Deal or not?"

"You aren't the captain," he concluded. "Are you even the one who should be making a deal like this?"

"Of course I can," I lied with a scoff. But if Ulrich went to James, he could back out, and then I wouldn't have the summer stone.

Ulrich finally exhaled and nodded. "All right. But I don't give it to you until my city and my people are out of the sea."

I frowned. It wasn't an ideal situation at all, but I made the deal, knowing I could just steal the stone if things got too dicey.

He held out his hand and I grasped it, giving a firm handshake.

With that out of the way, we swam around the palace to a row of buildings pressed side-by-side, and surprisingly still standing.

"You put them in buildings and give me a cave," I grumbled.

Ulrich chuckled. "If you can consider structurally unsound buildings a safer option than your cave, then yes. I did give them a better option to stay in." He swam up to the guards at the entrance to one of the buildings. "I need to speak with the captain."

James must have heard because he appeared in the dim light in the doorway. His eyes lit up when he spotted me, and he gave a gentle smile. "They didn't hurt you?" His eyes assessed me for any damage.

I shook my head. "Not at all."

Ulrich gestured. "Odette and I have come to an arrangement. You and your men will take me to Zelig to get help for my kingdom. In exchange—"

I coughed and cleared my throat loudly. "Sorry, I inhaled sea water." I patted my throat and earned a perplexed look from Ulrich and his men. "He's going to pay us for helping them."

"We can't go gallivanting around the sea saving people," James muttered.

"We're not," I said before Ulrich's open mouth could produce a sound. "We're helping people who deserve to be helped."

"We don't know what they did to anger the sea witch in the first place!" James argued.

I shrugged. "True. But Ulrich claims he doesn't know."

"I have no idea," Ulrich confirmed. "I only remember that once she had the contract in hand, my father acted like he knew her. If he had dealings with her in the past, I don't know about them."

"We'll just have to trust him," I said.

James rolled his eyes. "Odette, you can't make deals without consulting your *captain*." He gave me a disappointed look.

My jaw clenched and heart pounded. "Don't look at me like that. You've held a lot of secrets close to you, like maybe the fact all the men on your ship are sirens?"

He flinched. "I did tell you."

"As I was being pulled into the sea!"

"When was there another chance?" he argued.

"Maybe when I woke from my fever, or before that even happened, like when I got on your ship, or months ago after Castle Bay!"

James glanced at the others as if they would save him from my anger. "Odette, I wanted to tell you. We all did."

"And what stopped you?"

He hesitated.

The other men looked uncomfortable.

I gave an aggravated sigh. "Castle Bay?"

"More or less," he mumbled.

"Can we return to the concern of my kingdom?" Ulrich asked. "Are you willing to help or not?"

James let out a frustrated breath, little bubbles floated away from his gills. "We will take you to Zelig, and then we must return to our mission."

Ulrich nodded.

"Sire, the summer solstice is only a few weeks away . . ." one of the men reminded.

"I know," Ulrich said in a low voice. "Tell the people I'll return with help."

We began swimming to the surface. James swam up to my side. "Are you upset with me?"

"I just don't understand why everyone seems to know what happened that night, but no one will tell me."

"But you're right." He grabbed my arm. "There's so much more you need to know. It's not that we *won't* tell you. It's that we *can't.*"

I looked him over. "Is it anything to do with the sea witch? Can you tell me that much?"

He nodded. "That's all I can say right now." He swam ahead, quickly followed by his men.

I groaned and looked up at the surface of the water. "Why does he have to be so vague and complicated?"

"A lot of men are," Ulrich chuckled. He put his hand on my back, urging me forward.

By the time Ulrich and I reached the surface, James was already climbing up the ladder lowered to him by Sky.

"Where have you scallywags been?" Sky scolded. "We saw you get dragged below, and some of the sirens even tried getting on board the ship! We . . ." His gaze set on Ulrich. "We have a visitor?" He looked back at James.

James's fin had already melted away and he stood at the top of the ladder in all his glory. "Not now," he muttered, grimacing in pain.

I recalled the pain of transforming back into legs a few weeks ago and wasn't looking forward to it. I also wasn't looking forward to watching every man become naked before me, which also meant I would do the same.

Ulrich, however, watched as the men climbed the ladder one at a time.

"Why are you grinning like that?" I asked him, careful to keep my voice low.

"It's been a few months since I've been a human. I'm merely thinking how wonderful it's going to be."

Only four more pirates to go.

"Did you try to get to shore? I have the ability to return to a human form. Do you?"

He finally tore his gaze away. "Yes. And I will admit, I'm nervous about trying again because it hurt, but I was desperate. The town nearest to shore now is Layton. I made it a few blocks, but the pain of becoming human again was so severe, I collapsed. The people who found me didn't believe I was their prince." His jaw flexed. "They said I was a minion of the sea witch, beat me with clubs. Then dragged me back to the sea."

I felt a tad guilty helping Ulrich for my own needs. He was trying to do what was best for his people. I wanted what was best for me. But not guilty enough to conceal the bargain.

I reached out and took his hand and offered a little smile. "My crew won't harm you. I'll personally make sure."

"Your turn," he said.

"You best close your eyes," I warned.

He blanched. "You think . . . oh, no. No, I'm not interested . . ." He gestured between us. "But if it makes you feel better." He covered his eyes with one hand, holding on to the ladder with the other so he wouldn't float away.

"Thank you. James! Get me a blanket, I'm not coming up naked."

"Already have one for you," Sky answered.

I pulled myself out of the water with my arms, willing my fins to fade away. Unlike the other pirates, transforming back into a person with legs took me a little longer. Also unlike them, the pain seemed to hit me more, but I quickly remembered it was due to the still-aching wound on my leg. Any amount of weight on it made me grunt and yelp in pain.

By the time I reached the top of the ladder, I didn't care if anyone saw me. I just wanted to curl up in a ball and cry.

Instead, a blanket wrapped around me the instant my hands touched the railing, and strong arms hoisted me onto the deck. Sky smiled. "You made it up. I almost climbed down and got you. Your leg still hurt?"

I nodded, a little breathless. "I'd forgotten." And then I scowled and punched him in the shoulder. "How could you not tell me I'm a siren?"

"Ow. It wasn't my doing!" He rubbed his arm furiously.

I rolled my eyes and tried to limp to the stairs.

James suddenly appeared and scooped me up in his arms. "Not so fast. You've got to rinse that out again, and we need more medicine so you don't get infected again."

I glanced back at Sky, who glowered at James and shoved his hands in his pockets. "James, I'm feeling okay. I can sleep with the rest of the crew."

James ignored me. He set me on his bed and pulled the blanket aside enough to check on the wound on my leg. He finally exhaled and pressed his forehead to mine. "I was so worried when they took you into the depths. I worried Prince Ulrich had discovered you're the daughter of the pirate queen and feared he would hold you for ransom."

"That would have been a fun conversation for you to have with my mother," I said teasingly.

"Odette . . . we've had our differences." He pulled back so he could look me in the eye. "We've had our disagreements. But there is nothing more heartbreaking than having feelings for you and suppressing them."

My heart skipped and flipped in both elation and absolute panic. "You have feelings for me?"

"Yes." He quirked a grin. "I mean it too. I've had feelings for you for a very long time."

I reached out and touched the nub where his left hand should have been. "Can you please remind me how you lost your hand?"

Pain darkened his eyes and lined his brow. I expected him to pull away, as he always did whenever I brought it up. This time, he only said, "You were there, Odette. You were there when it happened. You just can't remember because it was taken from you."

I felt my shoulders fall and I rolled my eyes and tried to get off the bed. "Taken? Who would take my memories?"

James put his hand on my hip and firmly held me on the bed. "I want to tell you everything, I do. I swear on my life, I'd tell you now if I could. Can't you see that?" He peered up at me with one hundred percent honesty.

I couldn't resist. I reached out and touched his cheek. For a moment, I could have sworn he'd looked at me like that before. He'd pleaded with me, begged me to get help. My head began to throb like it seemed to always do when I tried to remember Castle Bay, but I wanted to hold on to the memory. I wanted to see that memory of James.

He held my face, the hot evening sun blaring overhead. He was begging me not to tell my mother something. He was worried how she would respond. I pushed him away.

That was all I could recall before my head felt like it would explode.

I pressed my palm to my forehead and drew a slow breath.

"You tried to remember something?" James's voice caressed my ear.

I nodded slowly. "Yes. You've looked at me like that before, and I pulled away from you."

"A few times."

I opened my eyes and saw a pained smile flicker across his handsome face. "Look at us. Quite the pair."

There was a knock. "Captain, we're ready to set sail," Sky called.

James rolled his eyes. "He has impeccable timing," he mumbled. "I'll be out in a moment!" he called.

"Why are you so hard on him?" I demanded.

"Because he knew of my feelings for you, pursued you, and rubbed it in my face," he replied stiffly.

I couldn't resist a smirk. "Your choosing him as first mate was intended to make him pay."

James grinned. "Guilty."

"You swear you have feelings for me?

He kissed my forehead and squeezed my fingers. "I swear on my one good hand."

FOURTEEN

The next day, after having my wound cleaned again and Gerard's magical medicine applied, I insisted on sitting on the deck with everyone. There was no way I'd allow myself to be confined to the captain's quarters when a prince was on board.

Ulrich had started a game of dice with Gerard, Sebastian, and another pirate by the time I made it out. Both Sky and James were busy with their duties. I took a crate beside Ulrich and watched.

"Why don't you join us?" Ulrich asked.

I snorted. "I'm not fond of dice games. They're all reliant on chance with absolutely no talent involved at all. Anyone can win. Anyone can lose."

Ulrich grinned. "That's why having magic is so fun." He rolled the dice, a wisp of white smoke— barely visible—wrapped around them, and the dice landed perfectly."

Gerard picked up the dice, rolled them between his palms, then dropped them on the barrel. They landed in the exact position as Ulrich.

Ulrich gasped.

Gerard smirked. "Unless your opponent has magic as well."

"Oh, this is going to be fun!" Ulrich's eyes lit up, and he rolled again.

"Where are you from, Gerard?" I asked.

He glanced in my direction. "Ashwrya." He looked away and toward the cliffs. "If you go that direction, we are north of Zelig, Griswil, and Arington. I'm from a small area called Somerset."

"What does Ashwrya look like?"

Gerard laughed. "My lady, it is an entire half of a continent. Your southern half has all four seasons, as do areas of my country. Of course, the furthest north is frigid most of the time, but there are summer months that come and go. They just don't get warm like Terricina."

"Wait, your seasons actually change?" I asked.

He nodded. "Ulrich, you cheat." He clicked his tongue and lifted one of the dice. "A hex? What kind of hex is it?" He lifted it closer to his eyes, and the small dice exploded in a small puff of smoke, spewing a rainbow of colored ash all over Gerard's face.

Ulrich fell off his barrel, he was laughing so hard.

Even I couldn't hold back a laugh.

Gerard sneezed and drew a handkerchief from his pocket to wipe off his face. "Your magic is quick," he observed.

Ulrich dried his eyes, still giggling now and then. "Yes, as is yours. I prefer fun magic, though my father wanted me to explore all of the options. I took a liking to the lighter side of things." He picked himself up and got back on his seat. "Your magic has more of a . . . dark tinge to it, though."

Gerard's face was still smeared with a vomit of colors that almost looked like he'd been splattered by a child with paint. "Yes. In my country, we have need for stronger magic." He let out a sigh of defeat when he realized he wasn't getting the ashes off his face.

"You may need a bath," I grinned.

"We can toss you overboard," Ulrich offered, gesturing to the side of the ship nearest him.

Gerard put up his hand. "If I wash off, you're bound to do something else. Throw dirt on me so it turns to mud?"

Ulrich gave an innocent shrug.

I leaned forward. "What arrangement do you have with James? What is it that makes him want to help you?"

"You'll have to ask him that," Gerard replied in an equally low tone. "It's not my business what your captain does or does not share with you."

"You were the one to prompt him to tell me about the pirates."

He shrugged. "I don't understand why he didn't tell you when he saved you from the kraken. You'd already seen him. In my opinion, it wasn't something worth hiding."

"Do you know anything else I don't?" I pressed.

"I'm afraid not, miss."

"You really don't need to be so polite."

Gerard's lips spread into a dashing smile, very similar to Sky's, but I wondered if Gerard used some of his magic to make it even more alluring. "In light of recent events, I have been reminded how to treat women with respect, pirate or not." He looked at Ulrich. "Are we done with this game?"

"Do you have a different one?"

Gerard grinned mischievously, reached into his pocket, and produced a deck of cards. "In this game, two people draw. If one of you gets a black card, you get to make the other person do something. If that person draws a blue card, they tell the truth. If they draw a green card, they do whatever you ask. If they have a white card, they get a pass, and if they get a red card, they get a favor to turn in later." He mixed the cards a few times, then lay the pile in the middle of the barrel.

I drew first and Ulrich picked up after. I flipped my card over to reveal a green card. Ulrich drew a blue. "What do we do here?" I asked.

"I'll draw." Gerard, of course, drew a black. "Look at that. All right. Odette, I want you to go give Sky a kiss. And Ulrich, the question I have for you is . . . do you prefer the company of men over women?"

Ulrich's face flushed bright red, which was answer enough. But he shook his head. "That isn't allowed in our country. I don't even know what my father would say if he found out."

Gerard grinned and turned to me.

I stood and patted Ulrich's shoulder. "I think you're amazing no matter what. And when I get back here, I'm demanding to know why you want me to kiss Sky."

"Because I enjoy watching both him and James squirm for you," he confessed with an easy shrug.

It was my turn to blush. But a game was a game. I found Sky watching the men switch out one of the ropes. I sauntered over to him and slid my arm around his waist, which drew his attention to me.

"Are you truly jealous of James?" I asked.

Sky's ears burned red. "No," he grumbled. "Look, you and I—"

I cut him off by pressing my lips to his.

Just as James headed our way.

I knew immediately Gerard must have used some of his magic to draw James's attention toward me and Sky. Unfortunately, the result wasn't pleasant, though a little funny.

James ordered Sky to climb up the rigging himself to fix the tangled rope, then turned to me with a sour look.

"Oh, James." I laughed and limped after him. "It's a game! I was playing a game with Gerard and Ulrich." I caught his arm and pulled him close. "You really are jealous of Sky."

He exhaled through his nose and shifted his glare to Gerard, who waved. He rolled his eyes. "I'd throw him into the sea now if I could."

I smiled, my heart leaping. I gave James a hug, enjoying the feeling of his muscled body against mine. He was jealous. James really did like me, and I suddenly felt more important than anyone else in the world.

"What is this game you're playing?" he asked.

"Come join us!" I started dragging him toward the stairs.

We explained again how to play, and his first draw he got black, and Gerard got red, which meant Gerard owed James a favor at some point. We played the rest of the afternoon, ignoring many of the chores we normally would have completed.

Over the next three days, nothing eventful happened. We headed northward and watched as shoreline gave way to cliffs. None seemed passable by ship or foot.

Finally, Ulrich pointed to a cliff. "That there is the east corner. We should arrive at the white cliffs by noon." He faced me with an eager smile. "Just a few more days and everything will be right."

"How are you hoping they will help exactly?" I asked.

Ulrich shook his head and looked back over the sea. "I don't know," he answered softly. "I know the queen is a sorceress or has one on retainer, and maybe she can come up with a spell or potion or . . . *something* that will help us. If she can't . . ." His voice trailed off.

James stepped up to his side, hands politely clasped behind his back. "It has been nice having you on board, I must admit. You've kept up the morale of the crew."

"You could come with me," Ulrich pressed. "Odette hasn't ever seen an inland country. It would be a fun adventure! Besides, what are you in such a rush to return to? Robbery and murder?"

James looked down at Ulrich. "That is your view of pirates?"

"Am I wrong?" he countered.

"Not all of us are murderers," I explained. "I have never personally killed another."

James shook his head. "Neither of those are the purpose of my current voyage."

"You really *are* cryptic, aren't you?" Ulrich replied.

James's brows furrowed in confusion. "I'll return when we get closer." He nodded with authority to Ulrich before walking away.

"I did have a question." Ulrich turned and leaned his backside on the railing next to me, folding his arms, and his gaze strayed from James to me. "You could have killed me and taken the stone at any point on this voyage," he said softly. He looked at me from the corner of his eye. "Why didn't you?"

"Despite what you believe about pirates, we are true to our word," I answered. "True, James may not have been pleased about my making the bargain without him, but like you said, he could have stolen the summer stone from you and thrown you back into the sea. If he knew you had it . . ."

"You never told him?" He blurted a laugh. "Why does that not surprise me?"

I shrugged in innocence. "I admit, I don't want to let you go on your own. I've grown rather fond of you."

Ulrich smiled. "I like you too. But I've traveled alone before, and I've been to Zelig at least once a year for their winter balls. Remember what Gerard said a few days ago about our seasons never changing? It's true. Arington is called the Fall Kingdom for a reason, and Griswil hosts the spring ball for the same reason we host the summer solstice celebration. I'm afraid we aren't prepared for Zelig's winter, however."

"What's life like as a prince?"

Ulrich brushed his hair from his eyes and his smile faltered a little. "It's very stressful, I'll admit. I imagine it also varies from kingdom to kingdom since each runs their lives very differently. For example, in Arington, they are starting to restrict the use of magic. Someone came through and attacked one of their towns with magic last summer. I heard the king was starting to force all magical creatures into the Weeping Woods. If anyone with magic enters their land, they're forbidden to use it, no matter the degree."

"What does that have to do with being a prince?" I asked.

The edge of his lip twitched up again. "Because I have to worry about how that will impact my kingdom. I have to wonder if that will start to force magical creatures and people into my land, and what sorts of individuals those may be. I also have to worry about the trade routes through kingdoms, the money our kingdom is losing because we've had no harbors the last few months, what has happened to our provinces, who is trying to usurp power, and what's going to happen when Delphi is returned to its proper place. We need to repair the palace and several buildings, including the harbors, and I'm in charge of all of it. Because I don't know whether or not my father is even alive." His throat bobbed up and down, and he averted his gaze, but I caught the sunlight glint off a streak from a tear on his cheek.

"All of that on your shoulders," I murmured softly.

"A bit pathetic, isn't it?" he asked. "That I'm terrified to rule my own kingdom when that is the very reason I was born?"

I snorted. "Of course not. I've been worried about running my own crew. I can't imagine being in charge of more than thirty men, let alone an entire kingdom." I leaned against his side. "It's totally normal." Maybe my mother was right after all. Maybe she didn't put a crew on my shoulders because she knew I would be overwhelmed.

There was a comfortable silence between us before Ulrich broke it. "Is it also normal that I completely trust you for some reason?"

I looked up at him. "Nope. Because I trust you too. I actually feel like I've known you forever. *And* you're one of the few men who actually seems to treat me with respect."

"The others don't?" Ulrich glanced back at the pirates.

"Not really," I confessed and rested my hands on the railing behind me. "Something happened a few months ago, and I lost my memory. No one, not one single pirate, will tell me the truth of what happened to make me lose my memory. Not even James. I remember pieces here and there, but that's it."

"No one will tell you?" he echoed.

"No." I looked down at the boots I'd been given. After the incident with the kraken, my new boots now lay somewhere at the bottom of the sea. "I wonder if I might have done something," I admitted softly. "If I did something unforgivable, it would make sense why no one will tell me the truth."

"Hm. That's unusual indeed." He gasped, pushed off the railing, and faced me. "I've got it! You can come with me to the capital of Zelig, to the castle. Queen Grimhilde will certainly be able to help you with your memories!"

I couldn't deny my heart leapt with anticipation. "You really think so?"

"Of course! That should be a relatively easy spell for a sorceress. Unless something blocks her . . . I don't know how that would work, though." He shook his head. "Come with me?"

I scowled and looked at the helm of the ship, where James stood, stunning and regal as always. "I'll have to convince him." I trotted up the stairs and stepped up to James's side. "I've got a bone to pick with you."

He glanced at me and sighed. "What now?"

"I need to go with Ulrich to Zelig's royal family."

"Come again? I must have saltwater in my ear."

I put my hands on my hips. "She can help with my memories."

James turned to me. "How in the deep blue sea could she help you?" He looked me up and down.

"Ulrich said she's a sorceress." I pointed to my head. "I need them back, and she can help."

He gave an exasperated sigh. "Odette . . . it's more complicated than you think."

"Well, *you* aren't exactly telling me, so I don't see another option here."

Our conversation was interrupted when the lookout shouted that the white cliffs were in view. All attention turned to the bow of the ship, then westward. In the distance, the darkness of the stone cliffs suddenly became a shocking white.

"Please, James," I said, taking his hand. "I want my memories back. I need to know what happened to your hand. I need to understand why things between us have been so . . . off."

He shook his head at me. "I'm warning you not to. You might not like what you remember."

"It's my right to have my memories whether or not I like them," I snapped back and dropped his hand. "No one else has the right to withhold them, and I'm getting tired of repeating myself."

"I know. I know." He removed his hat and ran his fingers through his dark hair. He drew a long breath. "It may do us some good to get on land. Besides, we are running low on food and will need to restock. Perhaps the queen would be willing to let us purchase supplies in one of her towns."

I threw my arms around him and hugged him tightly. "I've never seen another country. This is exciting!"

He chuckled and reluctantly wrapped his arms around me. "You're such a child."

"You love it."

"I do."

I jerked away and looked up at him. "Wait, really?"

A pink hue spread across James's cheeks, and he looked down at me with sincerity shining in his beautiful eyes. "Of course I mean it," he said softly. "I'd give up everything for you. Already almost have." He held up his hook.

I suddenly wished we weren't so close to the white cliffs, that we had another day where I could pester James until he sat down and talked to me. Instead, we only had about an hour or two.

I relaxed down on my feet. "Have we always been interested in each other?" I asked.

James glanced to his right, and I followed his gaze down to Sky, who was leaning to look over the sea at the cliffs. "Yes. And my feelings for you didn't change, even while you were with Sky."

I shook my head. "How could I forget something like that? I thought love was supposed to be strong enough to make it through stuff like that?"

"Or so storybooks tell." He chuckled. He turned to his crew. "All right, everyone! I've decided to join Ulrich to ensure he makes it to Zelig. Odette will be coming with me."

"And so will I," Sky stepped forward.

"I will go as well," Gerard offered.

"Sky, we will need to discuss this," James said. "You are my first mate." He then raised his voice. "I know others may want to join us, but I don't know how long it will take us to get there, and we need to travel light. Ulrich, tell us more about where we are going."

According to Ulrich, this was the only entrance from the sea inland, and it was heavily guarded. Of course, James ordered the removal of the Jolly Rodger immediately.

"It's not a full army," Ulrich explained. "Just an outpost. They remain hidden." He pointed to the cliffs. "Zelig has always lined the cliffs with cannons and arrows. I can't imagine much would have changed in just a few months."

James turned, opening his mouth to Sky.

Sky cut him off. "No. I'm not missing out on another adventure."

"You're the first mate." James frowned.

"Then I resign my position." Sky shrugged and folded his arms as if it were as simple as that.

"Sky, I need someone reliable on the ship." James frowned in disappointment.

Sky arched his brow and gestured at the other sailors. "You hand-picked every single one of us. I don't believe for a second that you wouldn't have chosen sailors you couldn't trust. Pick any of them. I'm going with you." He marched past James.

James looked at me, but I raised my hands. "I'm not taking the position of first mate now." I looked over at Sky. "I can't believe you're giving up."

"Fine. Sebastian?" He looked over at the round man with red hair.

The man grinned proudly. "Aye, cap'n!" He saluted and marched up to the helm.

"See?" Sky smirked. "That wasn't hard."

"I just can't believe you would abandon your post like this. You knew your responsibility as first mate when you agreed to be mine."

"Well, apparently, you need someone boring and not as adventurous as your first mate," Sky retorted and sat down at my side.

"Then you get to row," James countered.

Sky grumbled and took the oars.

"That's what you get for stepping down," I teased. I looked over Sky's shoulder to see the shoreline. "One thing is for certain. This time, you won't miss out on the adventure."

FIFTEEN

I kept my eyes on the cliffs as we neared the shore. They were far taller than any cliffs I'd seen before. I'd never sailed up the eastern coast because Captain Avery never did.

When we made landfall, it took Ulrich a moment to climb out.

"Are you going to be okay?" I asked, eying him.

He didn't meet my gaze but nodded. "I don't know what they'll say. I'm trying to remain positive. I wish I had thought to bring some sort of royal garment with me, but I don't even know if anything survived."

"You said they know you."

That broke his concentration enough that he finally looked at me and gave a faint smile. "Yes. Prince Mathias and I have been friends. I only worry if tales of Delphi sinking have already reached them. Because that means my people would have told them

I died." He shook his head. "We have a long way to travel, and without any form of land transportation, it may take us a few days to get to the castle." He began trudging through the sand.

"Days?" Sky gaped. "Days?" he repeated, looking at James.

"Well, you don't see a castle along the shoreline, do you?" James asked with a dramatic flurry. "Considering we don't have any transportation but our legs, you should have known it would at least taken longer than today."

Sky grumbled under his breath. "I don't like walking."

I laughed and gave Sky a playful nudge. "How hard could it be?"

"Don't say that." James flinched. "You know it's bad luck."

"You and your silly superstitions." I rolled my eyes.

"I wouldn't have them if things didn't actually happen." He inclined his head at me, eyebrows raised.

"Yes, well, I don't believe in superstitions," I boasted proudly, puffing out my chest for emphasis.

In the distance, thunder rumbled.

I looked to my right—northward—and spotted dark clouds in the distance.

James leaned to my ear. "Told you so."

I frowned. "You can't tell me *I* am the cause of those thunderclouds."

He shrugged. "You said it wouldn't be difficult. Now we have clouds coming our way."

"And it snows in Zelig," Ulrich added, looking over his shoulder at us. "Have you ever experienced snow?"

I shook my head. "We went through a hailstorm once."

He nodded. "Pretty, when we aren't stuck walking through it. It's lighter than hail, but the storms can be equally miserable. Like hail, we could get sick from being in the cold. But hopefully that won't happen." He glanced at the clouds uneasily.

"Great," I muttered.

The nearer we drew the cliffs, the larger they felt. I then spotted the pass Ulrich mentioned. It didn't look too deep but had a wandering road that reached the top, not unlike the zig-zagging pathway on the cliffs back home.

When we were almost to the pass, a mighty voice bellowed out to us, "Go back from whence you came! We don't allow strangers here."

Ulrich stepped forward. "I am Prince Ulrich of Terricina."

The voice didn't answer right away but soon came again. "If you are the prince, why haven't you entered from the southern side of the country?"

He sighed. "It's a long story, one I wish to tell the king and queen. I've come to seek their aid in a time of need."

"What sort of difficult time?"

"We're wasting time right now," I muttered.

Ulrich glanced at me. "Sir, I am sure if you allow me to approach, you will see I am the prince of

Terricina. I travel with these sailors because they are the only ones willing to assist me right now. With the storm coming in, we would prefer to get as near the castle as possible before we are forced to stop and find shelter."

There was no response this time.

Ulrich's gaze scanned the cliffs.

"Do you think they believe you?" Sky muttered.

"I don't know," Ulrich whispered back. "I pray they do. If we can't get Zelig to assist us . . . I will have to travel inland to Arington or Griswil."

"But you don't have time. The summer solstice is near," I reminded.

Ulrich gave me a look that let me know he was more than aware of how little time he had.

At the entrance of the pass, a small group of men appeared, led by a man in blinding silver armor with a beautiful yellow and orange feather sticking out the top. "You come most unprepared," the man said as he approached. "Not a piece of winter clothing or blanket?"

Ulrich sighed in relief and bowed his head. "Lord Tomblin. I'm afraid we didn't have time to adequately prepare for this journey."

"It seems so." The man scrutinized us, his piercing blue eyes rimmed with yellow. His gaze settled on me, and in the instant our eyes connected, I felt the air sucked from my lungs as I suddenly recalled rolling up the pirate flag before we left the ship. "You must truly be desperate to side with pirates."

I glared at him.

"They were the only ones willing to help," Ulrich reiterated.

"If you feel we are untrustworthy, you are welcome to accompany us to the castle," James added.

"What is in it for you?" Lord Tomblin asked. "Why do pirates join a prince on a journey that requires they come inland?"

Everyone turned to James, even Ulrich. And James looked at me for help.

Lord Tomblin locked eyes with me again.

"Because I need the summer stone, and Prince Ulrich is in possession of it," I blurted before I could hold my words back.

Lord Tomblin nodded and turned away. "Come along, then."

Ulrich followed without hesitation, but James faced me with his mouth agape.

"I couldn't stop myself!" I told him.

James leaned close. "He has the summer stone and you didn't tell me?"

"Was I supposed to?" I looked him up and down.

He rolled his eyes and looked at Gerard. "He's got the stone."

"I heard," Gerard frowned. "Let's get this done so I can get back."

"Wait, he wants the stone too?" I asked.

"Why on earth would Gerard want it? Why would you give it to him?" I grabbed James. "For once in your stupid life, will you be honest with me?"

James motioned for the others to continue. "Gerard joined me on my maiden voyage with the entire purpose to be finding that summer stone. That's what we've been searching for all along."

I shook my head. "Why would a landlubber want the stone? And why would you keep it a secret this entire time?"

James's jaw flexed. "He's giving me something in return."

"Oh of course." I rolled my eyes and shoved him. "You know, I guess I really am pathetic." I started marching after the others. "Just like you said. So pathetic not one person will tell me a single truth. I must have really messed up to earn such distrust."

"Odette," he tried to interrupt.

"No. No, I can't handle it anymore! I'm going to a foreign queen or sorceress to get answers because the man I'm best friends with and the man who claims to love me, don't have the balls to tell me!" I carried on, without any concern over who listened.

"Giving a stranger the stone I need so you can get something so mystifying, so secret you can't tell me? Can't tell me anything. Like the fact all the pirates are sirens. That's sort of a big deal, but don't tell Odette. No one should trust Odette! Born and raised a pirate, and *with* you nonetheless."

I was more than aware that every single pirate and soldier of Zelig was able to overhear me, and quite frankly, I didn't care. The whole forest, nay, the whole world could hear how cross I felt!

Behind me, James seethed. I knew because he couldn't think of a comeback sharp enough to spit back.

"Care to share how you made me reveal my intention with the stone?" I asked Lord Tomblin, hoping to add some other form of conversation now that thick awkwardness hung over us.

"I'm blessed by a phoenix," Lord Tomblin explained, gesturing to the feather in his helmet. "Part of that blessing is the gift of seeing through people's exteriors to their true intentions. It provides me the ability to interrogate without causing harm."

"Other than invasion of privacy," I sniped.

Lord Tomblin grinned over his shoulder at me. "I like you. But if you address the queen the way you just addressed your captain, she'll lock you up. Mind your words when we get to the castle." He turned away, but I didn't miss the muttered words, "I would never dream of speaking to a superior in such a way."

I managed to resist the urge to look at James and successfully avoided the nonexistent temptation to apologize. A handful of soldiers prepared horses for us at Lord Tomblin's request.

Ulrich nodded to Lord Tomblin. "We're going to have to double up on horses."

"Odette?" Sky jumped onto a horse and held his hand out to me. "Considering you're upset with James, maybe you should ride with someone who actually cares."

I snorted. "In that case, I'll ride with Ulrich."

"Ouch." Sky scowled.

"Odette, a word," James said unexpectedly.

Ulrich shook his head. "I'm riding with Sky." He looked at me and leaned close. "You need to resolve your issues anyway or it's going to come to a head, and you can't afford to explode in front of the queen." Ulrich took Sky's hand and climbed up behind him in spite of Sky's pouting.

I pursed my lips and pushed them to the side of my face before glowering at James. Unfortunately James was too busy trying to get on the horse to see my expression, and I had to give up and storm over to his side.

Of course he would struggle to get on a horse's back. He had one hand and a hook, and neither of us had ever ridden a horse in our lives. Luckily, with some guidance from one of the soldiers, James figured out how to get up. After struggling myself, the soldiers had to lift me on behind him.

An hour earlier, I would have relished the thought of wrapping my arms around James and holding on. But I was still furious at everyone for keeping secrets and wasn't about to let it go.

James intentionally waited for everyone else to lead the way ahead of us, then looked over his shoulder at me. "I didn't know you were looking for the summer stone. You didn't share that information with me. In contrast, it is not my duty to share what my intentions are in any voyage. You know that."

I looked away. "I just thought you would trust me. Considering everyone on your crew likely knew and I've supposedly known you better and longer."

"I do trust you."

"No, you don't!" I spat. "Don't lie to me, James! All you do is lie!"

James gritted his teeth, keeping calmer than I wanted. I wanted him to yell back so I could be justified in exploding on him. "Gerard needs the summer stone. I stopped asking why." He held up his hook. "In return, he will give me back my hand."

"Wait . . . why does he have your hand? And don't you dare say it's complicated!" I quickly added.

James shook his head. "The honest truth, I don't know. I don't know how he got it, why he has it, or how he will return it."

I slumped my shoulders. "Why couldn't you just tell me this?"

He opened and closed his mouth before glancing away. "Because I was nervous about what would happen if I did. I didn't want you going off on some adventure trying to get it."

I tilted my head. "Okay, I would probably do that."

"Why do *you* need the stone?"

"While we are sharing the truth"—I held my hands out helplessly—"because if I give my mother the stone, she will finally see I'm worthy to be a captain.

"You want the stone to give to your mother?" His eyes widened. "Why would you do that? Are you crazy?"

And like that, my anger was ignited again. "Maybe I am." I slid off the horse. "I'm so crazy, I'm walking." I started away from him, up the path after the others.

"Miss, it's quite the journey," one of the soldiers tried.

James nudged the horse and cut me off. "You can't keep walking away."

"And why not? *You* avoid my questions. Why shouldn't I avoid your calling me crazy?" I tried to go around the horse.

"I can't tell you the truth!" he said for the millionth time.

"Which is why I'm finding someone who can." I shrugged and managed to finally get past the horse.

"Why must you be so stubborn?"

I didn't look at him.

"Fine. If you want to get another infection or pass out from exhaustion, fine. You have no idea what I've sacrificed for you." James rode on ahead without me. "When we get help for Ulrich, I'll make sure to take you directly home so you can despise me the rest of your life."

I sassed him from behind.

As long as I stayed on the path, what could go wrong?

SIXTEEN

A lot.

A lot could go wrong.

I didn't realize how steep the incline of the trail was, how exhausting the back and forth of the path could be, the stones I'd have to step over, or that the entire three-hour walk was just to get to the top of the cliffs. To make matters worse, by the time I reached the top—out of breath—everyone else was well ahead of me.

Including James. I wished I'd swallowed my stubbornness and ridden with him.

I had an ache in my side, my leg was throbbing from the stitches, and I had to stop to grimace and swear silently at myself. It was my own fault. I'd proven it repeatedly. I was impulsive and rude.

Slowly, I took a seat on a boulder, and my heart dropped. I rubbed my hand up and down my aching leg. Why did I have to push people away? Especially James.

"Hey!"

I jumped to my feet and spun around so quickly my heel caught on a stone, and I lost my balance and fell.

The boulder I'd tried to sit on rocked back and forth and turned, revealing two large eyes that narrowed at me. Whatever the rock creature was, it had a mossy beard and clumps of stone and mud for hands.

"I . . . I'm sorry," I blurted. "I didn't know you were—"

"Course not. You're a fish. Why would you know a rock can talk?" it grumbled.

I studied the creature again. "I was trying to rest before catching up." I nudged my head in the direction of the others.

"Oh, young lad, you're falling quite behind."

"I'm a girl."

It was quiet a moment before asking, "Why are you walking? The others rode beasts."

"Because I was too stubborn to forgive someone," I mumbled. I was too tired to get back up and rubbed my hand over the wound again.

"Arguing with your lover, eh?"

"I don't know what we are," I confessed. "He claims he cares about me but keeps everything a secret." I shook my head.

"Perhaps he is protecting you from something? If not, find someone else to care about."

I felt my lips tug in a smile at the irony. I'd been with Sky too, and he hadn't shared anything either.

"Perhaps you are more upset about the situation itself and not this lover of yours?"

"Yes," I admitted. "Because . . . I guess anyone could have told me. My mother most of all. Maybe I should ask her instead of getting mad at them."

"There you have it. Go see your mother, fish lad!"

I chuckled. "There's no way. She's on the other end of the continent."

"Course there is."

I raised my brow and looked up at the stone.

"The mirrors!" It grinned, at least, I thought it was a grin. "Of course, you'd have to sneak into one. Queen Grimhilde isn't exactly fond of sharing her mirrors. But if you get through one, you can get to your mother and find out the truth once and for all!"

I gave the creature a skeptical smile. Maybe planning with a boulder wasn't the best idea. Travel through mirrors? "Thanks for the advice."

"You can't expect people to give you what you don't show them." It nodded. "Show a man trust, he'll return the favor."

"Easy for you to say. You're made out of rock."

"Not always." It sort of huffed, but I wasn't sure if it was because the creature was annoyed with my astute observation or because it was trying to make itself more comfortable before settling back into the ground. "A wizard made me this way. However, it was due to my own choices." There was a sound of grating stones. Perhaps a chuckle? Or a yawn? "He comes."

"He comes? Who?" I looked over my shoulder, and to my astonishment, James was riding toward me at a brisk pace.

He nodded his head when he was still a little too far away to speak, acknowledging that we'd made eye contact.

I chewed my bottom lip and got back to my feet, rubbing my hand again over my leg. When he was finally close enough, I called to him. "I'm sorry."

"Me too." He pulled on the reins, stopping the horse. "I'd get down, but I'm afraid I wouldn't be able to get back up." He quirked a grin.

I tucked some of my hair behind my ear and gave him a little apologetic smile. "I guess it's easy for me to get upset with you because you are the closest person to me. I'm not mad at *you*, though. I'm mad at everyone. I've just given you the brunt of my anger. Forgive me?"

"Of course." He reached his hand down to me and helped pull me onto the saddle behind him. "When you remember the truth, you're going to feel really bad about all this." He gave me a teasingly stern look.

I rolled my eyes. "Guilt trip right now, hm?"

"I have to pack it on, you know. Because you're the one who proved your salt months ago." He returned his attention forward.

I didn't understand *how* I'd proven my worth months ago. Because if I had proven I was worthy to be a captain then, why hadn't my mother allowed me to be given the captain's hat instead of James?

"Thank you for coming back to get me." I leaned against James's back and slid my arms around his waist.

"I didn't want to make you walk any further. Besides, I was warned the storm is about to hit."

Almost instantaneously, the wind blew harder and cut right through me. I shuddered and held on tighter.

He chuckled. "Maybe we should travel where it's cold more often."

"Shut up." I reached my hand up and twisted his nipple.

"Ow! Watch it." He reached his hand back and slapped my thigh.

Pain shot up my leg, and I yelped.

James flinched. "Sorry. I didn't mean to hit your cut." He looked over his shoulder. "You okay?"

"Of course. It startled me more than anything. Just get me out of this cold."

The wind was hardly the worst thing. Soon after, the icy snow hit—giant flurries like seagull feathers whipped around us, stinging my skin. I pressed my cheek to James's back, trying to hide my face away from the weather, but it didn't seem to matter which way I turned, the wind seemed to be able to reach invisible hands to slap me.

I shivered, and James's body trembled as well.

"We need to get some clothes suitable for this weather." He rubbed his hand over both of mine. "Hopefully Ulrich or one of the others has an idea where we can get something warm."

"My hands . . . h-have n-n-never been th-this cold," I said through chattering teeth. I tried to get as close to him as possible, but I was already as close as I could be.

He grunted. "They have a fire going, at least."

I peeked over James's shoulder and saw we were near the forest, and indeed a red fire glowed through the darkness. "Hurry and get us there." I sniffled and rubbed my nose on the back of my hand.

By the time we reached the fire, we were both shivering so hard we could barely stand. My teeth chattered so loudly I was positive everyone could hear. Ulrich was the first at my side and threw a thick blanket around my shoulders while Sky stepped forward to give one to James.

"You need to hold each other for warmth," Ulrich said.

"Where did you get that?" I demanded, eying his beautiful red cloak.

He grinned proudly and gestured. "Lord Tomblin has a cache here with spare blankets and cloaks."

I didn't think I'd ever been so grateful to see fire." I hurried over and sat down right in front of it, noting the wetness on the butt of my pants. James knelt directly behind me and wrapped his arms around me, adding the warmth of both his body and blanket to mine.

I leaned back against him. "I really am sorry I acted so . . ." I sucked my lips into my mouth, trying to find the right word.

"Rudely? Spontaneously? Impulsively?" James offered.

"Yes, all of those things," I mumbled. "I know I need to learn to change."

"Clearly."

I looked over my shoulder, and he smiled down at me. He lowered his head and pressed his cheek to mine. The cool touch of his cheek to my skin and the poking from his beard flooded my body with warmth. The rock was wrong. I didn't need to find someone else.

"Now everyone is bundled up, we need to continue," Lord Tomblin said, already on his horse. "We don't want to get caught here. We still have several hours before we reach a town with an inn for the night."

"It's not night yet?" I groaned, deciding right then I hated snow. There was nothing about it one could *possibly* enjoy. It was cold, covered everything, and made everything wet when it melted. I was positively miserable. It was bad enough James and I didn't get to enjoy the fire properly. We were forced to get back on the horses and move.

I was grateful when we arrived at the nearest town. By the time we reached the inn, my hair was soaking wet, the snow had seeped through the blanket and penetrated my clothing, and therefore my skin—even the horses—were drenched. None of us was in the best spirits.

But if there was one thing a pirate knew how to do, it was make the best out of the given situation.

Lord Tomblin had his men take care of the horses for the night, and we went into the inn to warm up. Unlike the inns back home, there was no music playing, gambling, or rowdy drunk men about to be thrown out. Everyone appeared to be a weary traveler, warming up their bellies with food and drink.

"I want a big mug of rum," I said as soon as I collapsed in a wooden chair. "And a warm bath. Do they have warm baths here?" I asked, looking at Ulrich.

He looked like a drowned cat and was trying to rectify his hair by combing his fingers through it. "They have running water here and enchanted tubs to make the water always warm. It helps in these winters to prevent the water from freezing completely. I hear they got the enchanted objects from a wizard."

Gerard scoffed. "Why would wizards enchant a bathtub?" Gerard had been so quiet on the journey I'd completely forgotten he'd joined us. Of course, I was mildly distracted by cozying up with James, so that didn't help either.

I reached into the small bowl on the table and picked up one of the nuts to peel at the outer layer of skin.

Ulrich looked at Gerard. "Why wouldn't they? If they have the power to enchant things, why shouldn't they want to better the world for those who don't have magic?"

Gerard snorted. "The gods didn't bless them with magic. They shouldn't have access to it."

Ulrich leaned back and rubbed the back of his hand against his nose. "I don't have the gift of enchantment to that scale. I am rather skilled at potions, though."

Gerard's brow twitched.

"Magic is restricted in Zelig," Ulrich warned. "I wouldn't dare use it without permission from the queen if I were you."

The round innkeeper made her way to our table with a tray of drinks, soon followed by a tray of stew and fresh bread. I'd never tasted bread so good. Of course, as pirates, we rarely got fresh bread, as it spoiled too quickly for long journeys.

"What are we going to do about the clothing?" I asked, wiping my face on my damp sleeve. "We're all soaked to the bones. We aren't going to be able to dress in these in the morning. Unless there is an enchanted way to dry them."

James leaned back to the next table, where Lord Tomblin and his men sat. "Are there any shops open we can purchase additional clothing? Or is it too late in the evening?"

Tomblin grunted. "There might be one shop open. Go out to the road, take your first right, and it's about three stores down." He picked up his mug and took another long swallow.

James nodded and got to his feet. "Come along. I can't carry everything on my own."

"Your coin purse will be rather empty by the time we leave," I pointed out as I stood to follow him.

"If he has enough in his coin purse," Ulrich slurred.

I glanced at him to find his cheeks rather flushed. "You're a lightweight."

"Am not." He giggled. "Maybe." He took a sloppy sip and dribbled some down his chin. He wiped at it with his fingers. "My father would be ashamed." He frowned.

I rolled my eyes and looked at Sky. "Keep an eye on him."

Sky scowled. "I'm not a babysitter."

I grinned. "You're not a first mate either."

Sky glowered at me, but a mischievous glint came to his eye. "I think I can keep him safe." He patted Ulrich on the arm.

"Just don't get us kicked out."

Gerard frowned. "I'll make sure he doesn't."

I followed James outside. And immediately regretted it. The frigid wind cut right through our damp clothing, making things a million times colder. Luckily we soon found the shop, and James loaded my arms with blankets and cloaks.

James walked to the counter. "How much?"

"Well . . ." The old woman filled her cheeks with air and started rattling off the price of each item.

James cut in. "I don't need to know how much each is individually. I need to know how much total." He raised a brow, studying the woman.

"Why, it's three gold pieces, plus four silvers."

James blinked at her. "What, are these made out of silk from a Sloth Toad's nest? Or silk and diamonds?" He narrowed his dark eyes.

"Things here are clearly more expensive than where you're from." She sniffled.

179

He dropped his coin purse onto the counter. "You'll take what I've got there and nothing more." He turned to me. "Come, Odette." He reached out and took the blankets from me while I carried the cloaks.

"How much money was in that coin purse?" I asked as soon as the door jingled shut behind us.

James rolled his eyes. "The equivalent of three gold pieces. I barely shortchanged her, and I still feel it was too much. Normally I would have continued to argue with her, but I'm rather exhausted and looking forward to some sleep."

When we pushed the door open, we both froze in the entryway.

The pointed tip of a sword poked between my shoulder blades, and from the corner of my eye, I saw James frozen in the same manner. A soldier finished locking Ulrich's wrists behind him. A couple of soldiers had their swords drawn on Gerard, who stood with both hands up. At first, I couldn't see Sky but then discovered him unconscious on the ground with a soldier's foot on his back.

Lord Tomblin was speaking to an equally high-ranking officer—I could tell because he also wore a phoenix plume in his helmet—in a language I couldn't understand.

"What is the meaning of this?" James interrupted loudly.

Lord Tomblin turned to us. "Someone sent for the royal guard. Claimed there was an individual impersonating Prince Ulrich"

"And is lies," Ulrich slurred, still tipsy. "You know it's me. I'm me."

"The party you travel with are not known friends of yours," the royal guard stated flatly.

"They want us to deliver all of you to the castle immediately," Lord Tomblin added.

"So much for getting sleep," I muttered to James from the corner of my mouth.

"Why are my men chained and unconscious?" He gestured to Sky.

Lord Tomblin opened his mouth to answer, but the other man spoke first. "He attempted to attack us, and so he was taken care of."

"How much damage could a drunk boy do?" I threw in.

The man didn't even acknowledge me. "As for this boy"—he gestured to Ulrich—"we need to ensure that he is who he claims to be. Impersonating royalty is a horrible crime."

"And imagine how embarrassed you will be, mister high and mighty, when you discover I speak the truth! And then you will answer for humiliating the crown prince of Terricina! Asides . . ." Ulrich smacked his lips. "You can see through me."

"Not while you are drunk. If you do not close your mouth, I'll have my men close it for you. Now, we will escort you immediately to the castle ourselves." He nodded to the men behind James and myself, but neither of us was going to allow whatever that nod meant.

Both of us ducked under their arms. I dropped the pile of cloaks by the door, rolled, snagged one of the chairs, and threw it with all my might at the captain of the royal guard. He easily stepped aside, a disappointed frown on his face. If he thought we were going down without a fight, he was wrong.

Then again, if I thought I was going to be able to take on the castle guard, I was wrong as well. The soldier nearest me drew his sword and stepped forward. I had only my boot dagger to defend myself, giving me quite a disadvantage. But I jumped back from his first movement. I slid closer to a table—whose patrons now stood pressed against the far wall—and snatched one of the candlesticks. I stabbed the hot wax end into the soldier's face.

He cried out and clutched his face.

I used his moment of distraction to draw my dagger, and when he attacked again, I locked my dagger up and under the soldier's hilt, grabbed his wrist with my free hand, and rolled inside. Without warning, I leaned up and kissed him on the lips.

He froze, eyes wide in confusion.

I promptly stomped on his foot, kneed him in the groin, then slammed my dagger across his cheek with all the strength I had in me. I didn't watch him slump to the floor. I turned to see James fighting two soldiers at once. His footwork had always been far better than my own.

I ran and leapt on the back of the man nearest to me.

Lord Tomblin heaved a sigh, and his voice rose over the noise. "Enough of this, Lord Wilfred. I already told you these men aren't a threat to the crown. You will have to pay any damages if you allow this to continue."

Lord Wilfred didn't seem too happy about ordering his men to stop.

They backed up, but James didn't dare put his sword away.

"They began the fight. My men were protecting themselves," Lord Wilfred said haughtily. He twitched his nose side to side in an arrogant manner. "What, with Selina showing up out of the blue, the queen is worried about keeping everything in order."

"Selina is here?" Gerard asked.

Lord Wilfred looked down his wide nose at Gerard. "Yes."

Gerard lowered his arms and rolled his eyes. "Take us to her immediately."

"And why should I follow your orders, boy?" Lord Wilfred sneered.

Gerard narrowed his green eyes. "Because *I* am Gerard Tovan D'Prei. Grandson of Madame Selina."

SEVENTEEN

Lord Wilfred's face slowly paled as his smug expression fell. Whoever this "Selina" person was, if she made Lord Wilfred stop at the mention of her name . . . then again, who was Gerard? To be able to throw his name and his relation to this woman around, he must have been far more important than I realized.

I looked at James for an answer, but he only glanced sideways at me and lifted his shoulders in a faint shrug. Apparently, even James didn't know about Gerard's heritage—whatever it was.

Lord Wilfred swallowed hard. "As you wish. Men, give each of them one of these cloaks or blankets and get them on the horses. We leave immediately."

James finally put his sword away and walked over to Gerard's side.

Gerard, however, held up his hand to stop James's question. "Now isn't the time to explain all of this. When we get to the castle."

"I shared intimate details with you," James quipped. "The least you can do is return the favor."

"And I shall, when there are not ears to hear." He nudged his head toward the terrified patrons huddled to one side of the room. "You understand the importance of being discreet."

James was clearly displeased, but with the soldiers ushering us out, he didn't have a choice other than to accept Gerard's request.

I snatched my cloak from the soldier I'd momentarily knocked out and glared at him.

"Easy, miss. We're just doing our jobs," he said with a nod of his head. He handed another to James and then stopped at Ulrich to tie one around his neck.

"You truly aren't going to unchain me?" Ulrich chided. "I am the *crown prince of Terricina*, in case you forgot."

"I'm following orders, Sire." He finished tying the cloak and adjusted the hood over Ulrich's head.

"You could at least chain my wrists in front of me so I can be of some use if my hood falls in the wind." He narrowed his eyes.

"I would have to agree with you." The soldier unlatched the key from his belt and unlocked one shackle from Ulrich's wrist.

"Florian," Lord Wilfred warned.

Ulrich didn't complain as he brought his wrists forward and allowed the soldier to re-attach the shackle. He mumbled a low, "Thank you."

The soldier nodded and hooked the keys back on his belt. "He doesn't pose a threat, father." Florian turned to his leader.

The rest of the men guided us back out into the still-blowing snow, though it didn't seem that snow came from the clouds now. Our breath puffed out before us, making us look like little chimneys in the dark, frigid air.

"Each of my men will accompany one of yours." Lord Wilfred adjusted his gloves. He then covered the lower half of his face with material.

"No, they won't," James quipped. He motioned for me. "Odette will ride with me."

"She can ride with me if it makes you feel any better."

"It doesn't." James slid his arm around my waist and guided me in front of him, then to the side of the horse. "I don't trust you. Or your men. What sort of man ambushes others in an inn while they eat supper?"

"The kind of man who is aware the daughter of the pirate queen is in our midst, as well as a pirate captain." Lord Wilfred arched his brow.

I felt the hand on my hip tense as I asked, "How would you know?"

"I make it my business to know." He straightened.

"And it's a gift of the phoenix feather, remember?" Ulrich added.

"Stupid enchanted items," I grumbled.

"Just get on the horse," James said in a low voice.

"I already said she would ride with me." Lord Wilfred reached his hand down toward me.

James didn't move.

I didn't move.

The man stared us both down. "We don't want to cause any further trouble tonight. Do we?"

Neither of us answered, and silence settled over the group. The lack of white clouds told me everyone was holding their breath.

"Very well," Lord Wilfred conceded. He reached behind him into the saddlebag and produced two sets of shackles. "You shall wear these. Captain." He tossed a set toward James, but James allowed them to hit the ground.

I understood, then, what was happening. He was testing James. Testing to see how hard he could be pushed.

James slowly turned, guided my foot into the stirrup of his horse, and then hoisted me onto the saddle. He had turned his back to Lord Wilfred, showing he didn't view the man as a threat at all, but my stomach climbed up in my throat.

James climbed into the saddle behind me. He looped the reins around the hook on his hand, then nodded to Lord Wilfred. "Lead the way. Sir."

For once, I didn't mind James being a little pushy or possessive. I didn't mind keeping my mouth shut either. I reached my hand up to touch James's.

Lord Wilfred didn't look too pleased, and I believed in my heart that if Lord Tomblin and his men hadn't been there, the second general—or whatever he was called—might have reacted more aggressively to James's defiance.

Lord Wilfred snapped his horse into movement with an aggressive tug and began leading us into the night.

My stomach finally settled, and I swallowed. I leaned back against James. It was then his body released the tension it had been holding, and he slid his hand across my stomach.

"That was frightening," he whispered in my ear.

I laced our fingers. "Thank you," I replied in an equal tone.

I checked on the others. Ulrich had been seated in front of Florian, Sky was flung over the back end of a horse, and Gerard rode with a third soldier. His jaw was set, and I wondered what he was thinking. If his grandmother was here, surely he would stay. Especially if he could get the stone from Ulrich before I had a chance.

The snow had stopped, but the wind continued to kick the flurries up from the top layer of snow on the ground and from the trees. I kept my cloak tight around me and couldn't help but feel I had an advantage, being shielded by James's body.

Out of the blue, James said, "I kept a secret."

I turned my head, holding the edge of the cowl from my face so I could see his expression.

He looked down at me, bags under his eyes. "That's how I lost my hand."

I turned the other direction to glance at the metal hook holding the loop of leather to control the horse, though the horse didn't need much encouragement or direction.

"How did keeping a secret lead to losing your hand?" I made sure to glance at the others to make sure none were eavesdropping. If they were, they gave no indication. Of course, it *was* the middle of the night, so everyone was likely too tired to care what we were talking about.

"The person I kept the secret from put a hook through my hand."

I flinched.

"It was a hook used for whaling, rather like this one I now wear."

"Why would they do that?" Bile crept up the back of my tongue.

"They wanted information."

"Did they get it?"

His silence was enough to tell me they had, and for a brief moment, I was able to imagine James hanging from one hand, feet on the ground enough to give him balance. But the weight of his half-conscious body pulled at the hook protruding from a bloodied and ruined hand. I could taste the tang of blood in the air and feel his warm, damp skin on my fingertips as I brushed the hair from his eyes.

Just as instantly as the image came, it was gone, and my head pounded as if someone had punched me upside the head. I massaged my forehead. "Was . . . I there?" and then my stomach sunk as saliva seeped across my tongue in disgust. "Was-was I the one who did that to you?"

"No. No, it wasn't you," he reassured, sliding his arm around my stomach and holding me to him. "You got me down, though."

"I cut off your hand?" My jaw dropped as I spun in the saddle, then tugged stupidly at the hood so I could see past it to James's handsome face.

He shook his head.

"You swear it wasn't me?"

"I already said no. Why don't you close your eyes and try to get some sleep?" James rested his chin on top of my head.

I looked down at the hook and ran my hand up and down his arm. I'd teased him relentlessly for months about being called "Hook," while all along someone had not only cut it off but tortured him by hanging him from it. No wonder why he hated the nickname.

The constant rocking of the horse was enough to at least lull me into a doze, though I kept my ears alert just in case.

"We're here," one of the men said.

I blinked away the frost on my eyelashes. I felt as if I'd barely closed my eyes, and we'd already arrived at the castle?

I lifted my gaze from the stony blue of the snow in the night and saw, through the gaps in the trees, we had approached stunning mountains. Sitting on an outcropping of stone, overlooking the valley below, was a magnificent stone castle. Behind the castle, the sun began to wake, casting its rays around the mountain peaks and giving the castle a yellow hue.

Initially, I was in awe of the castle—its high slender towers, peaked roofs, and beautiful architecture—was like nothing I'd seen along the shores of Terricina. But as we walked through the town to reach the entrance, I felt nothing but coldness. The same coldness as the snow.

"Feel that?" Ulrich muttered.

"I thought it was just me," I answered. "It's cold."

"It's winter," Gerard said stiffly, but behind his stoic mask, I could see the worry in his green eyes as he studied the castle.

"All weapons will be left at the door with the guards," Lord Wilfred ordered as we passed through the outer gates.

Soldiers stood overhead on the walls, looking down through ice-sheened helmets. If one hadn't moved, I might have believed them to be statues.

I licked my chapped lips and rubbed my dripping nose on the back of my hand. I couldn't wait to get inside and sit in front of a fire to thaw.

We passed through the inner walls to the courtyard, and Lord Wilfred ordered us to dismount. He then looked at Lord Tomblin. "You may return to your duties at the border."

Lord Tomblin's head tilted slightly. "My men and I shall rest up today and leave tomorrow morning. The others can watch the border for a day." He motioned for us to dismount and nodded to his men.

Ulrich had to wait for the soldier he rode with to set him on the ground. Ulrich shimmied his shoulders, rolling them to try and stretch. He walked over to my side and kept his eyes forward. "Something is very wrong."

EIGHTEEN

The inside of the castle felt somehow colder than outside. I pulled my cloak tighter around me, though the action didn't provide any additional warmth as I had hoped. Torches along the hallways flickered with a blue hue to them, which somehow made the place look like it was covered in a layer of ice.

I'd never been in a castle before, but this was hardly as exciting as I wanted it to be.

Sky held the side of his head and walked unbalanced. James had to hold him by the elbow to keep him upright. The men must have delivered a terrible blow to keep him unconscious so long, and I actually felt bad Sky was forced to now walk around after a head injury like that.

He groaned miserably.

We passed through the grand room—a room with a high ceiling, a balcony around the second floor, and a vaulted roof at least two stories high. With no torches lit inside, it was difficult to see much other than the shadows of shapes. Statues stood between the pillars holding the second-floor balcony.

We were directed to the throne room, a room to the left of the grand room, stripped of our weapons, and ordered to stay there. Lord Tomblin left us with a nod of reassurance. Lord Wilfred assigned two guards to stay with us and left to get the queen.

"*Kerling*," Gerard muttered under his breath. He walked to the fireplace, tossed a few logs in, and held his hand out. He whispered words I didn't understand, and a fire ignited.

"You're a sorcerer?" One of the soldiers drew his sword.

Florian, the soldier who had been kind enough to redo Ulrich's chains, stepped forward. "Relax. If he is the grandson of Selina, of course he is a sorcerer."

"Besides," Gerard added, rising to his feet. "If I wanted to cause any harm, why would I have waited until we arrived here?"

"Because you wanted to get here safely so you could injure the queen," he retorted.

Gerard rolled his eyes to us. "Non-magic folk are truly unbearable."

"Put your sword down," Florian said, swatting at his companion's hand. "He'd kill you with a word before you could take a step forward, and you don't want that out when the queen arrives."

James helped Sky over to the fireplace. Sky promptly flopped onto the hearth. He didn't look too good. His eyes were bloodshot, and I could see caked blood on the side of his head.

Ulrich crouched at his side. "Florian, he could use a doctor, or herbalist, or whatever you have that could help." He looked up at the soldier. "Unless you allow me to create a healing potion." He glanced at Gerard. "Do you heal?"

Gerard scoffed. "No."

Florian ran his fingers through his hair. "I'll see what I can do, but there's no guarantee. The queen has to approve."

"He's got a terrible wound." Ulrich frowned, straightening. "Your queen would deny that help?"

Florian glanced at the door and shifted his weight. "Things . . . aren't quite as they should be."

"I could sense it," Ulrich replied flatly. "What is going on?"

He shook his head. "I can't say. I don't exactly know."

It was good he didn't try and start because the door flung open with a rush of cold air, and a queen—as regal and cold as her castle—stepped into the room. Her pale face reflected the firelight, and her eyes were so blue, they looked like the deepest part of a flame.

"Queen Grimhilde," Ulrich greeted, bowing as a prince should, the best he could in chains, then straightened and rounded his shoulders.

The queen looked him up and down with a calculated slowness. She strode gracefully to her throne and sat. "Crown Prince Ulrich of Terricina. What brings you to my kingdom at this hour?"

Ulrich seemed to relax a little after her saying his title. "I came to seek your aid. My father . . ." He drew a breath. "He foolishly signed a contract with the sea witch. Only, at the time, he didn't know she was the sea witch."

Queen Grimhilde didn't blink. "And why is this my responsibility?"

"It is not. But we seek . . . *I* seek your assistance," he corrected. "And I'm sure we can pay you back some way. I don't know how to undo the contract. The sea witch has taken the capital city of Delphi and dragged it into the sea. All of my people who were in Delphi have been transformed into sirens, and my kingdom still on the land has been without a leader for months."

"A rather vulnerable position to be in." The queen inclined her head. "And you come to me for help."

Ulrich blinked. He'd already said it twice. He opened his mouth to answer.

"You think I have experience in magic enough to reverse your father's stupidity?" she continued. "He's dug his own grave. Let him lie in it."

"He already does," Ulrich said. "At least, I believe so. I haven't seen him since the city was dragged into the sea." He stepped forward. "But my people shouldn't suffer for whatever my father did. They should be on the land with their families."

"You believe it was he alone who upset her? Your people are purely innocent?" She flashed a smile, but there was no kindness in it. It looked predatory, and I couldn't help but think her face was masking a darker expression.

Ulrich was caught off guard. He stammered for an answer. "Your highness, I . . . don't purport to assume . . . I . . . we need help."

"Why not go to the sea witch herself?"

Ulrich turned to me. Evidentially, going to the sea witch directly hadn't occurred to him. He swallowed hard.

"You haven't done a thing to try and find either of them. Have you? Tsk."

Still, Ulrich hesitated. I saw his fingers flex. "Not exactly," he muttered. "We searched the debris for my father with no result. And I did send scouts to see what they could find, but no one could make it through Siren's Gate. *And* I've been looking out for my people. Surely, you understand. Perhaps you can find her for me, and then I can go to her?"

Queen Grimhilde's eyes snapped to me. Silently, she rose to her feet and approached. "What have we here?"

I sucked a breath in. I hadn't said or done anything. I hadn't even moved from James's side. Nothing should have drawn her attention to me.

The queen stopped inches from my face. Her eyes remained locked on mine, and her icy fingertips brushed my collarbone as she lifted my necklace onto her thin fingers. She chuckled, too light a sound for the tension in the room. "A spy in our midst."

"It's only a pearl." I tried to sound brave, but my voice came out differently.

"Foolish child." She plucked the precious pearl from my neck.

I gasped and put my hand to my chest, as though I could stop her.

James held my arm and gave me a firm shake of the head, preventing me from reacting.

"Please . . . it means a lot to me," I pressed.

"Keeping an eye on things, are we, Athena?" Her fingers caressed the gemstone. "Of course you would. But you're too frightened to use the mirrors." She chuckled again, crossing to her throne. Queen Grimhilde's gaze lifted to me. Her hand closed around my pearl. "She is protective yet disappointed in you, Princess Odette. Sent you to spy on me, did she? Well, you can return to your mother and inform her she won't get any secrets from me." Her eyes narrowed, began to glow blue, and the same glow enveloped her hand.

"No, wait!" I ran forward, but a tiny puff of smoke escaped the gaps between her fingers.

Queen Grimhilde extended her hand to me. The shattered pieces of my pearl necklace lay in her open palm. "I don't take kindly to spies. Men, lock them in the tower."

I reached out for the fragments, but the queen tipped her hand and dumped the contents onto the rug. My breath caught. It was gone. Worse, she knew my mother by name. How could she know my mother? And what had she sensed in my charm?

"We aren't spies," Ulrich tried. "I told you why I came!"

"And brought the enemy with you." She headed for the doorway.

"She needs your help as well," Ulrich said quickly. "She's lost her memories!"

"If I may, your serene majesty," Gerard's smooth voice said.

Queen Grimhilde stopped and faced him. She studied him with the same look she'd given Ulrich just moments ago, but her eyes narrowed. "I know you."

He gave her a dashing smile and bowed. "My name is Gerard."

"Selina's prodigy," she confirmed.

He nodded. "Prince Ulrich has something that may be of interest to you. The summer stone."

Her eyes locked once more on Ulrich.

"He is willing to offer it to you in return for aid." Gerard approached so calmly, he looked like a cat on the prowl. "Think of what having both the winter and summer stones could do to your power."

Her eyes flickered, and her lip curled. "Perhaps . . ."

Gerard gave her another dashing smile. "And you wouldn't even need to tell Selina. Keep it your secret." He added a wink.

Queen Grimhilde slowly turned to us. "I believe all of you are in need of warm baths, some breakfast, and sleep." She looked once more to her guards. "Take them to the East Wing. I will have the servants run their baths and bring breakfast to you. Oh, and do unchain Prince Ulrich. He's a mischievous one, and we don't need him causing damage to get back at us for those." She exited the room.

Ulrich let out a breath. "Thank you, Gerard."

Gerard looked at him sideways. "Be extremely cautious. She's more powerful than I thought. Not even I sensed that spell on Odette's pearl." He followed the queen.

None of us said anything as we were led up the stone steps at the back of the great hall. From there, the two guards each gestured to a room.

"You can have your own bed tonight," James said, giving me a nod.

My heart jumped into my throat, restricting my breath with panic. Just the thought of being alone made me almost lose my mind. How pathetic was I? "I would prefer you didn't," I said, the admission coming out in a frantic tone as I snagged my fingers on his hook.

He stopped. "Prefer I didn't what?"

"Leave me alone," I whispered loudly. "Not here, of all places. There could be hidden doors to secret passages! Someone could come in the middle of the night!"

"I think you listen to too many of the pirate stories." He grinned, a relieving sight, but nodded. "Can you manage without me?" He turned to Ulrich specifically, since Sky was still supporting himself on the wall.

Ulrich nodded. "I'll take care of him. Don't worry. It will be payback for last night."

I didn't care to ask what had happened when James and I left to get the cloaks and blankets.

Sky patted me on the arm, giving me a pathetic smile of his own. "Don't worry. No fairies are going to carry you away tonight. I think it's too cold here for those sorts of things."

"Actually, we have fairies for servants here," Florian, the guard, said.

"Oh great," I muttered.

Sky gave me an unapologetic smile, said, "Oops."

I dragged my thumb across my throat.

He laughed, then grimaced. As he stepped into his room, he waved his fingers at me unapologetically. Ulrich followed him. Florian closed the door behind them and turned to us. As James was closing our door, I saw Gerard walk on with the soldiers.

I turned to the bed just in time to see a beautiful woman in a shimmering green dress set another log on the fire. The beautiful four-post bed with pale-blue bedding embroidered with gold snowflakes stood to my right and had been turned down for us. The girl gave me a polite nod, lifted her transparent wings—I only saw the reflection of the firelight on them—and shrunk to a few inches tall.

My world froze.

The fairy flitted to the mantle, leaving a silver trail of dust trailing behind her. She moved a small dragon figurine aside, then disappeared down into the mantle itself. The figurine slid back into place.

I reached out and patted James's body, not sure what I was patting, eyes still unblinking. "Did . . . did you see that?"

"I saw the cozy look of that fire."

"You didn't see the fairy?" I looked at him with wide eyes.

He couldn't hold back a teasing smile. "I saw her. But you've got me here now. Nothing to worry about."

I rolled my eyes and frowned at him. "You sleep like a lump of wood. You're no help to me while you sleep."

"Then why do you want me here?"

I lifted my chin and shrugged, then spun on my heel and walked over to chair at the desk and dragged it over to the warmth of the fire. Deliberately, I peeled my wet shirt off slowly and set it over the chair. I then shimmied out of my pants and draped it beside my shirt. Standing in only my underclothes did nothing to help against the cold, but at least I would be warmer once I was dry.

I felt James's body heat behind me.

"You shouldn't tease," he said softly, his warm breath floating down to my neck and stroking my collarbone. His fingertips trailed down my hand—a ghost of a touch.

"If I didn't want you, I wouldn't tease," I said bluntly and turned to face him.

He shook his head. "We shouldn't."

"Why not?" I reached up and traced his lips. "Why shouldn't I want to be with you? James . . . I really don't know what happened those months ago, but you alluded to us already being together. I . . . want that feeling. I like that feeling of us."

He leaned down, but I kept my finger pressed to his lips, teasing him. His brows pinched in confusion.

I grabbed the bottom of his wet shirt and lifted it over his head. As I did, I leaned forward and kissed his chest. "Your clothes are sopping wet."

"Who cares?" He reached up and quickly tugged his shirt off all the way and threw it to the side.

He pulled me close and drowned me in kisses. His arms held me close, making me feel safe in a way no one ever could. His teeth pulled my bottom lip. I ran my fingers through his hair. He ignited corners of my heart I had somehow forgotten.

James felt so right. I thought Sky was my other half. But James?

He was my everything.

And then the damn broke.

Whatever spell had taken hold of me months ago broke.

I dug my nails into James's shoulders as the pain of memories hit me, taking my breath away as if I'd been dragged to the bottom of the sea. Memories that held the truth of the day Terricina's capital had been dragged into the sea.

Memories of James.

My James.

NINETEEN

Y"ou want me to what?" I stared at my mother, my jaw slack in shock.

She rested her forearms on the table, the parchment before me, and her green eyes slowly narrowed. "What part of that didn't you understand?" she asked.

I blinked and shook my head. "Just to be clear, you want me to usurp the throne of Terricina?"

"Yes."

"You want me to be the princess?"

"Yes." She let out a frustrated sigh and straightened in her seat.

"But . . . why?"

We sat at the kitchen table, having just finished a delicious meal I now realized had been only for the sake of preparing me for this conversation. It had been my favorite meal, after all—boiled crab over spicy lime rice with buttered clams on the side and even some red wine.

"I will explain everything once you are on the throne," my mother answered.

I pressed my fingertips to my forehead as I thought. My mother had just delivered a very frightening plan to take over the country of Terricina, and I didn't know whether to be impressed or terrified.

"Explain how this is going to work," I finally said, placing my free hand on the written contract before me.

"It's rather simple, really. I have already arranged a meeting to speak with King Eric. I will present him with this contract, which he will be unable to refuse. You see, this contract states that we pirates will leave the shipping lane open from Castle Bay and westward to Ashwrya's shore. Any merchant who flies the flag of Terricina will be allowed to pass to Delphi."

I gasped. "Are you crazy? That would ruin us!"

"Calm down." She chuckled. "This is why I say they will be unable to pass this opportunity."

"And why trick them with this? How does that get me on the throne?" I pressed.

"That part is simple. Once they sign the contract, the city will be dragged into the sea, and King Eric will have no choice than to sign away his kingdom to you."

"Mother, this . . . this is a foolish idea." I shook my head and pushed the paper aside. "Did you consider talking to him about why you're upset?"

She laughed at me. "Talk to him? No, this is revenge. I am taking everything from him."

I stared at my mother in disbelief. "Perhaps you could just ask him to give it up?"

"You want me to ask *him to have you rule the kingdom?"*

"Well . . ." I glanced at the paper. *"I suppose I meant* threaten. *Instead of dragging them directly into the sea, tell the king if he doesn't give you the throne,* then *you'll drag his capital into the sea."*

"Hm." She ran her fingers over the silver chain on her neck. *"And then when he refuses, do it anyway. Agree to bring the city out of the ocean if he surrenders the throne. I approve of this method."*

"Mother, how are you going to do this? We're sirens with the ability to take on human forms. We aren't magical beyond that."

Athena touched the parchment. "Through this contract. I've enchanted it. If King Eric signs it, it activates the powers."

"But . . ." I paused and shook my head. *"Wait,* you have enchanted it? Meaning . . ."*

She smiled.

My heart started to race. *"You have magic."*

"Our little secret." She winked.

"You . . . are the sea witch?"

"How else would I be able to enchant something?" She gestured to the contract, a proud smirk on her face.

I think she expected me to be excited, but I was terrified. My mother was the sea witch? *"Mother . . . I'm not even fit to be a princess! I don't know that I want to rule a kingdom at all,"* I objected. *"I don't want to."*

"Oh, hush. The decision has already been made." She got to her feet. *"I leave tomorrow with my crew to go*

to Delphi. You will follow at the end of the week with Captain Avery."

"Tomorrow?" I jumped to my feet as well. "Mother, this isn't a decision you should make so hastily."

"It isn't. This is something I have been preparing since the day you were born. Now you are eighteen, you are old enough to rule." She lifted her hat from the table and placed it on her head. "And when you rule Terricina, you will be able to help every pirate as well."

"Athena," I said firmly, knowing she hated when I called her by her name.

"It is done, Odette." She said each consonant sharply. Our conversation was over. She snagged the parchment and left the room.

I watched her, feeling helpless. I might have been raised a pirate, but not this kind of pirate. It was true some pirates were ruthless, but I had been raised to show mercy where it was due. Of course, that was mostly through Captain Avery's teachings and not my mother, whom I barely sailed with.

I licked my lips and went to the only person I knew I could talk to—James Barrie.

James was lounging on the beach when I found him, absently running his fingers through the sand, eyes closed, and face turned up to the sky. The sun was setting, and I couldn't blame him for enjoying a moment of peace.

I plopped down at his side in such a state of shock I could only stare across the bay. "My mother is leaving tomorrow."

He opened his eyes, a grin sliding to his face. "Ah. So you and I can spend some time alone." He wrapped his *arm around my shoulders. And then his smile dropped, and he pulled me to him. "What's wrong?"*

"She's going to Delphi. The capital of Terricina." I shook my head and dragged my knees to my chest. "She has this . . . insane idea that I'm going to rule the kingdom. She wants me to usurp the throne."

"Your mother?" He arched a brow.

I nodded.

James took my left hand in his left hand and traced my palm, his right arm never leaving my shoulders. "Why on earth would she want to do that? Isn't she content with what she's built here?"

I let out a sigh and shook my head. "She wants revenge. James, she admitted to me she's the sea witch."

His body went rigid.

I peered up at him.

"The sea witch? She's really the sea witch?"

"I don't know what to think," I admitted, throwing my hands up in dismay. "James, she's completely serious. She is going to drag Delphi into the sea if we don't stop her. There are thousands of people living in that city! She'll kill them all!"

"Okay, first you've got to take a breath." He demonstrated while I rolled my eyes. "There must be some way to stop her."

"The contract," I muttered. And then I gasped and grabbed his face. "You're smarter than a dolphin!"

"Uh . . . thanks?"

"All we have to do is burn the contract. If she doesn't have the contract . . ."

James's brows lifted. "Ah, then she can't go through with her plot."

"Exactly." I kissed him, then climbed to my feet.

"When is she leaving?" He grunted as he followed my lead.

"Tomorrow. Which means I need to get rid of the contract tonight." I wiped off the butt of my pants and turned to him. "I need you to distract her."

James laughed. "No, thank you. How do you expect me to do that?"

"I don't know. Get your father to try and make a deal with her for something. He's fond of that arrangement." I shrugged.

His brow twitched. "You're not wrong," he muttered. He dusted his hands on his pants. "Or you could just wait for her to fall asleep."

I tapped my lip. "That would work too." I opened my mouth to add something but heard footsteps and quickly turned to see who could be close enough to eavesdrop on our conversation.

Sky stopped in his tracks. "What'd I do?"

I breathed in relief. "Nothing. What did you need?"

"Captain Avery wants you." He pointed with his thumb over his shoulder. "They're gettin' ready to set sail."

My breath hitched. "Right now?"

"Yeah. Captain Athena wanted you guys to do one last mission before . . . something." His forehead scrunched in thought, and the scar on his cheek pinched. "I forgot.

I faced James with a helpless sort of silence. If I didn't leave, my mother would know I was up to something.

Then again, my mother was likely sending me on this red herring to keep me distracted so I couldn't interfere.

James stepped forward. "Don't worry. You go. I'll take care of it."

"Are you certain?" I asked, my voice low so Sky couldn't hear.

He winked and my heart jumped. "You can trust me." He leaned down and pressed his lips to mine, sending a rush of tingles to my toes. "I'll be here when you get back. Don't worry, everything will be all right."

I gave him a weak smile, not trusting that things were okay. My stomach rolled in unease, like a sea before the storm hits. I was learning to trust my gut—something Captain Avery always emphasized—and right now it was warning me not to leave James behind.

But I saw no other choice.

Begrudgingly, I made my way onto Captain Avery's ship.

He smiled at me. "Welcome aboard, Odette. We're heading off to pick up some cannons for the new ship. Shouldn't take longer than a few days."

My gaze shifted to the new ship in the harbor, the belly of the ship jutting from the land like the ribs of a skeleton. The keel was in place, like a spine, and soon would be filled in. In a few months, the new ship would be completed.

I'd speculated with James that he would be the next captain. He'd laughed and said it would be mine, for sure, since I was the daughter of the pirate queen. I had to admit looking at it at that moment, I had a sinking feeling in the pit of my stomach. I would much rather have been a pirate captain than princess of a land I wanted nothing to do with.

"Odette? Are you all right?" Captain Avery put his hand on my shoulder.

"Fine," I answered shortly and straightened. "I'm just not feeling well, is all."

"Getting back out to sea always seems to help." He offered me a friendly wink and turned to his helmsman. "Ready?"

"Aye, Cap'n!" Smee hollered back.

"Let's set sail!" Captain Avery walked away from me, seeing to the ship getting off properly.

I fell into place, climbing rigging to release the ropes around the sails. From my vantage point, I looked out at Port Mere. My home. James was down there somewhere, possibly walking up to my mother's house right at that moment. In a few hours, he would have the contract burned, and I . . . I would be out at sea with Captain Avery for no fewer than three days, depending on which port my mother decided to send us off to.

I was anxious the entire journey, and as I feared, something horrible happened.

When we arrived in the small Port of Gillsberry two days later, Sammy called down from the eagle's nest that there was someone in the water on the port side.

Everyone ran to the left of the ship just as Sky poked his head from the surface, breathing hard as if he'd swam all day and night to get to us. Which seemed to be exactly what he'd done.

"James . . . is gone," he panted. His fingers clung to the barnacles on the hull of the ship, and he didn't seem to care that his hands were being cut up.

"Get him up here!" Captain Avery shouted.

Men threw rope down and hoisted Sky onto the ship. His two-toned red and blue fin peeled from his body, giving into his land legs painfully slowly.

"Tell us what happened," Captain Avery ordered.

Sky shook his head, working through the pain to catch his breath. "Athena took him."

My heart stopped, and I dropped to my knees beside him. I grabbed on to his shoulders and shook him. "Tell me everything! Now!"

"I'm trying!" he yelled back, giving me a shove. "I don't know exactly what happened. I ran out and saw her dragging him down to her ship, spewing curses and saying something about getting her revenge. She left . . ." He paused and glanced at the sky, then finally shook his head. "The morning after you left. She took him. I don't know where. I didn't follow them. Probably should have, but they headed up the coast westward."

I looked up at Captain Avery and opened my mouth.

"Get us back to Port Mere now," Avery said before I could get a word out. "Put everything into her sails! And may the gods be with us. Odette, you've got some explaining. Does this have to do with you being nervous to leave two days ago?"

I swallowed the growing lump in my throat and nodded. "Y-Yes. I . . ."

He took me by the arm and pulled me to my feet. "You and I will speak alone. Reginald, help get Sky some clothing and get him to a hammock to sleep."

"Aye!"

Captain Avery took me to his cabin and closed the door. "Now we don't have prying ears, what is it?"

I explained everything I knew, about my mother's plan to have me rule Terricina, sink Delphi, my idea to burn the contract so she couldn't, and how I couldn't follow through because I was commanded to leave so James was going to do it.

I paced as I spoke, moving my hands in a dramatic fashion. " . . . so my mother must have caught James in the act. I don't know what her plan is with him. Do you think she'd hurt him?" I looked at Captain Avery but knew my mother well enough to know his sullen expression before I even asked the question.

Yes, my mother would harm James if he tried to intervene in her plans.

"Odette, I can't say what your mother did was right or wrong, or what she's going to do. It hasn't happened yet."

"But it will happen if we don't find some way to stop her." I let out a frustrated groan and put my hands against my temples. "I don't understand why she's even doing this in the first place. Yes, being a pirate is against the law, but we sort of deserve it. I don't think it's so traumatic that she would be angry about it."

Captain Avery rubbed his chin. "It might have to do with something that happened many years ago, come to think of it."

"And what is that?"

He shook his head. "I don't remember all the details. Time's washed them away, but I do know it has something to do between her and King Eric."

"You're so much help," I muttered.

He offered me a fatherly smile. "We're headin' back to Port Mere now. In a day and a half, we should make it if the wind's right and the current doesn't fail us, and then we'll find out about James."

I wasn't able to eat or sleep while we sailed back. It was agonizing, knowing James was in trouble and not being able to do a single thing about it. I knew I wouldn't be able to swim any faster than the Naiad, *so there was little point in trying.*

When we arrived back at Port Mere, in one and a half days as Captain Avery had promised, we were greeted by a pirate holding a letter with my mother's seal pressed into the blue wax—a siren.

Dearest Daughter,

I hope you find this letter before it's too late for your foolish lover. I offer you a choice and one only. Grimsby has been directed to give Captain Avery a letter of his own. As I am telling you, I am telling him.

James is in Castle Bay, held in the old boathouse. I trust you remember Castle Bay's reputation. Should you desire to go after him, I am not responsible for what the people of Castle Bay may do to you. I may have given them instruction to attack any ship pulling into port that isn't mine. I may have even told them the pirates were planning an attack on their very home.

You will find me in Delphi, the capital of Terricina. By the time you reach this, you will have just enough time to meet me there on Saturday. Join me now, and James will be released. Refuse me, and you'll never see your lover the same way ever again.

I will see you at the end of the week, Odette. Don't disappoint me.

Athena

My hands crumpled the edges of the parchment, and I struggled to swallow. Part of me wanted to shred it into pieces, and another part of me wanted to collapse to my knees and burst into sobs. I trembled as I turned to Captain Avery.

He ran his fingers through his hair and glanced at me. "James is in Castle Bay."

I nodded mutely.

"Your mother gave me explicit instructions to take you to Delphi."

"But James—"

"I'll send another crew to get him. You and I are going to Delphi." He motioned me back to the ship, but I didn't budge. "That was an order from your captain, Odette." His eyes narrowed, and his lips pulled downward in a frown.

I looked over my shoulder at the water. "I can swim there."

"Not through the Siren's Gate, you can't."

215

"*Then I'll go around it!*" *I shouted. I threw the paper at Grimsby, who didn't budge. "I'm not leaving James behind! He would save me if the roles were reversed.*"

"*Get on the ship, Odette.*"

I turned, but Captain Avery grabbed on to my arm.

"*I can't help if you don't trust me,*" *he said quickly and softly right in my ear.*

I put my hand over my mouth, stifling a pathetic sob. If anyone told James how dismal I was over his getting captured, I would gut them. But lack of sleep, starvation, and fear were taking its toll on me.

Captain Avery guided me back on board and ordered someone to get me food, then ordered me below deck for some sleep. "It's at least a day to Castle Bay, and you're useless to me like this."

I knew he meant it in the kindest way a pirate captain could, and so I complied. I ate all my food, discovering I was rather ravenous, found my hammock, and climbed in.

Sky rocked in his hammock, watching me. He looked much better than he had a day and a half ago. But he gave me a pathetic puppy-eyed look. "I'm really sorry about him," *he said.*

"*It's my fault,*" *I whispered back. "I sent him.*"

"*Sent him to what?*"

I closed my eyes. "It doesn't matter."

"*But—*"

"*I said it doesn't matter!*" *I snapped. "Now shut up or I'll cut out your tongue!*"

Sky clamped his mouth shut.

I fell into a fitful sleep.

TWENTY

The Naiad snuck into port as silently as a shark ready to strike. Only the moon pierced the darkness, and we had the added advantage—and danger—of cloud cover. Any other crew would have been nervous pulling into Castle Bay under such conditions, but we had no choice.

I ran my tongue impatiently over my teeth, unclenching my hands only long enough to stretch my numb fingers. My fingertips traced the crescent divots left behind by my nails now imprinted in my palms.

Captain Avery put his hand on my shoulder. "You know where to go. Get him and bring him back. Then we will head directly to Delphi and stop your mother before she does something we will all regret. I need not remind you of what could happen if we fail."

I nodded.

"Odette." He turned me to face him. "We will stop her. And you will save him."

217

"I know. Stop talking." I pulled away and marched to the railing of the ship.

Finally, we were close enough to the dock I could make my move. At the front of the ship, I jumped up on the bowsprit and sprinted its length. I launched myself into a dive and landed in the warm waters with barely a splash. I swam through the inky black of the sea to the shoreline.

As soon as I reached it, I scrambled through the impeding sand toward the boathouse built to the side of an old fishing dock. My green eyes scanned the darkness for any signs of men or women who might be on the sea witch's side.

I skidded to a halt as I reached the decaying dock and dilapidated wooden structure once known as a boathouse. Half the roof was gone, and the dock itself had splintered wood and was soft from years near the water. Luckily for me, that also meant my footsteps on the soft wood were muted.

My heart wanted me to run and burst in, but my brain won, and I moved with caution. I didn't know what kind of situation he was in, what traps—if any— had been left behind.

James had been in danger for a few days. I didn't know what to expect.

Creeping forward, I unsheathed my sword and kept my attention focused on the surface of the water—just in case. I heard nothing but water licking at the barnacles suctioned to the legs of the dock. I smelled nothing but the sea. I saw nothing but the gloom of night.

My heart hammered against my ribs, and I had to take steadying breaths.

When I reached the door, I licked my lips and cautiously tested the handle. I was only mildly surprised to find it unlocked and I gave it a sudden shove so I could catch anyone inside off-guard.

The door protested with a shriek of rusty hinges that shattered the silence of the night, and I flinched. I pointed my sword and swung left and right, but no shadows moved, and there was no light in the building, save the moonlight.

"James?" My voice sounded too loud, even at a whisper.

"Odette?" a gruff voice answered back.

I kept my sword poised, ready—just in case. The advantage to the roof being half blown off was the moonlight illuminating the inside of the abandoned building. But it revealed nothing but a damaged net hanging from one of the beams and old broken crates scattered about.

With a breath to calm my sickening nerves, I finally turned to look toward the rear of the boathouse.

James stood at the back of the space with one arm up, somehow bound to the beam overhead. He must have managed to get his right arm free but didn't have the strength to get his other arm free.

"You're crazy," he said weakly. "You've got to get out of here!"

"No, I've got to save you, stupid." I pushed my sword back into its sheath and marched over to him.

"Odette, no. You've got to run now. Stop . . . stop her." He held a hand out toward me as if that action alone would stop me.

"*You managed to get one hand down, I'll help you get . . . the . . .*" *My words faded, the sentence dying like a whisper on the wind when I caught sight of the truth.*

James's wrist wasn't bound to the beam by a rope. A thin whaling hook protruded from his palm, keeping him in place.

My stomach recoiled in disgust. I'd mistaken the darkness on his arm for a shadow. It wasn't that at all. It was blood. I didn't need the light of the afternoon sun to see James's hand was completely ruined.

I looked back down at his face. There was a gash on his eyebrow. Glancing lower, blood on his white shirt indicated a wound somewhere by his hip.

"*Odette, I told you to go,*" *he said softer.* "*You didn't need to see me like this.*"

"*I can't leave you.*" *I took a quick, deep breath through my nose, swallowed my disgust, and stepped forward.* "*No one else is going to save you.*"

I didn't have time to stop and think about what he must have gone through the past three days it took me to get to him. I had to get him down and back to the ship in time for Captain Avery and the crew to get us out of here. James needed medicine and rest.

I reached up on the very tips of my toes even though I knew how foolish it appeared. James stood several inches taller than me, and I barely reached his wrist. There was no way to reach the rope holding the hook in place.

"*Please,*" *James begged softly. With his right hand, he touched my side.*

"*I'm not giving up now.*" *I dropped to my heels and turned to find a crate to stand on. It took some effort to find one still intact but picked it up and carried it over. "You should know better than that. Besides, Captain Avery is waiting to take you home. I can't show up without you. What would be the point? I'm not failing him too."*

"You didn't fail me." His voice sounded so weak, so tired.

"It's my fault you were captured in the first place."

Even his scoff sounded more like a sigh of exhaustion. "You didn't cause her to take me, Odette."

I climbed on top of the crate and could finally reach the top of the hook. I pulled the dagger from my boot and tried sawing at it.

"Will you please listen to me?" James said, a hint of anger in his voice. "You're the only one who can stop her. You shouldn't be here. This is exactly what she wants! You distracted! No one else is willing to stand up to her."

"Look what she did to you!" I finally snapped back, stopping so I could look down into his handsome brown eyes. "She could have killed you! She definitely tried. She did this, and I only said no."

"She would have killed me if she didn't need me alive to draw you here. You've got to stop her." He tried to reach toward me and muffled a cry by biting his bottom lip. The movement must have twisted the hook in his hand.

I swallowed, but my throat was dry. "James, I'm getting you out of here." I started sawing again at the rope.

"Leave me the dagger. I'll do it myself. You go."

I paused. "But can you even reach?" I glanced between him and the hook.

"Of course I can. Look at my feet. I'm planted on the ground. If I raise up to my toes, I can reach. See?" To prove it, he got up on his toes and raised his right hand up to his left. His fingertips touched the hook, which caused him to gasp and quickly rest back on the wood. "S-see?"

"That was hardly impressive," I muttered.

"In a few short days, Delphi will be in the sea or worse. You're condemning hundreds of people to who knows what fate? Because you had to rescue me? I would never be able to live with myself."

I hated it when he was the rational one. Who was I kidding? He was always the rational one.

"I'll never forgive you if you allow those people to die because you had to save me."

I froze, then after a moment looked down at him.

His eyes were narrowed at me, and his split lips were pulled in a frown.

Slowly, I lowered myself to my heels. "Seriously?"

"I mean it. You have the potential to stop this from happening, and you're going to let it? Because I'm a little hurt? I'm not dying, Odette! Give me the dagger and get out of here!" His sudden anger hurt. I was only trying to help.

I stepped off the crate, my jaw tight, and I held my dagger out to him.

He wrapped his hand around mine and held me fast. "Get out of here. Now," he said firmly, his dark eyes burning.

I'd never felt more torn in my entire life.

Leaving behind the man I loved, injured and with the potential to get an infection and die, to save hundreds *of strangers I'd never even met wasn't my idea of a heroic action. Still, the sea witch had to be stopped one way or another. And he was right.*

I was the only one who could stop her.

The only one brave enough to stand up to her.

I grabbed a fistful of his shirt and pulled him down to meet my lips. The kiss was out of desperation, not passion as we'd once shared, and need. "You better get out of here alive, or so help me I'll find a way to bring you back from the dead so I can slap your stupid face."

James gave me a lopsided grin. "Are you going to say it?" He grinned bigger, this time his smile hopeful. "It's just three words. Two if you cut out the I."

"No. Because this isn't the last time I'm seeing you."

He chuckled, only to hiss and squeeze his eyes shut. "Well, I love you."

"I know." I blew him a kiss, wheeled around, and ran from the boathouse. Each step tore at my heart. I shouldn't have left him behind to fend for himself. She could have had a man waiting to stab him through the heart if I left.

And yet, I left.

I ran back into the darkness of night.

The citizens of Castle Bay had launched an attack as predicted. Many of my crew stood on the docks. I didn't know how long it would take to get everyone back on the ship or out to sea, and I knew in my gut that I didn't have much time. The only option I saw was swimming to Delphi, though that was an extreme length to try and swim. I needed the gods on my side.

Captain Avery must have sensed me because he looked in my direction. He gave me a short nod as a silent approval for a decision he didn't know I'd made.

I ran into the waters. And then I swam, not only for my life but the lives of thousands of strangers. Because it was the right thing to do.

In mere seconds, I was in my siren form swimming through the warm ocean current with as much speed as possible, using the eastern current and its momentum to carry me to Delphi.

I didn't know how it was possible, maybe I really had been blessed by the gods or something, because a green glow fell around me. I swam faster than I ever had in my entire life.

I did know one thing when I reached Delphi—I was positively exhausted.

But I couldn't wait.

I dragged myself out of the water. The transformation back into a human was always far more painful than returning to my siren form. I also had the tiny problem of being completely naked. Luckily for me, a group of men stood frozen nearby, staring at me with wide eyes.

It wasn't common to see a person climb out of the sea, less common to see a siren, and even less to see them transform into a human.

I pointed to the nearest man. "You there. Get me a shirt and pants." I gulped for breath.

The man looked stupidly at his friends.

"Now!"

He jumped and they all scrambled to find something. Eventually I was handed a shirt off a young man's back and large pants one of them pulled from a crate. I wasted no time dressing, ignoring the men watching, and took off toward the biggest building in the middle of the city that had to be the palace.

I ran down the street, holding my pants up, and when I drew near the palace, two soldiers stepped forward, blocking my path with halberds.

"I don't . . . have time for . . . this," I panted. "I need to see . . . the king."

"King Eric has public meeting days three times a week. Come back tomorrow."

"There won't be time!" I stepped forward. "He has a guest right now, a woman. Her name is Athena."

They exchanged an annoyed look.

"Look, miss, it's common knowledge that he has a guest," one of them said.

"He's in danger." I gestured. "The entire capital is."

"By this woman?"

"Yes."

The soldier on the left leaned to his companion. "She must be one of those nuts."

"Maybe we should let her see the king," he suggested. He cleared his throat, widening his eyes in a not so subtle way that cued me immediately that he had no intention of taking me to see the king. But if they took me to the palace, I could slip away and find my mother before she did something everyone would regret.

"Sounds great!" I clapped my hands. "Let's go!"

They turned and motioned me forward.

Get through the front doors and slip away. *I told myself.*

And that's just what I did. As soon as I was through the front doors, the soldiers tried to direct me down a hallway on the left, but I slipped past them and ran down another hall.

I flung doors open as I sprinted through the hallway. "Athena!"

The doors I opened revealed a closet, an empty bedroom, another bedroom, a study, and finally I flung a door open and my mother stood inside, rubbing her vibrant red lips together. She stared at me in shock.

The guards ran up behind me, but I swung the door shut. "You will let them know I'm your daughter and then you and I are going to talk!"

The door burst open, and I stepped over to my mother's side.

She held her hands up. "Relax. She's my daughter. You may leave."

I waved my fingers at them. "I told you."

The men apologized to my mother, gave me a hesitant look, and then left us.

The instant the door was closed again, I faced my mother. I drew a big breath. "So. James. You locked him up in a boathouse."

"And you were supposed to find him and try to rescue him. I am about to meet with the king for my final meeting, and you're not about to stop me."

"Athena, you're going to destroy an entire capital. It will ripple and destroy the entire kingdom," I argued.

She smirked. "They would deserve it. But I won't allow the entire country to fall. That's why you are going to be on the throne." She lifted a black veil and placed it over her face. "We shall speak when I'm done."

"I won't let you do this." I stepped in front of her.

"I'm doing this for *you," she growled. "I'm making your life better! Preparing your future! I would think you would be grateful."*

"I am grateful. You've done so much. But this? Destroying a kingdom? I don't want that! You shouldn't want this as your legacy."

My mother held up her hand. "It is a shame you aren't on my side. There is only one way to fix this. You will forgive me with time. Once you understand." She began to chant the words of an unfamiliar spell.

I looked frantically around the room for a way to stop her. I couldn't stab my own mother through the chest, but if I could distract her long enough to break her chanting, the spell wouldn't complete.

But long delicate fingers wrapped around my mind.

I gasped at their touch and turned to see the fingers weren't physical, but magical. "Mother, stop!"

She didn't.

The fingers pulled away from my mind. Memories from days before peeled away one layer at a time and started to fade. A glowing yellow orb in the clutches of the spirit hand curled together, swirling until it solidified into a beautiful white shell.

And then there was darkness.

TWENTY-ONE

The memories slammed into me like an angry wave, leaving me struggling to catch my breath. I could have sworn I saw my mother sitting at her desk in her bedroom, twiddling with the white shell around her neck, then suddenly looking down at it and letting out a gasp. I was almost positive the white shell shattered into a million pieces, just like my pearl necklace had done under Queen Grimhilde's power.

"Odette?" James cupped my face, his brow lined with worry. "You're back. You went pale and your eyes rolled up into your head."

"I remember," I whispered. I shifted my gaze from the ceiling to his face.

He studied me. "Remember what?"

"All of it." I smiled and let out a little laugh. "I remember you." I touched his scruffy jaw. "I remember being a siren. I remember being a pirate.

I remember . . ." I licked my lips. "I remember my mother is the sea witch and she wanted to sink Delphi because she wanted revenge on the king."

"But you remember me?" James reiterated.

I laughed again. "I already said that."

James leaned down and pressed his lips to mine a little tighter than usual.

"Why didn't anyone tell me, though?" I asked when he pulled away.

"We couldn't." He rubbed his thumb over my cheek. "After your mother came back, you didn't remember me. I ran to you, and when you looked at me . . . saw my hand . . ." He swallowed hard. "You pulled away in disgust. I thought I'd done something wrong until your mother told the entire city what she'd done. She told us she took your memories and if we tried at all to help you remember what occurred that week, we would suffer the same fate."

I clenched my teeth. "Of course. What did she say to you in the boathouse? What did she do?"

James licked his lips. "When she had me in the . . ." He drew a deep breath. "In the boathouse, she said she was going to turn the king into the figurehead on her ship. She said he would watch his city sink and be forced to see everything while being completely helpless, just like she had been. But I didn't know what she supposedly went through."

I scooted a little more into his arms. "Did she mention the spell at all? How to break it?"

He shook his head.

I took his left arm and rubbed my hand where his hook normally sat. "I teased you relentlessly about your name being Hook without realizing the nickname was given to you because you got a hook through your hand. Not because you wore one."

James shrugged a shoulder. "I suppose I was a little too sensitive about it. I think it hurt more knowing you didn't remember that night at all. It was the first time I told you I loved you."

I softly bit my lip and looked up at him. I didn't know if I could say those three words yet. I didn't know if I deserved his love.

He quirked a smile. "You're not going to say it, are you?"

I changed the subject. "If my mother is the sea witch, does that mean I have powers too?"

"I'm the last one you should ask. I think you'd need to speak with Ulrich."

I bit my bottom lip. "What if he hates me when he finds out?"

"He knows about your memories. I'm sure he'll be all right." He reached up and touched my chin.

There were three rasps on the door before it flung open and Ulrich marched in, followed by a weary-looking Sky, and a young man and woman I assumed were the prince and princess.

"Get up. We don't have time to rest," Ulrich ordered, motioning us to get up from the bed, not caring that I wore only a nightgown and James wasn't wearing a shirt. "Crown Prince Mathias. His sister, Princess Tavia."

Mathias and Tavia were clearly twins. Both had hair the shade of shadows and copper-orange eyes with gold around the outside, giving their eyes a glowing appearance. They had had time to get ready for the day, while we were still exhausted.

Tavia stood nearly as tall as her brother—a good four inches taller than me. She wore a simple but rich black dress with a silver shimmer and a red ribbon around her ribs tucked just beneath her breasts.

Mathias, on the other hand, had a strong jaw, his hair was neatly trimmed on the sides, and his eyes glinted with boyish curiosity. His thin lips curled into a smile as he sized me up with those dangerous eyes. "Perhaps we should give them a moment to dress?" he spoke to Ulrich, though he didn't look at him. I couldn't help but feel Mathias could see right through me like Lord Tomblin could.

I gritted my teeth, matching the intensity of his glare, but held the blanket up to my chest.

Tavia's smooth voice said, "Brother, don't be so rude. They are guests." She walked to a door beside the desk and opened a closet. Seconds later, she produced two robes, one for me—a beautiful blue that shimmered in the firelight—and one for James—a bright red the color of blood. She approached me first and held out the blue robe.

I quickly stood and put it on. "Thank you, Tavia."

"You may address me as *your highness* or *Princess*." She turned smoothly on her heel and held the other robe out to James. Her gaze deliberately trailed over his exposed chest and bare arms, drinking him in like a tall bottle of rum.

"Heya, Princess." I tapped to the corner of my lip. "You've got a bit of drool right here."

Her eyes darted to me and narrowed with sudden anger that flared behind her strange eyes. She rolled her shoulders back and returned to her brother's side.

James chuckled while he pulled his arms through the sleeves of his robe.

I shrugged innocently and walked around the bed to his side. "So why did you wake us, Ulrich?"

"*Prince* Ulrich," *Princess* Tavia corrected.

Ulrich waved his hand dismissively. "Titles don't matter right now. I brought you in here because there is clearly something wrong with Queen Grimhilde. She isn't acting as she normally does."

Mathias' lips tightened, and Tavia's fingers stretched.

"You know," I stated, looking from one sibling to the other.

Mathias glanced at me. "Yes." He returned his look to Ulrich.

Tavia ran to the bed, seized the small blanket at the foot, and ran to the mirror over the fireplace. She flung the blanket, and it landed on top of the mirror's frame, successfully covering the reflective surface. "You know better than to speak of these things without the proper precaution, Prince Ulrich," she said quickly, voice practically a hiss.

"Yes. I'm sorry." He drew a breath. "I don't know what to do. I mean . . ." He threw his arms up in the air. "My city is at the bottom of the ocean, my country is without a leader, my father is likely dead, and I come here for help, and your mother . . . she almost threw me in the dungeons! Them, I understand, but me?"

"Hey," Sky scowled.

Mathias glanced at his sister.

I stepped forward and put my hand on Ulrich's shoulder. "We don't have time to worry why her behaviors are different. You have less than two weeks now to get Delphi back."

Ulrich turned to the twins. "If Delphi isn't raised by the summer solstice, we will be stuck there forever. Terricina's main port is completely decimated, no one is running the kingdom, and we're more vulnerable than we've ever been."

Mathias ran his fingers through his wavy hair. "I don't know how we can possibly help you. Our powers are limited."

Ulrich held his hands up helplessly. "I didn't know what else to do. Maybe you can decipher the contract? Find a way to help undo it?"

Tavia looked at him with such pity it actually broke my heart. "Prince Ulrich," she said, her voice low. "We can try. When you have rested. At lunch or dinner, we will speak with our mother and all of you present. If we can't find a way to help you, we might be able to offer help some other way." She walked forward and hugged him, not long and deep like a lover, but gentle and short like he was a good friend or maybe brother.

Ulrich tried to smile but failed. "You're right, I suppose." He straightened and rubbed at his eyes, and I could have sworn I saw the glint of a tear on his cheek. "Forgive me for waking you." He swallowed and flashed another smile, this one coming easier.

I couldn't imagine knowing his entire kingdom's fate rested on his shoulders and that there was absolutely nothing he knew to do to help them. To think I'd selfishly thrown a fit about being a captain, and here was Ulrich willing to throw everything he wanted aside for the safety of his people.

"Can I speak with you alone?" I asked Ulrich before he could leave.

He nodded, and I waited for Mathias and Tavia to clear out before I dared speak.

Sky cleared his throat. "Can I stay?"

I nodded. "Yes." I turned to Ulrich. "I remembered everything."

"That's great!" Sky exclaimed.

"My mother, Athena, is the sea witch."

"What?" both Sky and Ulrich exclaimed in unison.

I explained what I remembered to all three of them. Ulrich listened with silent anticipation, his expression growing more and more stern.

When I finished, he sat down on a chair in front of the fire, staring at its flames. "Your mother is the sea witch. You never knew?" He glanced my direction.

I shook my head. "Not until she told me."

"And she sunk my city. You tried to stop her."

I nodded. "I didn't know what else to do. I don't want to be on your throne. I was happy being a pirate with my friends."

He leaned forward, rested his elbows on his knees, and put his face in his hands. "Maybe I need sleep," he mumbled into his palms. "I'm trying to figure out so many things and . . . can't think."

"That's not a bad idea," Sky reassured. "Once we've rested, maybe we can sit down together and try and come up with some ideas of how to break this contract of yours?"

Ulrich heaved a sigh before groaning to his feet.

I walked over and gave him a hug. "We'll figure it out."

TWENTY-TWO

James woke first, and I reluctantly peeled my eyes open and blinked furiously against the morning light as he pulled the curtains back.

"In spite of how cold this place is, the view is breathtaking." He stepped to one side so I could look out over the white snow-covered trees and valley below.

I rolled out of the bed, dragging the blanket with me, and shuffled over to his side. He was absolutely right. The vibrant colors of the rising sun reflected off the snow, casting fractals of light upon the trees and houses. Chimneys puffed heavy smoke into the sky. Everything looked like a painting.

After we'd washed up, the servants brought us clothing to wear. James, a handsome black and red suit, with fancy stitching, expensive buttons, and unnecessary frills on the wrists. I was forced into an awful pink and white dress that made me wonder if Tavia had chosen it herself. Even worse, the servant made me do my red hair up in a large pink bow.

Yes, a bow.

A pirate wearing a bow in her hair like some curly-haired, freckle-faced child.

So what if I had curly hair and freckles on my face? I was no child!

I walked out of the bedroom, a scowl deep on my expression.

James turned, hands politely behind his back, and his conversation with Sky died. Sky looked much better after getting some rest and cleaning up.

"Don't say a thing." I raised my hand. "I look like a tent! I feel like . . ." I patted the preposterous petticoat that puffed out the bottom of the dress. "A sheep!"

"That's an unusual comparison," Sky chuckled. "I would have said a blowfish."

I gave him an unamused blink.

James snorted a laugh but quickly recovered. "Odette, I was going to say you look stunning."

I tilted my head, looking up at him. "James, lying is your strong suit, but I've learned to see through it. I'm a redhead. In a *pink* dress!"

"What color dress would you rather be in?"

"I don't know. Green?"

Someone cleared their throat, and we all turned to see Ulrich. He wore a stunning suit of blue with golden accents, but he had dark bags under his eyes and his complexion was pale.

"Ulrich, are you okay?" I asked quickly.

"Of course." He straightened. "I just didn't sleep." He rubbed at his eye with a gloved hand. "I'll recover once all of this is done."

"I can't imagine you could sleep much right now."

He gave me a crooked smile and shook his head. "It's one thing after another." He gestured to his right. "Shall we? I believe everyone is waiting for us for lunch."

"And I'm starving," I added.

We made it to the bottom of the stairs and saw two wide doors open, revealing a massive dining hall with a hand-carved table that was as long as the room. Three chandeliers overhead gave the room light, along with two fireplaces. Three stained glass windows stood from floor to ceiling at the end of the table, and the table was decorated with a lace tablecloth. Gold and silver plates and flatware were organized with precision.

"I'm surprised they didn't hide their expensive cutlery so we poor pirates didn't steal it," I joked.

"They did."

I jumped out of my skin and turned to see Mathias over my right shoulder.

He flashed a smile. "The normal dishes are pure gold." He gestured. "Please come sit."

"He's joking," Ulrich mumbled. "Mathias just has a dry sense of humor."

I still didn't know how to read Mathias. He was smooth, not quiet like Gerard, flirtatious like Sky, or bold like James. But still, he *was* handsome in his own way. With a thin face, pointed jaw, nose like a bird's beak, *someone* would find him attractive. He just wasn't pirate-y enough for me.

Ulrich led us to one side of the table, and Prince Mathias and Princess Tavia walked to the other.

Mathias stopped at the chair nearest the one at the end of the table, which was undoubtedly reserved for the queen.

Luckily Ulrich chose at the seat nearest her. I stood at his side, then James, and finally Sky. If the prince and princess weren't yet sitting, then neither was I.

"Where is Gerard?" I asked.

"He will be joining us shortly. He . . ." Tavia turned her attention to the doorway.

Seconds later, it opened. Gerard held it and gestured with a bow so graceful, it made me realize he, too, had been raised alongside royalty. He was definitely comfortable here.

Queen Grimhilde entered first, and I wished I'd asked Ulrich and Mathias for some tips on how not to offend the woman. I felt out of place, and I knew James and Sky did too. None of us had been around royalty like this. None of us had been trained how to act. We'd never even been close to a castle, let alone eaten a meal with the queen, prince, and princess.

Following behind Queen Grimhilde was a slender woman with high cheekbones, deep-set eyes, and thin lips. I couldn't help but compare her to a skeleton.

Ulrich nudged me with his elbow, and I realized he was hinting for us to scoot down and move out of the way so this woman could take the seat he'd gone to. So I elbowed James, who then nudged Sky, and with a ripple of movement the royals probably frowned at, we moved.

"Do not fret, Prince Ulrich. I will take Prince Mathias's position this morning," the woman said. She must have been Selina.

Mathias's lips quickly flashed upward. "As you wish, milady." He and Tavia moved two chairs, so Gerard could take the seat beside his grandmother.

Gerard pulled the seat out for her and pushed it in as she took her seat.

Ulrich inhaled sharply when she sat before Queen Grimhilde and he turned his face to Mathias and Tavia, who didn't respond. Apparently, that wasn't customary.

The queen took her seat next, and Mathias motioned for us to take ours.

"We have spoken," Queen Grimhilde said, beckoned with her hand toward the stranger. "The only help I can offer you are a handful of fairies."

Ulrich's brows shifted. "Fairies, Your Highness?" His gaze finally darted to Mathias and back to the queen. "I'm afraid I'm unfamiliar with the magical properties of fairies or how they could possibly assist us in getting Delphi out of the sea."

"That's up to you." She raised her hands and clapped.

The mirrors on either side of the room shimmered and fairies flew out in an orderly fashion. As they landed on the floor, they grew to human size, and each of them carried a tray of food, which they placed on the table before disappearing again.

Mathias turned his head toward us. "Do not serve yourself until the queen has served herself and begun eating. You are not royalty and therefore are the last to eat."

I successfully bit back my words and instead tightened my hands around the napkin on my lap.

"Lady Selina is visiting us from Ashwrya," Tavia explained, watching Mathias serve her some sausage, a beautiful large scone, and some cheese.

"Gerard did tell us that's where he is from. It sounds lovely," I said.

Selina smiled at me in a way that made my blood run cold. "Yes, dear. What else has he told you?" Her dangerous look moved to Gerard.

Gerard didn't flinch but set his goblet down after a sip. "I told them about our rolling green hills, stone architecture, and changing seasons."

Her expression softened. Perhaps that was a look all mothers gave their children because Athena had given me that look a few times. And I also thought to myself how odd it was that Selina was Gerard's grandmother at all. She was much younger-looking than I expected. She didn't have a gray hair on her head.

"It's a pity we can't help you more, Prince Ulrich," Selina added before taking a bite of her food.

Ulrich nodded silently.

"After all," I cut in. "We're on the same side, aren't we?" I'd phrased the question intentionally. I needed to see how she would answer because I didn't know if we really were on the same side. I didn't know Gerard's angle, or Selina's, or even Queen Grimhilde's, for that matter.

"Side?" Selina answered.

"Did you not send Gerard to James to have him collect the summer stone?"

The room went silent. I suddenly felt as if I were balancing on shards of glass.

Gerard straightened in his seat, slowly lowering the napkin from the corner of his lip. He moved calmly, yet I saw how tight his hands were and realized I should have kept that information to myself.

"You sent Gerard to get the summer stone?" Queen Grimhilde asked, looking to Selina with the clearest look in her eyes I'd seen her with since we'd arrived.

"The girl doesn't know of what she speaks," Selina scoffed. "Gerard was there for a reason that has nothing to do with her." Selina's cold gaze shifted to James before returning to the queen.

"If it doesn't have anything to do with me, it must have something to do with James. After all, Gerard sought you out specifically, didn't he?" I looked at James, and my stomach dropped.

James's lips were tight, his face paling, and for the first time in my life, I saw genuine fear on his face. "Odette, stop," he said. He looked at me, his eyes full of anger. "Now. Don't say another word while we eat."

"James," I said softly.

"I mean it," he snapped. "Not another word."

The harshness of his words stole my breath. I wanted to press for an answer, but I was so shocked by his sudden hostility, I didn't know what to say. His anger at that moment was more intense than at the boathouse.

My stomach churned with unease, and I found myself staring at my empty plate. I hadn't even put food on it yet.

"You may serve yourselves now," Tavia instructed.

I was no longer hungry.

From the edges of my vision, I saw James scoop food onto his plate, and he reached to put some on mine, but I leaned back against my chair and set my jaw. I wasn't in the mood to look at him.

Mathias cleared his throat loudly. "Perhaps I should introduce them to the fairies after breakfast, Mother? Explain to them how fairies *are*, you know?"

"That's a wonderful idea," she approved.

Tavia added to the shift of conversation by asking Gerard about his adventures at sea. "You must tell us all about it. I've never sailed on a ship."

James reached under the table and put his hand on my knee, but I swatted it away. He tried again, and I stood up so sharply the chair nearly fell.

Again, all eyes were on me.

I cleared my throat and bowed at the waist. "Please excuse me. I'm not feeling that well. Must be all the time away from the sea. Thank you for opening your castle to us. It is lovely. And it was wonderful meeting you all. I hope we won't bother you for staying too long." I straightened and marched from the room.

I wanted James to follow so I could slap him across the face, but I also wanted to be alone. I just wanted to get back to the sea, get back to doing pirate things, like finding a ship to steal. I didn't like remembering my mother was the sea witch who sunk an entire city, or that I was stuck in this freezing land trying to get help from a cold-hearted queen, or that James had unnecessarily scolded me.

I wanted to go back to the life where all I wanted was to be a captain.

All this gallivanting around to save a kingdom made me long to go back to how things used to be. Maybe my mother was right after all, and I just should have listened to her and been compliant all along.

The castle was so quiet the sound of my skirts rustling sounded like an entire army of women in dresses following behind me down the hallway. Eventually, I found myself at a corner of the castle. It curved outward, and I knew the upper floors stretched up into one of the towers. But here, there was a little alcove. Sitting in the center of the alcove was a wooden stand with a wide top covered in silver velvet.

And upon that velvet sat a stunning blue stone.

I reached out and poked it. "You must be the . . ." I looked around at where we were. "The winter stone. Are you the reason it's winter here all the time?" I tilted my head and ran my finger over the finely polished surface. "If I stole you, would the winter disappear?" I picked it up and tossed it from one hand to the other, feeling the weight.

It was rather small, about the size of a thumbnail. It didn't appear to have any significant features, aside from being just another gemstone, except something seemed to chill my hands. It radiated from the center of the winter stone. I drew it closer to my face, wondering what it was that gave me a sense of numbing cold in my hands. It was something intangible, like . . . magic, if I imagined magic to feel like anything.

"You are a curious girl."

I wheeled around, smoothly sliding the gemstone into the glove on my hand. "That's the second time today!" I snapped.

Mathias leaned his shoulder against a wall, strange orange eyes watching me.

I put my hands on my hips. "And you're nosey. I doubt lunch is over with. Why did you follow me?"

"My instincts told me you were up to no good." He reached his hand out toward me.

I raised my brow. "No good? Because I'm a pirate or because I'm a girl?"

"Both." He grinned, but it didn't reach his eyes.

"What happened to your mother to bring you such unhappiness?" I asked in a cautiously low voice.

His smile dissipated and he looked around. "You shouldn't ask such questions." Yet, when he looked back at me, the mask of solemnity was gone. "It's Selina. I don't know how or why or what her play is, but Mother hasn't been the same since she arrived."

"How long is Selina planning on staying?"

He shrugged.

"Where is your father?"

Again, Mathias shrugged.

"You're not too great at this whole conversation thing." I gestured back and forth between us. "Usually one person asks and the other person answers."

"I don't feel like I have to impress you." He shrugged.

"That's good."

"It wasn't a compliment." He straightened and tugged the bottom of his jacket to adjust the wrinkles that weren't there.

I rolled my eyes. "Of course not."

He twitched a brow. "I don't know you, and therefore how I answer your questions is irrelevant. You're of no significance to me, and there's no need for you to know what's going on in my life or my kingdom."

"What have I done to offend you so?" I glared. "I just barely met you, but both you and Tavia look at me with nothing but disdain, which I have done *nothing* to earn."

"Perhaps because we know your true heritage. Is Ulrich aware that the answer to his problems stands right at his side?" He folded his arms across his chest. His eyes narrowed at me, and my blood ran cold. "Or aware your mother is the one who sunk his city?"

"No. I'm *not* the cause of his problems. And yes, I already told him about my mother. Why must I be forced to answer your questions, yet you offer nothing in return?"

Mathias studied me a moment. The silence between us tightened like a string, which he finally cut. "You missed the fun part of the conversation at lunch. You're all leaving before dinner. Mother sent for the servants to pack your horses with some supplies, and you'll leave with our fairy allies."

"Slaves," I corrected.

Mathias arched his brow. "Selina was right about one thing."

"What is that?"

"You're amusing."

"I'm glad I can be a piece of entertainment for you." I rolled my eyes and walked past him.

Mathias reached out and snagged my arm. "The stone, Odette."

"What st—"

"The one hidden in your glove."

I turned my face and met his orange-eyed gaze, and I knew he could see right through me. I pulled my arm away, held up my left hand, plucked the glove off, then held up my right hand and did the same.

"I must have dropped it," I said flatly, careful not to think of what I'd really done with it. "Oops."

Mathias shook his head. "I can't let you leave with that stone. You can give it to me willingly, or . . ." He lifted his shoulders.

"Or what?" I snapped.

"You're brave, I give you that." He chuckled. "But do you truly want to see why my eyes are orange?"

"I don't have it," I repeated firmly.

Mathias crouched to the hem of the dress. He snapped his fingers and flame quickly engulfed my skirts.

"What are you doing?" I screeched.

I tried to stomp out the flames, which completely failed considering I was wearing the thing. With no choice, I reached behind me, grabbed the ties holding the skirts on, and released the knot. I dropped the skirts to the ground and stepped out, at the same time dropping the stone that I had slipped discreetly into the waistband.

Without so much as a word, Mathias reached over the smoldering skirts, plucked the stone from the ashes, and straightened.

I glowered at him, wishing the look were enough to strike him dead.

"Thank you," he said. "I trust you can find your way back to your room without a personal escort."

I gritted my teeth.

Mathias winked.

TWENTY-THREE

"Poke him in the face, I will," I muttered as I made my way back to my room. I didn't care if any fairy saw me in my indignant dress, considering it was *their* prince who had done this to me. "I've got my dagger. I could land a carefully placed jab under his ribs. Pretend I tripped," I carried on.

I pushed the door of my bedroom open and stopped dead.

My mother stood in the center of the room.

She looked every bit her normal self—black pants, white shirt, green corset to match the same color as the scale tattoos on her chest and neck. She didn't wear her hat but had her red hair in dreadlocks tied back in a green bandana. She rested the tip of a sheathed sword on the floor at her side.

She smiled. "Odette, I'm happy you finally showed up. You and I need to talk."

The last person I wanted to see at that moment was my mother. My attention locked on the silver chain that should have held the spiraled seashell with my memories inside. Yet the chain was empty. She was only there because I'd somehow broken the spell that took my memories.

Whatever she had to say, I didn't want to listen.

"No, we really don't need to talk," I said with calculated slowness.

"We really do," she answered in the familiar "don't argue with me" tone. "Close the door and sit." She gestured to the couch beside the fire.

I looked down the hallway on either side. No sign of James or anyone else. My mother had already shown she was willing to take everything away from her own daughter.

With no one was there to back me up, I realized I had to face her alone.

So I met her gaze. I rounded my shoulders. I stood my ground. "How did you get here?"

"The mirror." She gestured to the fireplace. The mirror that had once hung above it rested on the hearth and was no longer shielded by the blanket. "It's complicated, and we don't have time for me to explain it right now." She approached me and lifted the sword at her side into both hands, presenting it to me.

It was my sword.

The one she'd given me for my sixteenth birthday two years ago.

My eyes widened. "You had it repaired?"

She nodded.

With my eyes locked on Athena to gauge how dangerous she was, I took the sword from her hands. After all, a sword was a far more effective weapon than a dagger or candlestick. I pulled the handle, and the sword slid out from its sheath. The torchlight bounced off the sharpened edge. It looked just like it had, in pristine condition. There was no hint I'd taken it to a tree weeks ago.

"I thought it was beyond repair," I added.

She let out a sigh. "I realized I did everything wrong with you," she explained. "I know you remember." Her fingers ghosted over the vacant spot on her neck. "When I tried to speak with you seven months ago, I should have tried harder to explain why I chose to do what I did. I should have had you at my side through all of it. So I'm asking now for your help."

I lifted my gaze to her. "Help with what, exactly?"

"Revenge," she replied so simply it made my blood run cold.

I swallowed hard. "You mentioned that. But revenge for what?"

Athena gestured to the couch. "I must explain everything so you understand. Otherwise, you will never agree to such a thing. Your inability to understand my motivation is why you attempted to stop me before. Please sit?"

I needed to know.

"I do want to change out of this first." I gestured to my pantaloons and corset combination.

Athena gave me a quick smile and glanced at the door, nervousness adding a tight edge to her pristine smile. Perhaps she didn't want Selina and Queen Grimhilde to know she was there. She definitely wouldn't be happy if James or Ulrich interrupted.

If I could somehow let them know . . .

"You can speak as I change into something proper if you'd like." I tugged off what was left of the dress—the corset with too much ribbon.

"You remind me so much of myself." She chuckled, and I looked over my shoulder at her. She traced the stitch on the back of the couch with her fingernail. "When I was your age, I thought I had the world figured out too. I knew what I wanted and would do whatever it took to obtain it." She lifted her eyes to me as I shed the pantaloons. "I was a princess, Odette. The *rightful* princess of Terricina."

"You were a princess?" I hopped on one leg as I pulled on my pants, not exactly sure I believed her. "Then how did you end up a pirate?"

"I was born and raised in the palace," she continued. As she spoke, she walked the length of the couch. "Everything changed when I met a man . . ." The corner of her lip strained at the sad memory.

I pulled on my shirt and tucked it into my trousers. "How could a man take all of that away?"

Athena leaned back into the couch. "He swept me off my feet. He was handsome, smart, brave." She heaved a sigh. "James reminds me of him. You remind me of me. Which is why I didn't want you and James together in the first place. I was trying to protect you from my mistakes. For that, I believe I must apologize." There was a stiffness to her words, indicating she didn't really want to admit she was wrong.

I folded my arms. "You shoved a whaling hook through his hand, tortured him, and left him to die."

She raised her shoulders in a shrug. "I already said I didn't do things the right way before." She straightened. "I reacted in anger and fear. I wasn't going to allow him to cause you heartbreak, and he needed to be punished for trying to burn my contract."

"So you removed him from my memory, our relationship, completely?"

She shrugged. "I couldn't have you repeating my mistake. When I took your memory, I wiped away your relationship with him as well. Sky is much better for you."

I shook my head, flabbergasted. "You punished him for what I told him to do, then ran off and sunk Delphi. To make things worse, you kept the truth from me, *and* forced the pirates to keep it all from me or they would lose their memories as well." I put my hands on my hips. "Did I miss anything? Oh. And turned King Eric into the new figurehead of your ship."

Athena's eyes narrowed into the same glare Selina had given Gerard.

Gerard had shown poise over and over, and I used his example to stay calm. I relaxed my stance. "Tell me more about why you wanted revenge on the king?"

Mother relaxed a little. "Once King Eric and I were wed, things began to change. Then I got pregnant with you and . . ." Her lip quirked. "You were a difficult pregnancy. I was ill through nearly all of it, which put me in bed. But I discovered, through loyal advisors, Eric was making deals without my consent. He had created alliances and trade routes with people I didn't normally associate with, lands I didn't trust. I was foolish enough to confront him." Athena walked around the edge of the couch and slowly sat. "He assured me he was 'securing a more powerful kingdom,' as he put it. I tried to reaffirm *I* was the queen of Terricina. He might have been its king, but I was the ruler, not him."

I shook my head. "How did he get away with it?"

Athena scoffed. "He had the ability to turn a phrase in such a way anyone would do anything for him. I believe magic was involved. My own people turned against me."

If this man was as horrible as my mother said, he deserved to have his kingdom taken from him. And then something struck me I hadn't caught onto right away—I was actually a flesh and blood princess. Luckily, Mother carried on while the weight of the new knowledge forced me to sit in a chair.

"King Eric became upset with me when I got rid of a contract before he could officially have it signed. In retaliation, he took me to the seashore. You see, many of my loyal subjects had begun to go missing, such as my advisors who warned me about Eric in the first place. I knew he was behind it, but I couldn't figure out how. And then Eric revealed he had taken possession of the summer stone. He showed me that every person who had gone missing, he had transformed into sirens at his will."

"He used the summer stone to transform everyone into a siren?" I gasped.

"And he did the same to me, and you, when I refused to reinstate the contracts." She sighed warily. "Every person who had been at my side was thrown into the sea, turned into those creatures. I gave birth to you in the ocean and raised you on my own. That's why I always told you your father was dead. We remained in the sea until Timbony discovered we could set foot on land. It was then we became pirates." Athena reached over and took my hands. "If I could do one thing to hurt King Eric, it was steal his kingdom."

I watched my mother. Her story felt completely true yet completely surreal.

"What other questions do you have?" she asked when I hadn't spoken.

"I . . . I don't understand the pirates being sirens."

"Ah." She nodded. "After we were banished to the ocean, I asked everyone to side with me. When Timbony discovered we could walk on land after all, we also learned we did better on the sea in boats. As a result, I set up Port Mere, and others stayed in the sea."

I rubbed my hands on my knees and looked at the fire. "The sirens who stayed behind?"

"Became more like the creatures they surrounded themselves with." She smiled. "I could have remained at Eric's side as his wife. I do regret not giving you the best life possible." She reached out and put her hand over mine. "But I don't regret my decision to stand by my people. He doesn't deserve to live a happy life in the kingdom that should be mine. He doesn't deserve to have luxury while we fight for everything. Are you willing to help me?"

I licked my lips. I had been hoping to help Ulrich get his kingdom back in order, to restore Delphi. Yet my mother had revealed I was the rightful heir to Terricina's throne. It was no longer that she felt I deserved it. It was my birthright.

What would Ulrich think?

"Odette?"

"I need a moment." I stood and began pacing the room.

I mulled through her information in my head. My father was the king. If Ulrich was indeed his son, then we were at least half siblings. Ulrich would probably love that. If I took the throne, I could raise Delphi, somehow freeing the sirens from their curse.

If I took the throne.

"We should leave now." Mother rose to her feet and walked to the mirror, an eager spark in her gaze similar to the one she had months ago when she first told me she was going to sink Delphi.

"I need to think."

"We don't have a—"

"You just told me my father is alive *and* that I'm a princess. James, Sky, and Prince Ulrich are here. I can't just leave them. And . . ." Something dawned on me. "You knew I was here because of the pearl necklace I wore," I murmured.

"I have to keep an eye on my daughter."

"But you only showed up *after* I somehow broke the shell holding my memories. I used magic, didn't I? It was magic that broke your spell over me."

"Odette." Athena walked around the couch toward me, her movements cautious—like how one would move when trying to corner a frightened stray dog.

I backed away. "I have magic." I stared at her, face pale, palms clammy. "Yet another thing you never told me. What other lies do you hide?"

She stopped. "We must leave before Grimhilde senses I am here. We must get back to Delphi and put you on the throne."

I had to choose my next moments carefully. There was something I was missing. A piece of the puzzle I couldn't see. There was a reason she needed to get back to Delphi so quickly. *It must have to do with the summer solstice.* It nagged at me.

"If you are the queen of Terricina, why do you need me? And why are you afraid of Grimhilde discovering you?"

"It's *your* throne by birthright." Mother's eyes narrowed dangerously.

"Did you ever stop to consider what *I* actually want?" I stepped closer to her. "Mother, I want James. I want to be a pirate. You know, in a lot of ways, I am your daughter. But this is not one of them." I shook my head. "I appreciate you wanting a better life for me. I truly do. But I'm quite content being a pirate if that means a boy—who has been raised his entire life to be the king and actually knows what he's doing—is on the throne. I'm done with you manipulating my life."

My mother's lips thinned, and she rounded her shoulders. I knew that was the end of the conversation by her body language alone. She was furious with me. "You were so obedient without your memories," she muttered and drew a shell from her pocket.

I snatched my sword and ran for the door.

"If you step out of this room, you are no longer my daughter," Athena said. Her voice was as cold as the ice dangling from the window outside.

Her words seeped through me, like the melting snow, as I put my hand on the chilly metal of the doorknob. I turned my head to look at the woman who had raised me, the mother who had taught me everything I knew. "If you go through with this, I don't want to be your daughter anyhow."

And with that, I opened the door and stepped into the hallway.

I ran as fast as I could down the stairs, playing on the gamble my mother truly wanted to avoid Queen Grimhilde. If she followed, she'd easily catch me, and I wouldn't have a chance to escape.

Just as I rounded the top of a second flight, I spotted James at the foot of the steps with Ulrich, Sky, Mathias, and Tavia. They were mid-conversation when I jumped on the railing of the stairs and slid down. I landed lightly on my bare feet and seized James's arm.

Tavia gasped audibly. "Odette!" she practically shrieked.

I ignored her. "My mother is here," I said, out of breath.

His eyes widened and snapped up the stairs. "How?"

"The mirrors. She went through the mirror in the room we were in."

"How is that possible?" Ulrich asked before I could.

"The only way possible is if she has one of the enchanted mirrors," Mathias quickly said. "You can't just walk through any mirror, there are only certain ones you can enter. Stay here." He started sprinting up the stairs, skipping one step with long, easy strides.

James pushed me to Ulrich and took off after him.

"I said to stay!" Mathias scolded.

"I'm not a dog, and you don't know what Athena is capable of," James retorted, his voice fading as they continued down the hallway.

I put a hand to my lips and realized only then how terribly I was trembling.

Ulrich watched me with concern. "Did she do something?"

"Is there a way to know which mirrors are enchanted?" I asked Tavia, facing her. "Because she's on her way to Delphi, but I don't know what her plan B is."

"Did she mention anything about my father?" Ulrich interrupted.

"Yes, but wait." I looked again at Tavia.

Finally, her icy exterior melted a little. "I can't go to an enchanted mirror and ask it where it's companion mirror is," she explained. "They could be scattered anywhere in any country. I'm sorry."

"Is there a way to know if a mirror is enchanted?" Sky pressed, finally making his presence known.

"Not for you." Tavia's voice dripped with disdain. "Only magic users can sense magic. Since you're a pirate, I doubt you have any abilities."

Ulrich rolled his eyes. "Tavia, she's a siren."

"And my mother is the sea witch."

Tavia's breath hitched. Her hand flew to the collar of her long, elegant gown.

Soft voices and footsteps drew our attention back to the top of the stairs. I drew my sword, Tavia took a defensive stance, her hands held out to her sides like claws, and Ulrich took a step back. Sky patted his hip for his sword, but the guards had taken them when we arrived at the castle. My feet stung on the chilly stone floor, but I didn't dare move.

James appeared, and everyone but me relaxed. Mathias appeared next, and they both shrugged as they walked down to the main floor.

"I destroyed the mirror," Mathias explained to Tavia.

"She's gone," James added, giving me a nod.

I sheathed my sword.

"What, exactly, happened?" Mathias asked as he made it to the bottom.

"I returned to my room," I explained. "My mother was in there. She said she came through the mirror. And then she explained to me why she's doing all of this."

Mathias sighed. "If we are to help, we need to know—"

"Absolutely nothing," I said sharply. "You've done nothing to help Ulrich and his situation, and you have known each other your entire lives. Your *hospitality* toward him shows me I have no desire to give you any amount of information because I. Don't. Trust. You."

Tavia straightened, the same cold expression as her mother's taking shape.

Mathias exhaled through his nose.

James cleared his throat. "If Athena is going to Delphi, we need to get out of here as soon as possible. Could she have one of those mirrors in Terricina somewhere?"

"Of course it's possible," Tavia said haughtily. "But it is impossible for us to know. I already explained to Odette that we can't trace them."

"Only our mother knows," Mathias added. "We aren't able to enchant."

"But there is a way for magic users to trace the magic in a mirror," I said. "Tavia spilled that before you came down."

"Which does you no good," Gerard said from the shadows.

Everyone turned to face him. Clearly, I wasn't the only one who didn't trust Gerard, because we went silent. He was as unreliable as Queen Grimhilde in my opinion. I still didn't understand whose side he was on, with the back and forth of the summer stone.

Gerard must have sensed our distrust because he let out a sigh. "There is another way to help Delphi and its people, without using the mirrors. Princess Tavia already explained that the mirrors are risky and dangerous. Even if you found a mirror to walk through, there is an entire world on the other side. The mirror realm isn't like anything you've seen before. And then you have to find your mirror's companion, which is even more difficult if you don't already know its location. This is why Queen Grimhilde is able to use them—she's the one who placed the mirrors."

"Then what's your suggestion?" I demanded.

He gestured to Ulrich. "Prince Ulrich, you have the summer stone. We can get back to the ship, and if you use the power from the stone, you could get us down to Delphi before Odette's mother finds a way through the mirror realm. And with that same summer stone, you can defeat her."

"And how do you propose he does that?" I asked before Ulrich could. "How could using the stone possibly be faster?"

"Because the mirror realm is vast," he continued. "It isn't like she can just walk from one mirror to the next. She has to find the right one."

"How do you know all this?" Mathias asked.

Gerard rolled his eyes and head simultaneously over to the prince. "I know a thing or two about magic and enchanting. I'm a necromancer myself. Trained by Selina, remember?"

"Fascinating," Mathias grinned. He opened his mouth like he was going to ask a question.

I didn't let him. "Great. Back to the ship. We need to ride as hard and fast as we can. Mathias and Tavia, thank you for letting us stay in your home." I bowed my head to both of them, not caring a piece of silver that I didn't properly address them.

"Wait, you said you were going to send us with fairies," Ulrich said, snagging Mathias by the hand.

"Ah, yes. Of course." Mathias walked over to a small table pressed up against the wall under a tapestry. He lifted a vase, pulled out the dried flowers, and spoke directly into it. "Please send the lost boys to me immediately." He replaced the flowers in their vase.

"Lost boys?" James asked.

"You'll see." Mathias directed his attention toward the floor under the small table.

Tavia rolled her eyes and folded her hands in front of her.

A piece of the floorboard suddenly flung open like a small door, and seven small fairies marched out in a line. I stepped up beside James for protection. They hummed an unfamiliar song, their little arms swinging the same direction, save one toward the end, who ended up hitting hands with the fairy in front of him. That fairy turned around, scolding him in a voice I couldn't hear, then bopped him on the head!

Mathias cleared his throat. "Take on your human forms. You will be traveling with these lovely people and will listen to Captain Hook."

The fairies stopped, looked at each other, and promptly grew in size. Their little wings disappeared, but their pointed ears remained.

To my complete amazement, they were children.

James raised his eyebrow. "You want to send children to help us?" He looked at Mathias. "Is this a cruel joke? What on the five seas are we supposed to do with seven children?"

Mathias shook his head. "Don't let their appearances fool you. Fairies age differently than we do, and they are going to be very good." He finished the sentence by looking at the fairy boys. "And you should each introduce yourselves." He nodded.

The one who had swung his arms the wrong direction stepped forward. He had curly blond hair, piercing blue eyes, large cheeks, and a narrow, pointed nose. "I'm Nibs. The twins are Happy and Grumpy." He put his hand to the side of his mouth. "It's the only way we can tell them apart."

Happy and Grumpy were identical to the point I couldn't see any defining differences at first. Both had piercing blue eyes and blond hair.

"I'm Curly!" another boy announced, jumping forward like a rabbit. He had the same sparkle to his eyes, but with a shade that was more lavender than blue, and jet-black hair.

"That's Slightly," Nibs continued, gesturing to the smallest of them. "He's really shy."

Slightly cowered behind Curly and wiggled his fingers in a weak wave of greeting. His brown hair shielded his brown eyes, almost as dark as James's, though James's eyes were broken with copper and chestnut tones.

Curly threw his arm around Slightly's neck and used his other hand to gesture to a fairy with white hair and eyebrows and red eyes. He was picking at one of his buttons, attempting to get it in the right spot. "This is Tootles. He's brilliant but deaf." He poked Tootles, who quickly snapped his gaze up.

Nibs used his hands to make some shapes and then gestured to us.

Tootles' eyes lit up, and he grinned.

"Hopefully, they're saying good things?" I muttered.

"That's Bins," Nibs threw in, pointing out the last of the fairies—a boy with a round belly, freckles on his nose, and black hair with an almost blue tone.

"Can we go now?" Ulrich pressed.

James grumbled under his breath. "I can't believe I'm bringing children on my ship. All right, everyone. Out! We need to get back to my ship as soon as possible."

TWENTY-FOUR

Tavia took some mercy on us and provided us with warm clothing to wear on our ride back to the sea. "In spite of what you think," she said, helping me pull on thick gloves, "I think you are brilliant."

I lifted my gaze.

"I envy you," she added softly. "Perhaps when you've helped Ulrich return his kingdom to normal . . ." Her lip tugged in a small, hopeful but beautiful smile. "Never mind."

"You should smile more often."

Her orange-gold eyes lowered to mine. "Why is that?"

"Because it's rather beautiful." I offered her a smile of my own and received one of hers back in response. "I do know what it's like to have a mother who has lost her senses, after all. If you were going to ask for help, I'll gladly return if you truly wish. And I know Ulrich will as well."

She gave my hands a squeeze. "We don't know what else to do to help you. Please understand that. Please. And return as quickly as you can. One more thing. Use caution around Gerard. I don't know about him yet. I can't see him like I can you, so I don't trust him."

I nodded.

She let go, and Mathias led us through the castle to the stables at the back. As he had promised, the horses were already laden with heavy saddlebags full of supplies. He even went to the man standing off to the side puffing on a pipe and spoke with him in a hushed voice.

"What's he doing?" I asked.

"Asking if the horses have enchanted shoes," Tavia explained. "They can run faster if they do."

The excited "lost boys" ran about the stalls, ruffling the horse's manes and getting into the tools.

James scowled. "Oy!" he called.

The boys jumped and all spun to him—except Tootles, who needed a nudge from Curly.

"You behave yourselves or you're staying here," James demanded. "If you're coming with us, you'll listen to my orders, understood?"

They all nodded. Happy turned and explained to Tootles using his hands.

"I'm your captain," James continued. "My word is law. Even more so than the prince and princess. If you don't do what I say, you could end up injured or killed, and I won't be responsible for a death aboard my ship because of children being foolish."

"We got it, old man," Grumpy grumbled, folding his arms over his chest with a huff.

"Old man?" James muttered.

I elbowed him. "Relax. They've probably been stuffed in the floorboards their entire lives. Let them have a little fun."

Mathias pulled his collar tighter to his neck and puffed his breath into his gloved hands as he returned to us. "They are ready for you. All horses have been granted swiftness." He turned to Ulrich and held out his hand. "I wish you all the best of luck."

Ulrich smiled warily. "I'm afraid I will need more than luck on my side."

"You've got me," I grinned, looping my arm through his. I hadn't had a chance yet to tell him we were related.

It came as no surprise that the fairies had never ridden horses.

Fortunately, the royal family was kind enough to provide more horses this time. The fairy boys were placed on two old mares, and three sat comfortably in a row. The seventh fairy, Grumpy, wanted to sit with James.

"I want to ride with Odette," James tried to explain.

"She can ride too," Grumpy argued.

"There's not enough room," James frowned.

Grumpy scowled—his expression making him look like a ninety-year-old man.

"Good luck!" Mathias waved from afar. He and Tavia had taken shelter in the doorway, and at that wave, he put his hand on Tavia's back and guided her back into the warmth of the castle.

I climbed onto the horse behind Ulrich. "Don't worry, James. I get to ride with my baby brother." I hugged Ulrich.

He turned in his seat. "What?"

"There's a lot my mother said while we spoke," I explained. "Including that your father and my mother were married, and she was pregnant with me when he banished her into the sea."

Ulrich cocked his head. "That doesn't make sense. Remember that tapestry you saw in my memory? That was my family. I had a mother *and* older sister in that tapestry. So if you're my sister and Athena is my mother . . ." He sat back with a confused expression on his face. "If my mother is your mother, and she's the sea witch, does that mean I'm actually a siren too?"

I clenched my hands into fists, stunned. My mother had lied to me again. How could I not remember the tapestry? *How am I supposed to trust anything she told me?* I wondered.

"I always wanted a brother or sister." Ulrich smiled at me again, clearly trying to alleviate my sudden change of mood.

"Happy family reunion, now let's get out of here!" Sky said from the front. "You can be happy when we're on the ship and safe."

Happy tilted his head so sharply to the side I thought he was going to slide right off the horse.

Somehow, he kept his balance. "I don't understand," he mumbled.

"They aren't *actually* going to be you," Nibs pointed out. "They mean the expression."

"Oh." Happy gripped tightly to the mare's mane and started tugging. "Let's go! I want to see the ship!"

"Be nice to the horse," James scolded. "Do you like it when people pull your hair?"

"Let's find out!" Nibs suddenly grabbed a fistful of Happy's hair and yanked.

Bins, who sat behind Nibs, gasped. "Stop, Nibs!" he shouted and tugged on the back of Nibs's shirt.

Grumpy sprinted the short distance to the horse and tackled Nibs to the ground, landing blow after furious blow until James jumped down and scooped up the boy, still clawing and growling to get after Nibs, who was now crying in hysterics.

"That'll show you to mess with my brother!" Grumpy yelled.

James plopped Grumpy onto his saddle and looked down at him. "You pull a stunt like that again, and I'll lock you in the brig the entire voyage at sea and you won't be able to see any part of it."

"What's a brig?" Grumpy scowled.

"It's a dungeon on a ship."

Grumpy's shoulders lifted, and he lowered his head.

I sucked my lips into my mouth, trying not to break into a smile. I failed when James got back on the horse and made eye contact with me. The corner of his lip tugged in a smile while he rolled his eyes.

I smiled and chuckled in response.

Sky was wiping off Nibs's face with a handkerchief and got him back on the horse. "Don't worry. You'll fit right in with the pirates." He patted the boy on the head. "You quite all right?"

Nibs sniffled dramatically one more time and nodded.

"Good. *Now* can we leave? No more distractions?" He looked at each of the seven small fairies. He nodded with finality and we were on our way.

Even with the enchanted horseshoes and guidance from Lord Wilfred—who met us in the courtyard—the journey to the ship still took us the rest of the day. Lord Wilfred even took us down a road he said was designed for such fast travel.

The sun had begun to sink into the sea by the time we reached the outpost at the top of the cliff's face we'd climbed only two days before. Down below, standing starkly as a shadow in midday, sat *The Sea Devil* with her lanterns aglow.

And the familiar peace of the sea enveloped me.

James let out an audible breath of relief and looked over at me. "I can't wait to get back on the sea. It's more predictable."

I laughed. "Not when we try and provoke it with the summer stone."

"Ah. Yes, I'd nearly forgotten . . ." His eyes shifted to Ulrich.

Ulrich reached a hand up and rubbed his eye. "Don't worry. Though, I am positively exhausted."

"We should have made you sleep the ride down," I said.

"Hm." He shrugged.

"I'm hungry," Slightly said softly from behind Tootles.

"Hopefully Louis will have some dinner ready when we arrive," James said.

We began the descent down the winding pathway and were greeted down below by the soldiers who had helped us on our way.

Ulrich was the second to dismount, behind Gerard. "Prince Mathias wanted us to leave the horses here. He said the royal guard should be down in a day or so to collect those horses that should return to the castle. Thank you, Lord Tomblin."

Lord Tomblin smiled. "Good to see you again."

"I'll be on my way with my men," Lord Wilfred nodded. "Good evening."

I helped Sky get the boys from the horses. It was rather amusing watching Sky with the children, and I imagined it was due to his own childish ways.

Tootles reached out and touched Sky's cheek, brows pinched in question.

"I got it from a sword," Sky explained, pointing to the sword on his hip and making an action across his cheek with his finger. "Protecting Odette." He pointed to me.

Tootles widened his eyes and stepped away from me.

"No, no." Curly hurried over. He stepped in front of me, pointed to himself and then Sky, and pretended to hold a sword and fight in the air. He finally pointed to his cheek and made a hissing noise of pain.

Tootles relaxed.

"He thought you meant Odette had given it to you," Curly explained to Sky.

"Ah." Sky nodded.

James heaved one of the horse's saddlebags over his shoulder, then walked to the next horse to retrieve that one as well. Sky also had a saddlebag laden with supplies on his shoulders, and he handed one to Gerard to carry. Ulrich retrieved the last one.

"Wow, *that* is what you sail on?" Slightly gasped. He then remembered he was supposed to be shy, clamped his mouth shut, and darted behind one of the twins.

"It's pretty amazing," I answered, bending over at the waist to smile at him. "Just wait until you get on board."

"I won't have you running about tonight," James quickly added. "We're getting on board and going right to sleep. Do you understand?"

"James, they may look like children, but—" I started.

"Oy, we're older than you," Grumpy snapped, using James's attention-grabbing exclamation himself. "Don't treat us like we're stupid."

James narrowed his dark eyes. "As long as you obey my orders, there won't be a problem. Got it? There are a lot of dangerous things aboard *my* ship, and I won't have any of you getting hurt because you refuse to listen to me. Remember?"

Grumpy rolled his eyes and took his brother by the arm.

Happy started to skip. "Look at that ship! It's bigger than any boat I've seen! Maybe tomorrow we can go swimming too. I haven't been swimming in ages!"

One of the boys yawned loudly.

"This is going to be just . . . great," James muttered.

I slid my hand into his. "We're almost to the ship. One step closer to everything being righted."

"What else haven't told us?" he asked.

"Apparently *you* remind her of my father," I revealed. "Handsome and cunning."

He looked down at me.

I explained how she felt wronged by him. Ulrich listened eagerly about how my mother said they met, how he took everything from her, and all with a dashing smile and sly words.

James frowned. "Is that why she left me in the boathouse?"

"Apparently." I heaved a breath and looked up at the crystal-clear sky, relieved to be back in the warmth. "And your father *is* alive, Ulrich. Sort of, I suppose. He's the figurehead of my mother's ship. The wooden statue on the front."

He sighed. "At least we know where he is."

"I would love the chance to meet my father."

"That's unusual to think about," Ulrich said with a chuckle.

I looked back at him. "Tell me about it." I smiled. "Good thing I didn't sweep you off your feet with my dashing looks."

Ulrich chuckled. "No love at first sight for us, huh?"

He waited for me to climb into the rowboat we'd left on the shore when we arrived before he stepped in, followed by the "lost boys." They stacked on top of one another, scrambling to get a seat where they could peer into the dark water. James climbed in next, and Sky and Gerard were kind enough to wade into the water, pushing us past the break of the waves before they climbed in and helped row us to the ship.

Ulrich's fingers went to the necklace resting on his chest. "I admit, I'm frightened to try and use this. If it is as powerful as the stories state, I could do something irreversible."

"We have to try." I reached out and grabbed his hand, giving him a comforting smile. "Besides, if you're going to be the king, shouldn't you practice using it? Your father did."

His smile faltered. "If your mother is telling the truth, it was very dangerous for him to do something like that. As for being the king . . . you're the eldest. The birthright falls to you now."

I shook my head quickly. "No way. I'm not taking that from you. You've worked your entire life for it."

"You're honestly a princess?" James asked, pinching his brows tightly together.

"Relax, I'm not leaving this life of piracy for frilly dresses, gilded dishes, or proper manners any time soon." I smiled and kissed his jaw.

"No, but you *could* change the law."

"And make pirates legal? We steal and plunder. It's not exactly honest work."

He frowned. "You mean you want me to become a *proper* merchant captain?"

I grinned. "With a triangle hat and everything."

James rolled his eyes, but a smile played on his full lips.

"While we're sharing truths," I turned to Gerard. "Whose side are you on?"

"I stay on whatever side I need to get what I want," he replied flatly. "You needed Queen Grimhilde on your side, so I tried to volunteer something she might want. The summer stone. I still need the stone myself, but we need to get Delphi from the sea first."

"Why are you helping?" Ulrich pried. "You could have taken it."

Gerard sighed. "I'm not as coldhearted as I seem."

My eyes widened. "And why didn't we get James his hand back while we were there?"

"He hasn't fulfilled his bargain," Gerard replied simply.

I frowned. "How *did* you end up with his hand?"

"I couldn't get down," James answered, his eyes focused on the nearing ship. "You left the dagger with me, and I . . . couldn't reach to get down. The only option I saw was to try and tear the hook through my hand . . ." His jaw flexed.

"You cut off your own hand?" Nibs gasped in morbid fascination.

"No. His grandmother did." He looked back at Gerard. "She showed up out of nowhere. She used

276

magic and seared it off right at the wrist." He pulled the hook off to reveal the nub. "She took my hand and said she would return it if I helped her procure a certain magical stone. If I failed . . ."

"If you failed, what?" I pressed.

Gerard answered. "With magic, you can manipulate someone if you have a piece of them. A hair, nail, blood—"

"Hand," I concluded. "So you showed up, threatening James, and—"

"I didn't threaten him." Gerard held his hands up. "I came to get the summer stone. That is all."

"I don't trust you."

"No one does." He shrugged matter-of-factly.

"Cap'n is back!" Sebastian hollered from the deck. "Get the ladder and the ropes! We need to hoist the boat back up here after we get them all on board."

I found that I had grossly misjudged Gerard. He'd been on board James's ship for over a week, right alongside me, and I hadn't asked much about him. It was likely Gerard trusted us as much as I trusted him. He was, after all, the foreigner on our ship.

The fairies climbed up the ladder one at a time. I followed right after them and grinned when Sebastian gave me a worried look.

"We have . . . guests?" he asked.

"Yes," I chuckled. "Don't worry. They're curious, but they're going to be good. Has Chef Louis made food?"

"Down below."

I turned. "Lost boys, come on. This way. We're going below deck to get some food." I motioned for them to follow me. I then turned to Sky, James, Ulrich, and Gerard who had made it on board. "Gerard, why don't you join us?"

He arched his eyebrow in sudden surprise.

"Maybe we can talk about less serious things?"

Gerard looked at James—for permission or help, I couldn't decide. He nodded once and followed me down to the galley.

"Why the sudden interest?" Gerard asked, caution written all over his face.

"Because I . . . might have realized I've been so consumed by my own problems that I haven't stopped to look at anyone else's." I glanced over my shoulder at him. "For example, not even knowing what you like to eat." I heard Louis squeal and rolled my eyes. "Boys! Go sit down now!"

The seven fairies stopped pulling at Louis's clothes and ran over to the tables. Tootles hopped down from the counter and Grumpy got his nose out of the pot. They looked at me sheepishly.

"Did no one teach you manners?" I asked.

"Well, we've been servants of Queen Grimhilde since we can remember," Curly answered. "We thought maybe . . ." He looked at Nibs for support.

Nibs sighed. "We thought being with you might be different. We're sorry."

I walked over. "It is different. We don't plan on making you wash the ship or anything like that. But you should know better than to climb all over Chef

Louis, especially when he was so kind as to make you all food without knowing you'd even be here." I looked at Louis. "Do you have enough for all of us?"

Louis adjusted his apron. "I 'ad a feeling you vould be back tonight."

"We bring supplies," James announced as he stepped into the galley and dropped the saddlebags from the horses to the side of the room.

Gerard set his down in the same spot, followed by Sky and Ulrich.

We sat and just talked. It turned out Gerard wasn't fond of our food at sea even remotely. He was smart, enjoyed his time on the ship, though he couldn't wait to get back on land and into nature. He'd also studied magic his entire life.

"With my mother being the sea witch, I should have magic?"

He shrugged. "Not always. It can skip children. But yes, it's possible, especially since Ulrich has magic. I'm afraid I'm no teacher." He took his final bite. "I recommend finding someone as soon as possible."

I leaned over and looked at Ulrich. "Hey, brother. Who teaches you magic? I want to start lessons."

Ulrich grinned. "After everything is back to normal."

"That will take a century," James said under his breath.

I elbowed him and, when I made eye contact with Gerard, shrugged. "I'm a horrible friend."

Gerard gave a little smile. "I'm afraid I don't have much experience with friends. I haven't had much time for friendship. But, if it helps, from what I've seen on board this ship, you all seem to get along for the most part."

"Other than my abrasive personality," I added.

He twitched his brows and took another bite of his food.

"Why don't you have many friends?"

"Necromancers don't exactly draw people to them," he answered.

"Why not?"

"The whole *dark magic* aspect."

"Oh, I suppose I didn't realize . . ."

James picked up his empty plate. "Up on deck. Ulrich will use the summer stone and get us back to the bay which is *supposed* to be the city of Delphi. If your mother isn't already there, we can try and figure out how to turn the spell that made all of us sirens. If she is there, you can try and talk to her one last time."

"One last time before what?"

James didn't answer right away.

"Before you do what? James, she's my mother!"

"And we all know what she's capable of."

I stared at him, stunned. "James, she's never murdered anyone. She turned the people of Terricina into sirens when she could have killed them."

"If she has the ability to change Terricinians into sirens, why hasn't she changed us back?" He gestured to the pirates. "Think about that. She told you it was King Eric who transformed everyone?"

"None of this really makes sense," I answered softly. "I mean, if Ulrich and I are brother and sister, why lie about it?" I put my elbow on the table and rested my forehead in my palm. "There are so many questions I didn't think to ask."

James put his arm around me. "It doesn't do you any good to stew over it now."

Ulrich pushed his empty plate forward. "I'm ready. Everyone else?" He looked around at the rest of us.

Sky got to his feet next. "I am. Come on, Odette. Let's see what this sea witch is truly up to." He held his hand out to me.

I reluctantly took it, and he pulled me to my feet and hugged me.

"You're the bravest person I know, Odette. With all of us working together, we'll be able to stop her. Just you wait." Sky kissed my forehead.

I faced James. "You want to bolster me too?"

"Nah." He shrugged. "I've got to cheer Ulrich on, though." He winked at me and patted Ulrich on the back. "Come on, mighty prince. Let's get you to your kingdom."

I looked at the boys. "You can have one more plateful each, and then I want you to find hammocks and get some sleep."

"But we want to see everything!" Grumpy objected.

"It's nighttime. You can't see anything on the ocean at night anyway."

"Except the stars," countered Happy.

I sighed. "If you come up to the top deck, you must stay out of the way."

"Yay!" the boys cheered and scrambled up the stairs without their second helping of dinner.

When I reached the top deck, all the pirates had gathered around to watch Ulrich. The prince stood at the bow of the ship, looking down into the sea. My brother. At least, I really hoped he was my brother. I'd grown fond of Ulrich, and the thought we could truly be family made my heart jump.

I walked up to his side and nudged his shoulder with mine. "You've got this."

He looked up from the stone glowing green in his hand. "Using it to recall memories is far easier than what I'm about to do. My father always warned me to be very careful with its magic."

"What better way to use it than to help him?"

He nodded and lifted his gaze to the sea once more. "Take us home!" he called. He raised the stone in a fist high above his head.

Suddenly, the ship began to lift from the sea.

The waves had transformed into seahorses, which raised us far above the normal waves of the sea as though we were flying. An unfelt wind snagged the sails from behind and drove us forward with such speed I'd never before experienced. The green glow from the stone swelled inside the sea horses, somehow running beneath us and at our sides, keeping us moving.

A few men lost their balance and fell to their knees. Others steadied themselves on something nearby. A few sailors, like myself, anticipated the sudden lurch forward and somehow kept our footing. I caught Ulrich by his arm and kept him upright.

"It worked," he breathed.

"I told you that you could do it." I grinned.

He smiled back at me proudly.

Beyond him, the cliffs flew by, a blur on the horizon. We would arrive at Delphi before dawn at this rate.

"And now you need to sleep," I insisted.

Ulrich looked at the stone in his palm. "Will everything be all right if we sleep?"

"James usually has a few lookouts stay awake all night so we can be safe. I'm sure they'll let us know if something happens with the spell."

James suddenly started yelling at Tootles to get down from the rigging while Slightly scrambled up after him.

I grinned. "Those boys are going to give him gray hair before he's twenty."

TWENTY-FIVE

I woke when Sky burst into the room and shouted, "Captain, you've got to see this!"

I had been snuggled against James's chest with his left arm around me. He'd had a bath in Zelig and smelled amazing. But being rudely woken by Sky yelling, James tore out of the bed so fast I didn't have time to be groggy.

We made it out onto the deck to see thousands of seagulls flying overhead. Their little black bodies stood out from the moonlit sky, and their anxious caws were almost deafeningly loud as they neared.

"That's not a good sign," James muttered.

Gerard stumbled up the steps with a few other sailors, pulling a shirt over his head. "What do you mean?" he asked, his tone annoyed. "It's a bunch of birds."

"Flocks of them," James corrected. "Seagulls don't fly at night, and only like this if there is danger.

Typically, creatures will flee if danger is coming, such as a hurricane or tsunami. Or something bigger."

I patted James's arm. "Look at the sea." I pointed.

White-tipped waves had drawn my attention. Not typical waves from the rough seas, or the green-tinged enchanted waves from the summer stone flying us to Delphi, but movement as if all the sea's creatures were fleeing as well.

My theory was confirmed when the white waves reached us and we spotted the humped backs of whales, arching dolphins, and even some fish jumping as they swam away.

I swallowed hard.

The sound of the creatures faded behind us, leaving behind a deafening silence broken by the steady rush of the waves propelling us forward. We had made it around the southernmost tip of Terricina, and the shore was in sight.

Ulrich stepped forward, his face paling. "I see why they fled. That's Delphi."

"What?" I blurted with Sky at the same time.

"He's right," James confirmed. He held a looking glass to his left eye, balancing it on his hook. "I can see the shoreline. It's no longer a gaping hole. Water rushes down the street and into the ocean."

"We need to stop the ship now," I said, grabbing Ulrich's arm.

He didn't hesitate to remove the stone and rubbed his thumb over it. "We've arrived. Halt." He shrugged at me, likely unsure if what he said would work.

Luckily for us, the ship gradually slowed until it rested at a normal pace.

"Close the sails. We need to stay out of sight as much as possible," James ordered. "Why would your mother have raised the capital? I thought that was her play to get Ulrich to give up his throne?"

I shook my head. "She must have decided to take the throne herself. She doesn't need us."

"She actually does," Ulrich disagreed. "She isn't the one born on the throne. My father was. He's a descendant of a line of kings centuries old."

I scoffed. "That's not what my mother told me. Why didn't you say something earlier?"

"Because I was too tired to think. Look, you know what your mother told you, I know what my father told me. Either way, someone is lying."

I opened my mouth to object, knowing in my heart I truly couldn't believe anything my mother said anymore. After all, she'd lied to me before, and she'd already done it again. She would say anything to get what she wanted.

"Okay, then." Ulrich rubbed his hands together. "Best time to take her by surprise will be at night, under the cover of dark. Especially right now, since she likely isn't going to think we made it here so swiftly." He turned around and faced us.

"We have a couple of hours before dawn," Sky added.

Gerard cleared his throat. "If I may, you're all sirens, are you not? Whether she's sent for the other pirates or not, you could intercept them and tell them what is really going on. Get them on your side."

"I'll do that," Sky offered.

"Maybe we should wait to approach her until we have all of the reinforcements," James tried. "It does us no good to try and attack her without additional support."

"Unless we don't want her to know we have additional help on its way," I threw in.

He shrugged a shoulder. "I suppose that's true." He rubbed both eyes with his hand. "I'm trained on attacking ships, but this? I have no experience."

I placed my hands on my hips and let out a sigh. "I wish we knew what she was doing."

The fairy boys scrambled up the stairs, each looking disheveled. I wondered if the boys had stayed in their hammocks or chosen to return to their fairy size and sleep somewhere else.

I walked over to redirect them downstairs, but Bins darted around me.

"We can help!" he proudly announced.

"Oh?" James crouched, trying his best to give the boy a smile, but I could tell he was annoyed by the thought of listening to the ideas of a child.

"We're fairies, right? Fairy dust! You just think happy thoughts, and you can fly!"

I glanced at Ulrich.

He shrugged.

Gerard chuckled. "How is that supposed to help us? They can all swim to shore."

Tootles stepped forward and moved his hands.

Curly stepped forward to explain. "He's saying that she might expect you swimming, but not flying. You can get through the city a different route."

"Huh. That's not a bad idea." James rubbed his chin.

"Fairies are very common in my country," Gerard said.

James rose to his feet and gestured with a hand for Gerard to carry on.

"Fairies actually have more magic than you think. Because of this, they are often sought after. Also because of this, they tend to be captured. Seeing one as a servant is quite a way to show off your status. Having seven or more?" He shook his head. "It's downright distasteful."

"How does one even catch a fairy?" I asked.

"That's a discussion for a different time. And, to be honest, I don't know that I would tell you," he confessed.

"You believe this can work?" James repeated.

"Yes." Gerard nodded. "If you believe in their magic, they can do practically anything. But we need a little more of a plan than just flying and entering Delphi from the north or whichever direction."

James inclined his head. "Sky will swim to Port Mere. Hopefully, he will spot some of our people along the way. I want three men to go with him. You will speak with the other pirates and *request* they join us to stand up against Athena if we must. Some pirates are best to avoid, including my father. I trust you can figure out the others on your own. They are loyal to

Athena, and the last thing we need is them somehow letting her know our plans." He turned to me. "I will go with you and the rest of my crew. We will approach your mother in the least threatening way possible. Give her an opportunity to back down one last time."

I raised my brow. "Absolutely fantastic. All we have to do is say Ulrich is the rightful heir and demand she returns home. Sounds easy!"

James frowned.

"She's wanted this my *entire* life, James." I sighed. "I don't think it's going to be as easy as a conversation."

"You won't let us take her by surprise and kill her," James said softly.

"Let me go in alone." I exhaled, feeling a heavy weight on my chest as I spoke. "You and your men stay outside of the palace, away from the guards. Don't let anyone know you're there."

"Let you go in alone?" James objected.

"Then I am the only one who will be hurt, or whatever might happen."

He ran his fingers through his hair, something he always did when he was worried. "How will we know if you need help? How will I know when I need to step in and help you fight?"

I looked over at the fairy boys and grinned. "Hey, Grumpy. Why don't you accompany me?"

"An adventure?" His face went from completely stunned to the biggest smile that rivaled his brother's. "Yes!" He pumped his fist in the air.

"I'll carry him in my pack," I explained to the others. "If I need help, he will fly and get you."

"That's smart," Gerard said.

Grumpy rubbed his hands together eagerly and turned to the other fairies. "Everyone, fairy form! Let's sprinkle fairy dust on this smelly lot!"

All seven of the boys transformed into rather small human-shaped beings with translucent wings of varying colors. Happy and Grumpy had blue-green wings with Happy having more green in them and Grumpy having more blue. Curly's wings matched his lavender eyes, Nibs had green wings with a red and purple undertone, Tootles' were a vibrant red with glittering pink in them, Bins' wings were as black as his hair, and Slightly had shockingly bright wings that shimmered every color, rather like a hummingbird.

"They all come from different regions," Gerard pointed out. "I understand why they called them the lost boys. Who was the boy with the black wings?"

"I'm Bins!" the boy shouted at him—though it sounded more like a squeak due to his size. He flew around Gerard in a spiral up to his head.

Gerard smiled. "I meant no offense. You're the rarest one here. Midnight fairy, am I correct?"

Bins landed in Gerard's extended hand and puffed up his chest.

"Mathias said they were children but older than us?" I asked.

Gerard nodded. "Very much so. Equivalent of a typical human's six or seven-year-old child. I'd wager they're equivalent of around sixty to seventy years old. I'm ready to fly, Bins."

Sky walked over to me while the fairies set to work covering everyone else in fairy dust, one at a time. He took my hands. "I know you're more fond of James than you are of me. I can respect that."

"Sky."

"Let me finish." He gave me that genuine, dashing smile that had stolen so many hearts. "He's better for you than I am. I also want you to know I'm sorry for everything that's happened. After your mother took your memory and separated you from James, I finally saw my chance. But I think we're better friends. I hope you'll be able to help out both sirens and humans in your new position."

I rolled my eyes. "If I even take the throne."

He shrugged. "Good luck." He gave me a big hug. "Whatever you do, remember your mother is a siren too."

"What's that supposed to mean?"

"It means there's a reason she's been able to manipulate so many people for so many years." He tapped his lips.

Of course. A siren's song. If a siren could lure a man—or foolish pirate girl—to their death with a simple song, what was my mother capable of?

Slightly fluttered over to me and covered me in dust.

I watched Sky jump into the inky waters, followed by three other pirates, and they disappeared.

"Now, think of something happy and we'll be on our way," Grumpy said, fluttering just a few inches from my face.

Around me, pirates floated in the air, their arms outstretched, laughing at the feeling of flying. Even James hovered in the air, grinning like a child.

What was the happiest thought I could imagine?

I tried to imagine being a pirate captain and how happy that would make me, but my feet didn't leave the deck. I tried to imagine myself as a princess and that didn't help either. I thought about being a siren, being out at sea, sailing under Captain Avery, and even being with James. None of these worked. Every memory from my childhood had been blackened by worried thoughts. My mother had manipulated me my entire life, and facing her alone a second time terrified me.

If I failed, who knew what she would do to get her way?

James landed at my side and took my hand. "What is it?"

"I can't imagine something happy," I confessed. "I'm too worried."

"Not even me?" He pouted.

I blushed and tried to look away.

James reached out and touched my cheek. "What about the family you never knew you had? A father you might get to meet, and a brother . . ." He gestured with his hook toward Ulrich.

I felt my heart swell, and my feet lifted from the wooden planks. However, that joy and happiness was immediately masked by fear. "What if he doesn't like me? My real father?" My feet hit the deck again.

"What if I can't even talk to my mom, and then it will be my fault she won."

James cupped my face in his hand and hook. "Odette, there is a lot to be afraid of right now. But there is joy in every trial. What is something right now, right in this moment, that makes you happy?"

I looked around. Pirates had become braver and were flying about the ship, laughing. I pushed aside what they might be thinking about to help them fly and focused on James.

"The touch of your hand." My voice sounded soft. I closed my eyes and tilted my cheek into James's hand. "The joy I felt when I remembered you. How you make me feel safe and wanted. You've never had any expectations for me. You've never demanded anything from me." I pushed away all fear, all doubt, all worry, and opened my eyes. "James, I love you."

His handsome face spread into a beautiful smile. He kissed me. "Look down."

I peered down to see I floated a good four feet in the air. I beamed at James. "That worked."

He kissed my forehead. "Now we all get to know what the birds feel like."

I laughed. "I suppose we do."

"This way!" The fairies darted ahead of us.

I leaned forward and we shot across the sea faster than we could have swum. We flew across the land, over the darkness of the broken mountain and thick forest. Within the hour, we set foot on the edge of Delphi.

The buildings were in even worse shape than I had thought when I'd seen it in the sea. Piles of rubble resided in perfect squares in a row on a street I knew had once been homes, and everything was covered in a mossy sheen.

We were completely exposed without buildings to hide behind.

The fairies spread out and searched the spaces where a pillar still managed to stand or the corner of a building that had forgotten to fall. We didn't see any signs of people until Tootles came back with a *zip*, his hands moving furiously.

I didn't know what he was saying exactly, but the size of his eyes and the movement of his body signaled he'd found some kind of guard or soldier, or perhaps a really tall man with sharp teeth and—wait.

I jabbed James with my elbow.

"Ow! Careful!" he whispered, rubbing his arm hard.

"It's a siren. He's saying she turned the sirens into guards."

Curly blinked at me. "You're right. You catch on fast."

"Wonderful," James said sarcastically.

"You all need to find somewhere to lay low." I turned to the one spot of light in the city—the palace. I opened the pack I'd flung over my shoulder. "Grumpy?"

The little fairy darted in, then rested his arms on the edge and peered up at me. "My name is really Michael, you know. My brother's name is John."

I winked. "I'm glad I have you coming with me, Michael."

He flashed a bright smile, then disappeared into the bag. I gently closed the top and hoped I didn't jostle him around too much as I headed for the palace.

I made it to the next road over before two men ran for me from either direction. One was bent at the waist like an old man, trying not to move his upper body as he loped toward me. The other sort of scampered sideways as if he were afraid to get too near me. As humans, they were barely more attractive than their siren ancestry. They were both bald and had the same elongated faces as the sirens.

I had felt threatened and afraid in the water, but seeing them on land, I knew I had the upper hand in this fight. My hand instinctively rested on my sword hilt, but I made no move to draw it. "I demand to see Athena."

The one to my right jerked his head a little unnaturally. He tapped his teeth together. He jabbed at me with a metal spear.

I rolled my eyes and continued on my way, followed—not quite escorted—by the two siren men. I ran my hand over the soft leather bag at my side as if I could somehow comfort myself by comforting Michael, though I didn't know if he even knew what was happening.

The nearer we drew to the palace, the better the buildings had been kept together. I recognized the row of buildings in which Ulrich had briefly imprisoned the pirates, and then we turned onto the main road which led to the palace doors.

The men who greeted us at the doors must have been Ulrich's original palace guard because they looked and acted far more human than the sirens behind me. They also wore armor with their helmets open-faced. Beneath the arch of the brow of the helmet, I saw the men's pupils dilated in fear.

I nodded to them each. "I am Odette. Ulrich sent me," I said as softly as possible to still be heard. I didn't know if the sirens understood human speech or not, but I needed to let the humans know I was on their side.

The one to my right looked beyond me, then back as if to ask where his prince was.

I managed to nudge my head to my right before one of the sirens jabbed me with the back of the spear. I continued past the pointless palace guard and into what had once been the glorious throne room lined with massive pillars. The open roof I had seen in Ulrich's memory was wider now. Cracked and splintered pillars lined all the way back to the moss-covered throne.

Athena stood in front of it, her hands clasped in front of her, and for the first time in my entire life, she wore a dress. The garment was amethyst so dark it was nearly black. A long train flowed behind her, and the right side had a slit up to her hip where a glorious silver and diamond crested octopus brooch was pinned. The gown glittered like the stars overhead.

I stopped several feet away. "Mother."

"Odette." Her hair had been washed of the dreadlocks and pulled from her face up into something black that made her elegant red curls dangle over the back of her head. "It didn't take you long to get here."

"No." I put my hands behind my back to prevent myself from picking at the strap of the bag or hint at any threat by rubbing the hilt of my sword. I took a step forward. "I wanted to speak with you. I had time to think about what you told me."

"And?" Her cold fish eyes studied me.

"It's a lot to take in." I gave a short laugh. "The prospect that this is my real home?" I looked around the palace. "This has never been a dream of mine."

She laughed at my expression and waved her hand dismissively. "With you at my side, we can rule this kingdom." She approached me, and my heart raced faster. "I've put King Eric in a new form as added entertainment for the guests." She gestured to her right, drawing my attention to a green-yellow glow.

I thought it was residual bioluminescence from Ulrich's attempt to help his people navigate the buildings in the dark of the ocean. In fact, it was a tall prison of glass, and locked inside was a gray-green-brown octopus pressed into the far corner. I gasped. "You turned him into an octopus?"

The sound of Athena's laughter echoed off the empty walls. "Wonderful, isn't it?"

I closed my mouth and thought of Sky and how easily he smiled. I slid a smile onto my face and looked at the woman who had given birth to me. "Positively cruel." I walked more casually up to her.

"I was afraid when I came in. I thought you would be mad at me."

"For what?" Though she phrased it as a question, I knew it hung like a noose around my neck. One wrong move and she'd kick the bucket out from under my feet.

"Saying I wasn't like you. I thought about your wanting to be the queen, and why I shouldn't want to be a princess. A life in a palace?" I raised my hands and turned a circle. "Not being forced to be at sea for weeks or even months on voyages that may or may not result in a bounty. How many times have we gone with empty bellies"—I faced her again—"because we ran out of supplies while stuck waiting for a merchant ship to pass? Or because we were caught in a storm or marooned? Who wouldn't want to stay on land where life is stable?" As I spoke, I realized I actually meant what I said. Every pirate had that deep desire even if the ocean itself called to them for a period of time.

My mother held her hands out to me. "I would love to rule with you by my side. And I will teach you everything I know."

I stepped forward and took her hands.

She gripped on to me, her grip crushing my hands to the point I gasped. "Odette. I am the queen of the sirens. You may have been raised the siren princess, but you cannot deceive your own mother."

"Y-You're hurting me," I gasped. I tried to pull away, but somehow her hands tightened. "Ah! Mother, please!"

Michael suddenly darted out from under the flap of my bag and flew as fast as he could for the open roof.

Athena's gaze locked on figures in the shadows. "Follow him. Bring them back to me."

TWENTY-SIX

I was careful to make sure you didn't know a thing about your magical abilities." She tugged on the skirt of her dress and somehow peeled away a long piece that evolved into seaweed. She wrapped it around my wrists and the seaweed tightened until I was securely bound.

"Athena, I was being truthful!" I tried. "I do want to learn to be the princess!"

"Of course you do." She smiled. "I'll teach you how to do all of it. I will fix it, just like before. We'll be just as happy as we were before you foolishly broke your seashell." She held up a hand, and in that hand was the shell she'd revealed in Zelig.

"No you don't!"

My mother seemed to have forgotten I hadn't been raised a lady. I'd been raised a pirate. And one thing my mother herself had taught me was that pirates don't fight fair.

With a growl, I turned my hips, hooked my leg, and kicked the back of her knee, both breaking her concentration and dropping her. She had no choice but to let go of me. The ridiculous dress she wore did nothing but restrain her movements—slit or no slit. With that, I had the upper hand.

I slammed my bound wrists down on the back of her head, spun on the still-damp floor, and ran for the open doorway just as James ran in. "Go, go, go!" I yelled.

He skidded to a halt, sword at the ready, and paused a moment in confusion. Gerard was right on his heels.

My mother shouted in a language I didn't understand, and Gerard's eyes widened.

"Get out!" I yelled again.

"She's summoned help," Gerard said. He grabbed my arm and sliced his short blade through the seaweed, releasing me. "Get your sword and fight!"

"How do you know what she said?"

"Spellcaster, remember? Not to mention she's speaking the same language as the northern lands!" He wheeled around just then, as though sensing something.

It was a humanoid form of a shark appeared. He had legs and arms of a man, but a gray fin protruded from crude clothing, and his head wasn't shaped quite right. He carried a scythe in his hands and swung it at Gerard.

Gerard jumped back, bumping into me hard enough to make me fall. I rolled to my knees as a man looking like a killer whale stomped down at me. He carried some kind of war hammer in his massive hands. These were mutated sirens my mother had combined with sea creatures to give them human abilities.

Gerard kicked the shark man in the stomach, then turned and held his hand out toward the center of the floor between me and Athena. He spoke words with the same intonation as my mother had, and a gaping hole appeared in the ground. From that hole began to climb skeletons.

I screamed. I'd somehow forgotten Gerard knew how to summon dead things, or perhaps it hadn't really hit me until I saw the creatures themselves climbing out of the ground.

He jumped and looked at me in genuine surprise. "You're scared of skeletons?"

"They're dead people! They used to be alive!"

He rolled his eyes. "At least I didn't summon zombies. Look—" He ducked another swing of the scythe. "They won't attack you and can't die. Much better option for an army."

James backed up, fighting a fish creature with two heads and a claw. I heard other battles outside and wondered how my mother had summoned these creatures to her aid so readily. Perhaps she had them ready all along or had been experimenting with spells the last eighteen years so she could get her revenge however she wanted.

"It's futile, Odette!" she called to me over the sounds of the battle. "You won't win. You cannot defeat me when I haven't shown you everything I know."

"If Athena gets enough time to cast another spell, she will take away my memories!" I shouted.

I grunted when the whale-man kicked me in the hip but used the momentum to roll out from in front of him and jumped up behind. I drove my sword through his back. He released a distorted scream that tore through my chest and made me cover my ear with my free hand. I wanted to apologize to the creature I'd killed. The whale was completely innocent.

Instead, I turned to face my mother.

She was successfully fending off Gerard's skeletons with a nearly bored expression. She flung bursts of water from her hands. When she struck a skeleton, it slammed into a pillar and exploded into pieces.

I ducked under the arm of another sea creature I fought and glanced over to see the shell back in my mother's hand.

"No! Please, Athena!" I started running for her.

I knew Gerard said the skeletons wouldn't attack me, but I couldn't help but think that these skeletons had once been *inside* a living being. I could have been beside a handsome lord, a mother, a merchant, or even a fellow pirate. There was no way to tell, and it terrified me. I sucked in a breath, determined to not give in to my fear over having my memories stolen, and ran past them.

I'd made it past the second row of skeletons when I heard James grunt in such a way I instantly knew he'd been hurt. I glanced over my shoulder. A stingray's stinger protruded from his right shoulder, the only arm capable of fighting back. If I didn't turn back to help him, the siren man fighting him could kill him.

The siren yanked the stinger out of James's shoulder, earning another cry, and James dropped to his knees. But if I stopped running, my mother could wipe my memories, and I couldn't bear the thought of forgetting James ever again.

I tightened my grip on my sword and ran again.

Ulrich showed up out of nowhere and got to my mother first. He struck her hand, sending the shell to the ground and shattering it.

She let out a sound I'd never heard, a scream mixed with a roar, and turned to face him. "You little toad!" she snapped. "You'll pay for that!" My mother's attention turned to my little brother.

Giant tentacles of seaweed broke through the stone floor and wrapped around Ulrich's legs. He let out a cry of surprise as he was forced to his knees. He tried batting at them with the sword, but even as he cut them, more sprung up and quickly wrapped around his arms.

"Mother, please don't!" I shouted.

She backhanded Ulrich across the face, then seized his hair. "Where. Is. The. Stone?"

"Gah!" James cried.

I stopped beside a skeleton and wheeled around as the stingray creature roughly bound James's hands behind his back. Three creatures now fought Gerard, and some of the skeletons at the back of the group ran over to help him.

"How *dare you*!" Athena shouted. My attention snapped back to her. Blood dripped from her hand. "Foolish, foolish child!" The spittle from her words landed on Ulrich's face.

He struggled against the seaweed. My mother slapped him again, and I spotted his necklace—with the summer stone trapped inside—fly through the air and into the boot of the skeleton two skeletons away from me.

"Stop this!" I shouted with all the strength of my voice.

She turned her face to me, baring her teeth in a way that made me see the siren she really was. "You bring your friends to fight me? Friends who should be loyal to me!" Her glare landed on James. "They should be fighting by my side!"

I slowly sheathed my weapon, my hands trembling. This woman couldn't possibly be the mother I knew. I put my hands out. "Mother, I came to you because I wanted to be the princess. I said that when I arrived."

"You wait until it is convenient. When your life is threatened!" She sounded hysterical, her eyes were wild. "You have no idea what I've been through to gain my power!"

"No. No, I don't. I don't know what it's like to have any power at all, Mother." I slowly released the belt on my waist and set my sword on the ground, presenting myself as completely powerless to her. "But you can teach me. You can show me."

My mother laughed manically, which slowed until her typically evil smile appeared and some of the insanity left it. "I will teach you all I know."

"And you don't even need to make me forget anything. If you do, I won't remember how far you've come. What you've done to give me so much." I stopped so close I could have reached out and touched Ulrich's shoulder. "Just . . . let him go."

Athena's jester-like smile turned to Ulrich. "Not until he tells me where the summer stone is."

"He doesn't have it," I stated.

"Oh?" Her brow raised, but she didn't move her eyes.

"Neither does James." I looked over at them to see even Gerard had been overpowered now, as well as most of the other pirates. Whatever I said would put all these men at risk. I swallowed hard.

"I assume you want me to let them go? I already told you, darling. Not. Until. I have. The stone." She seized Ulrich by the hair again and yanked his head back.

"It's in the skeleton's boot!" I blurted, holding my hands out.

Athena rolled her eyes to me. "The skeleton?"

"Yes. I saw it."

Ulrich's eyes widened. "Don't, Odette. She'll destroy everything!"

"I'll get it. Please . . . please don't harm him." I took a step forward.

"Oh, I have a much better plan for him." She waved her hand, speaking a quick curse.

"Odette," Ulrich croaked.

His face compressed and elongated, his skin turned green, his arms curled up and legs curled in. His bones popped, skin shrunk, and all the clothing and hair disappeared from his body until my mother stood with a fat green frog with purple spots in her hands.

I put my hands on my cheeks.

"If you want your brother back, I suggest you obey every single thing I say." She turned to face me, presenting the frog like one would a crown.

A frog.

My mother had turned Prince Ulrich, my little brother, into a frog.

I lifted my gaze to her. Before, I had clung to a shred of hope that my mother couldn't possibly be a monster. My mother had raised me, trained me, held me when I cried, nursed me to health whenever I fell ill. She made me the strong woman I was.

Yet, in that instant, I lost all respect for her.

Whatever hope I had that she would relent faded.

My mother wanted one thing in her life and one thing only: power. I decided at that moment Athena was no longer my mother.

Athena lifted her chin. "Men, send Gerard back to Selina." Her gaze shifted to him. "And Gerard, darling?"

He grunted as he was dragged to his feet, his arms bound behind him now. "What?"

"Your grandmother will hear of this." She lowered her chin, brows raised, smirk playing.

Gerard narrowed his own glare. "Go on. She's the one who sent me here." The creatures dragged him out the front door.

My mother's lip twitched. "Bind Odette again."

A half-dolphin man stepped up and pulled my arms behind me. The skeletons were beginning to follow Gerard—the six that were left. One of those six had the summer stone in his boot, and I needed to get it.

Whoever possesses the summer stone possesses the power of the sea.

"As for the pirates . . ." she continued.

I looked around, hoping to catch sight of something to help me. And then I spotted the lost boys, all in their fairy forms, on the edge of the ceiling watching from above. *You don't need to wait for her to teach you magic. It's innate. You were born the siren princess. You were born to possess the summer stone.*

"Bind them. Lock them up, even if it's a cave in the bottom of the sea. I want them out of here until I have the summer stone in my possession and I am on the throne."

"Odette," James objected, a pant of pain lingering at the edge of my name.

I looked over my shoulder at him, my heart racing. "James! Please, Mother. He's injured. He's bleeding." My heart welled up in my throat.

"That is a shame." She stroked her fingers along Ulrich's head and spine. "I'm afraid he will likely die. If not from bleeding out, then from infection."

Ulrich's throat puffed out like a blowfish, and he croaked noisily.

The dolphin bound my wrists together with the seaweed rope.

I looked up, aiming my gaze at the little lost boys. "But I told you where the summer stone is!" If they could get the summer stone out of the boot of the skeleton and get it to me, we might have a chance.

They got the hint, elbowing each other before springing into action and disappearing into the night sky.

My mother stopped in front of me. "I now have you as an ally. The pirates will be reminded of my power. And you . . ." She took my chin. "You will be my daughter again."

"Y-Yes," I hesitantly answered. "Just like before."

Her lip curled in an insane sort of curl. "Yes . . ." She let go and turned her back.

I ran for the front door. Grumpy flew around the edge of the doorway and right to me.

"What are you doing?" my mother demanded.

I jumped over my wrists, bringing them in front of me, and held out my hand for the pendant that belonged on Ulrich's neck. The green magic glowed brightly and filled me with warmth to my core. Like I felt with the winter stone in Zelig, I could feel the magic, but the feeling was a thousand times more intense.

It tasted like the salt of the sea, smelled like a summer afternoon, and felt like warm arms of a loved one around me. Each of those sensations held precious memories for me.

The first time I'd ever sailed with my mother, she held me up on the railing by the helm, my tiny feet teetering on the edge of falling, but her hands had balanced me. She laughed with me, telling me how someday I would grow up big and strong like her, that I would have friends and family.

The summer afternoons I spent with my mother, in the heat, under the tree in the back of the villa where she made me practice for hours to get my footwork just right. She'd taught me how to hold a sword, strike a blow, dodge, and anticipate. She'd praised me, told me how proud she was, over and over.

And finally, her warm arms as we stood on the porch overlooking Port Mere and the ships below. She told me someday I would be my own captain, chart my own course. I would conquer the sea and everything she'd ever been afraid of. It was that moment she told me she first mentioned how we can only outrun our pasts a short time. I never could get out of her what she meant.

And then the voice of the stone echoed through my chest and into my mind:

> *Hardened by the passage of time.*
> *Stolen by the longing of dreams.*
> *Crumbled by the passion of lovers.*
> *Imprisoned by the slander of crime.*
> *A finer prize can no man have,*
> *Than the heart of a woman fair.*

But to take the heart of a woman
Is to lay your soul out bare.

I had no other choice.

I kept my eyes on my mother and dug deep into my heart. I wished for my mother to be transformed into her most useless form. I didn't take time thinking what that might be or how that would impact anything else. I just acted.

With the summer stone in my hand, I held it out, directed at my mother.

Athena looked up at me in a panic as the green wave of magic hit her. "What did you do?" She gasped and dropped Ulrich from her hands. "What did you *do?*" she screamed and ran at me. But as she did, she took on her siren appearance before shrinking further and disappeared into the folds of her dress.

TWENTY-SEVEN

I panted, tears in my eyes, then ran over and moved the dress aside. A fish as big as my hand flopped helplessly on the ground. I quickly scooped it up and sprinted to the glass tank with the octopus. I promptly dropped my mother inside.

The octopus scrambled up to the top and I scooped him out.

"Sh-she said you were my father." I trembled as I looked down at the summer stone. "Let's see if I can fix this." I licked my lips and the summer stone sent out another wave of magic.

The octopus's arms shrunk in, his body elongated, and just as quickly as my mother had been turned into a fish, the octopus transformed into a man. King Eric stood before me in sopping wet, royal clothes. Ulrich looked just like him. He had the same short chin, wide nose, gentle eyes, and dark hair.

"In all my days . . ." he said on a breath, looking me up and down. He smiled at me. "My little Odette." He walked over and stopped in front of me. "I don't suppose you remember me?"

I shook my head, still trembling.

"Of course you wouldn't. You were so young when she took you." He ran his hand over his face and looked over at Ulrich as he hopped with little *slaps* across the wet floor. He crouched and picked up the frog. "Ulrich, I am sorry."

"I've got to turn her back," I said in my panic. "I . . . I didn't mean to turn her into a fish." I looked at the stone and back at my mother.

"Not yet," King Eric said. "Think about everything that has happened. We need to learn how to help her before letting her go."

"Your plan is to leave her in there?" I stared at him with wide eyes.

"It's the best we can do until we discover what has changed her." He put his hand on my shoulder. "I know you have no reason to trust me. I don't imagine she's said many good things to you over the years. Not that I gave her many good things to say." He looked at the fish in the tank with complete and honest sorrow. "I should have been a much better man to her."

"She told me you betrayed her." I pulled out of his grip. "That you made bargains behind her back and when people who were loyal to her told her, you threw them all into the sea!"

He blinked and then sighed. "There are two sides to every story, but that is not true."

"Then what is it?" I demanded.

"The truth is, she seduced me. I knew she was the siren queen, and I knew she wanted power. It was sort of a double-sided arrangement. Her people would no longer attack my ships. My men would no longer kill her people." King Eric's lips flashed in a smile. "We most certainly didn't think we would fall in love with each other."

"Then how did she end up a pirate?"

He walked over and sat on his throne, looking around at the damage. "She began trying to pass laws without my seal of approval. She wanted to move her sirens to the land, have them live among my people. She even snuck three of them into the castle as servants. One of them was your nanny." His jaw flexed. "I saw them as vile, murderous creatures and didn't want them around you children. I made a terrible mistake."

I felt the stone grow warm as if to confirm his tale.

"I ordered my men to kill those sirens." He let out a heavy sigh and closed his eyes. "Their . . . executions put too much strain on your mother, and she gave birth to Ulrich a month early. He barely survived. After that, she refused to speak to me no matter my attempts to reconcile. When I caught her stealing the summer stone, I had no choice." He looked up at me and I saw tears streaming down his cheeks. "I had to return her to the sea. Knowing I needed an heir to the throne, she took my firstborn child. You."

"All she ever wanted . . . was for her people to be safe?"

314

He nodded, again lowering his head in shame. "I am truly ashamed of the man I was. I searched for you for years. I kept the trade routes open she made, ensuring my men wouldn't cross pass with the sirens and kill them on accident. When the pirates began to show up, I even requested over and over to meet with them. I had no idea she was their queen until the end of last year. It was then I truly sought to meet with her. I failed."

King Eric looked so small. Feeble. Useless. He didn't look like the arrogant king I'd heard him to be or even seen from Ulrich's memories. He'd been beaten down and now was completely helpless to help his own son, his wife, and his kingdom.

"I don't want riches," I stated.

He lifted his dark eyes to me.

"I don't want pearls or goblets of gold. I don't even care if I have a roof over my head!" I heaved a breath. "All I ever wanted was a family. People who love me. All I wanted was for my mother to see what I'd done and be proud of me. Ulrich was the same, you know. He did everything seeking your approval, and you ignored him when he warned you about the contract."

King Eric nodded. "I know. I pushed him away when I found he preferred the company of men." He shifted the frog Ulrich so Ulrich could see his face. "I never should have done such a thing. You are my son. I've always loved you and always will. When Athena made me her figurehead on her ship, I realized the errors of my ways. I want to be better." He looked at me. "Truly. When she used her powers to sink Delphi,

315

I did the only thing I knew to protect my people. I used the summer stone to turn them into sirens."

I lowered myself to one of the broken pillars in the middle of the room. "You made your own people sirens?"

"It was all I could do to save them."

I drew a big breath. "We need to get the pirates and find out how to make them humans. I don't know if the summer stone can help with that, but if all Mother wanted was for them to be a part of the kingdom . . . I think we should try and integrate them into the kingdom."

The king smiled softly. "I agree. Perhaps I can hire them to rebuild Delphi." He looked around the palace. "We need some repairs before the summer solstice in two days. I suppose it's too soon for you to call me father, so why don't you call me Eric for now?"

I nodded with a weak smile, but jumped to my feet. "I've got to go get James and Gerard!" I spun on my heel and sprinted from the room, all the way down to the beach.

The sea creature men were pushing the pirates into the surf while a few were giving a hearty fight.

"Wait!" I shouted. "Stop!"

All eyes shifted to me.

"Athena is gone, but I can help." I raised the stone up in my fist. "You will all be made into men, human men, where you will be properly hired. The king has offered to help give you jobs and homes. I command you to take a human form."

The dolphin shed away from the siren's back and landed in the shallow waters with a heavy splash. The siren looked down at himself, completely confused, as the scales shed from his skin, hair grew on his head, and a rather handsome man in his thirties took form. He turned to the dolphin, took him by the tail, and dragged him into deeper water so he could swim away.

This happened to each of the creatures. Whatever they had been combined with separated from their bodies, and human forms took place. I wasn't exactly sure what my mother's hopes were, but this was a start.

"Now, release the pirates," I commanded.

They followed my orders, cutting through the seaweed ropes with swords the pirates wore on their hips, then returned the swords to their owners.

James ran to me and pulled me close with his left arm. "Don't you ever scare me like that again." He pressed his lips to the top of my head. "What happened to your mother?"

"I . . . sort of turned her into a fish." I flashed a nervous smile.

"A fish?" He raised his brows. "I didn't see that coming."

"Your shoulder." I bit my lip. The wound was horrible.

He looked down at it. "Yeah. That."

I shook my head. "I have to get Gerard."

"Already got him!" Nibs announced proudly.

I turned and saw the fairies in their human forms, marching in a row with Slightly holding on to Gerard's hand. I gave him a relieved smile. "I was worried about you. I wasn't certain they would actually take you away. I was worried they were going to lock you up somewhere."

Gerard twitched his brows. "I thought they were going to execute me, to be honest." He stopped in front of me. "What is the plan now?"

"Fixing him." I pointed my thumb at James.

"You have the stone." Gerard motioned with his eyes.

I faced James. "Oh. Right. Why do I just have to wish what I want? Why don't I have to use a spell?"

"I don't know," Gerard answered. "I haven't had a chance to study them."

"Oh, that gives me comfort. You just barely found out your mother was a powerful witch and now you think you can use magic too," James teased me.

I grinned. "I am my mother's daughter. In a way."

"Let's hope you don't do the going crazy part," Gerard said.

"I have a question for you about that," I said. I placed my hand on James's wound.

He hissed and turned his face away, bearing a grimace on his face.

The summer stone's green magic spread through my body, into my hand, and into James's wound. Slowly, the grimace on his face faded, and he turned his head back to watch in astonishment as the power healed his wound.

"Wow," he said. He lifted his shoulder and moved his arm. "That's incredible."

"Let's go turn Ulrich back to himself!" I said. I took off running. The boys fell into step along with me. I reached the throne to find my father fast asleep with Ulrich on his lap.

Ulrich began croaking when he spotted me and hopped off our father's lap.

This caused King Eric to jerk awake with a snort and sit up.

I fell to my knees in front of Ulrich. "I know just what to do." I held him in one hand, and just as I'd healed James, I tried to fix Ulrich.

Only, it didn't work.

I frowned and tried again.

Nothing.

"She must have put a curse on him," Gerard mumbled. He crouched and picked Ulrich up himself. "Ah. Yes. It's an old curse, and pretty typical. Also, very easy to solve. These sorts of spells can be broken by true love's kiss."

"He's my brother. I love him." I pulled Ulrich from Gerard's hands and kissed him on top of the head.

"Not that kind of love," Gerard clarified. "Real love."

I looked down at Ulrich, then up at James. "We need to find a true love for him."

"Don't look at me." James put up his hand and hook.

I rolled my eyes. "I wasn't saying loved him."

Battle cries sounded before the sound of running footsteps followed.

I grinned. "Sky is here with the others."

James headed for the door and held up his hand. "Oy! We're all safe!"

"You mean you had the battle without us?" Sky whined.

"It didn't last long, to be honest." James shrugged.

Grumpy, or Michael, leaned against my side. "I'm sleepy."

"Me too." I wrapped my arm around his side and pulled him close. "We'll get to bed soon enough. We just have to figure out where to sleep. And you did great."

Luckily, curious people from the nearby towns showed up within the hour. There was much joy with the city of Delphi being returned, along with their king, though no one could understand why pirates would be willing to help. We were directed to nearby houses with spare beds or shops with empty attics, sheds, and so on.

The people of Delphi, who had been turned into sirens and back, were able to travel to family or were also given places to stay.

I found myself, however, sitting on the beach, watching the sun rise. Ulrich sat in my lap with his eyes closed behind transparent eyelids. I looked over my shoulder and watched James walk over.

He sat at my side and drew me to his chest. "Told you that you were brave."

I snorted. "I was absolutely terrified if you must know."

"I could see it. But you overcame that fear and saved us all."

I shrugged.

"We get to stay for the summer solstice," James said. "We have to help Ulrich find his true love. Want to know the best part?"

"Hm?"

"I get to see you in a dress again."

I groaned.

James kissed my head.

TWENTY-EIGHT

The next day everyone worked on cleaning up as much of the debris as possible. The square in front of the palace was cleaned first and prepared for the summer ball. Word traveled fast, and soon hundreds of people carted away rotten and broken wood or chunks of stone.

Women began to put up colorful triangles of fabric and ribbons, strung on ropes, between poles that had been erected around the square. They painted the skeletons of houses in vibrant colors while men worked on ensuring the palace was structurally sound.

I saw the appeal of living in a city.

I had worked in the palace all day, helping to clean out the guest rooms, haul new furniture in, and hang curtains in the windows since they no longer had glass in them. Luckily, that also meant the coolness of the sea would help the temperature in the room at night.

By the time the sun set that night, the palace was actually decent. We had rooms to sleep in with proper beds. I kept Ulrich with me at all times, keeping him safe.

When I woke the next morning, my heart jumped. It was the summer solstice, and that evening would be the summer ball. I was put in a green sleeveless dress, the servants pulled up my reckless red hair, and an emerald necklace was draped on my neck. Much better than pink.

I looked at my own reflection in a small temporary mirror. I looked . . . beautiful.

And then I realized it was because I saw me as the princess. *Crown* princess.

I didn't want to admit how excited that made me feel. I almost felt guilty for feeling such joy. I'd insisted I wanted to be a pirate the rest of my life, but I actually had a chance to live in a palace. And I wanted it more than anything.

I exited the palace, relieved the sun hadn't reached its hottest point, and easily found James in the crowd. He stood beside Sky, who had attracted a group of girls, as per the usual. One of the girls even flirted with James, flipping her blond locks over her shoulder or curling them around her fingers.

I stood behind her with a bemused grin on my face until James spotted me.

His face lit up with a smile, and my heart fluttered. "Excuse me." He put his freshly shined hook on her shoulder and moved her aside so he could approach me. He bowed at the waist. "You look positively stunning." He took my hand with his and kissed the back.

I laughed. "What was that?"

He pouted. "Is it so terrible I have manners?"

"No, but you don't need to be so formal." I pulled him close and planted a kiss on his lips.

"Pardon me, Princess Odette," a young man said.

I swung my head to look behind me and spotted a young man. He was handsome, with the sides of his head neatly shaved and the top of his hair parted to one side, a boyish smile, and beautiful blue eyes. He was a little older than me, but I couldn't tell if he was older or younger than James.

"Can I help you?" I asked.

"Yes." He nervously shifted his stance. "My name is Prince Keltin. I am from Arington. I wondered . . . have you seen Prince Ulrich?" He glanced around. "I've been searching for him everywhere."

"Are you his true love?" I gasped.

Keltin's eyes widened in horror. "Pardon me?"

"Odette," James scolded.

"Forgive me." I let go of James. "I'm afraid he's under a curse. Come with me." I motioned for Prince Keltin to follow and led him to my bedroom, which he nervously entered.

Ulrich, in his adorable frog form, sat in a lump on the nightstand. He started croaking louder and louder when I entered, but when I reached for him, he hopped onto the bed and then from the bed to the floor.

Keltin took a step back. "What is this?"

"That's Ulrich," I explained. "Remember how I said he's under a curse? He's been turned into a frog. Gerard said he will remain like that until someone breaks the spell with true love's kiss. I tried, but apparently it doesn't work with siblings." I shrugged.

Keltin's nose wrinkled in disgust. "This is a horrible joke." He backed out of the room.

I frowned. "Why would I joke?"

Ulrich hopped after him.

Keltin shook his head. "I'll ask someone else." He turned and left quickly.

Ulrich's croaking became more frantic, and I picked him up.

"Don't worry. We'll break your spell before midnight! Now I know who you have a crush on," I teased.

Ulrich gave out one mournful croak.

"Stop being so dramatic. I'll chase him down."

I rejoined the party, carrying Ulrich in my hand. James didn't think anything of it. I passed poor Ulrich to Sky when I wanted to dance, and then he handed Ulrich back to me when he wanted to dance.

After another hour, I found Prince Keltin standing beside a girl in a dress cut off at the knees. It was blue with an iridescent sheen of gold on top. Her brown hair had been tied up in two buns at the top of her head. Somehow she'd gotten pearls to stay in her hair as well.

She greeted me with a beaming smile. "You must be Crown Princess Odette. I'm Princess Ismae. This is my brother, Crown Prince Keltin."

325

"Crown prince?" I smiled. "You failed to mention that."

He shrugged. "It's unnecessary to give titles constantly," he muttered.

"Am I to understand correctly, Prince Ulrich is your brother?" Ismae carried on, her eyes alight like the stars on a summer evening.

"Yes, he is."

Ismae stepped up to my side, prompting me to begin walking. "I wonder if you could put in a good word for me. I've liked him for some time, and I believe his father had started to ask him about who he is interested in?"

I blinked at her and looked between our shoulders to her brother, who had a sheepish blush to his cheeks and pretended not to hear us. "Are you unaware . . ." I started, but Ulrich croaked. I sighed and held him up. "This is Ulrich."

"Good heavens!" Ismae gasped. "He's a frog?"

"Turned into one yesterday. Err, the day before. Perhaps you could give him a kiss?"

She blushed madly but bravely leaned down and kissed the top of Ulrich's head.

Nothing.

She bit her lip and looked at me. "If that's not truly Prince Ulrich, that was a mean trick."

I rolled my eyes. "Why would I make you kiss a frog?"

"Because you're a pirate? And the siren princess?"

James rejoined my side. He nodded his head to Ismae in greeting. "Good evening."

"Good evening, sir. Have you come to ask me to dance?" Ismae grinned and seemed to suddenly have a problem with her leg because her entire body leaned to one side and she reached up and patted her hair.

He gave a courteous smile. "No, I came to inform Princess Odette everyone is gathering at the table to eat."

"Don't you dare start calling me princess."

"Or what?" he challenged, looking down at me. The look made my heart forget to beat, my lungs forget to breathe, and for a moment, I was positive I was stuck with my mouth open. He leaned down and brushed his lips against mine. "Cat got your tongue?" he whispered.

I came to my senses only because a herald announced dinner was served.

I swallowed and straightened. "Not in front of Ulrich." I shielded Ulrich away from James's body.

James laughed and slid his arm around my side. "I think I could get used to seeing you in dresses."

"It doesn't seem real," I admitted and ran my hand over the silky material.

We walked to the long table, and I was directed by a man in a long tailcoat to sit beside my father. I set Ulrich down on the table, and he stretched his chubby little legs before plopping to the plate across from me. He climbed onto it and wiggled his body down.

The woman beside that chair blinked at him, then looked at my father. "King Eric, I've never seen such a thing."

"That's because you've never seen Ulrich cursed," he answered.

"Good heavens!" she gasped. "Poor Ulrich!" She leaned closer to him. "Do you know what is to break the curse?" She took her goblet and poured a tiny bit of water onto the plate, which seemed to make Ulrich very happy because he wiggled his little body into it further, practically squashing flat.

I looked down the row of people beside her. A man sat to her opposite side, then Keltin, and finally—as I predicted—Princess Ismae. I grinned a bit to myself at how similar Ismae was to her mother.

King Eric explained the exact same thing I'd tried to explain to multiple people that night. Only, this woman actually believed it.

She picked Ulrich from his little water bath and handed him—dripping—to her husband. "Give him to Keltin and have Keltin give him a kiss on the head."

Keltin's ears and neck grew red.

The king turned and passed Ulrich to Keltin. "You heard your mother."

Keltin looked down at the little frog in his hands. "If this works, I'm sorry I didn't try earlier." He leaned down and kissed the top of Ulrich's head.

As quickly as Ulrich had been transformed into a frog, he took his real shape with proper arms and legs, a human face, and his same messy sun-kissed brown hair. He sat on the table in front of Keltin, legs to either side. His clothes were wrinkled and disheveled, and his hair stuck up.

But he was grinning. "Stupid," he said to Keltin.

328

Keltin pushed his chair back so he could stand and wrapped his arms around Ulrich. "I'm so sorry I didn't try. I didn't believe her."

The few of us who saw the transformation began applauding.

King Eric had the same man in tailcoats direct Ulrich to his quarters, likely so he could bathe and dress in something proper.

Ulrich grinned and waved to me. "Thank you, Odette! I'll be right back, all of you."

James chuckled. "True love's kiss, huh?"

I smiled. "I think it's adorable."

My father stood and clapped his hands, silencing all the chatter. "I have an announcement I would like to make. I would like to clear up some of my misdeeds and create some new laws. Many of you may know I fell in love with the siren queen nineteen years ago." He glanced at me. "She bore me two beautiful children, Crown Princess Odette and Prince Ulrich." He faced the crowd again. "A lot has happened these past few months, but even longer still. I would like to propose we allow the sirens to join us on land, allow them to purchase property, work at our sides, and become citizens of Terricina."

The crowd began to murmur.

"I know this will be a change, especially considering Delphi was just returned to its former location. However, they should be treated as part of our country like each of you. They will be expected to follow our laws, of course. I know this will take time. For now, enjoy the rest of your evening. Happy summer solstice!" He raised his goblet.

Everyone grabbed theirs and did a cheer before taking a drink and resuming their chatter.

I leaned toward my father. "This should make Mother happy. I think we should return her to her true self and talk with her."

He nodded. "I believe that may be the best thing as well."

Ulrich pranced back into the room wearing a white suit with golden accents. His hair was still damp but brushed nicely. He walked down to Ismae and leaned to her ear, saying something only she could hear. She nodded and took the chair meant for him, and he took the seat she'd been in.

A servant removed the dirty plate and returned with another.

All the dishes, silverware, and goblets were mismatched, many of them borrowed from nearby people. The food had also been made by everyone in the surrounding towns, and it tasted positively delicious.

When we finally got a moment, after eating our fill, I led the way to the fish tank where my mother lazily moved in the water.

Ulrich stepped up to my side. "You think she's ready to be let out?"

"I think we have to try."

We glanced at each other.

I patted my dress and then neck. "I don't have the stone."

"Don't look at me, I've been a pitiful frog the past two days," Ulrich complained.

I looked at James, who shook his head, and then my heart dropped. No one from our party—not Sky or my father, not anyone—had the summer stone. I ran to my room and tore it apart looking.

"Gerard!" I shouted.

EPILOGUE

James Hook would like his hand back," I said casually, stepping out of the black hole that led to the underworld. I kicked off a skeleton hand grasping at my boot. Once on solid ground, I waved my hand, and the portal closed.

Selina sat at a desk in the corner of her room and didn't even look up from whatever she was writing. Her long black hair was braided over her right shoulder and glistened nearly blue in the evening light. "That's unfortunate. I don't feel we are done with him. Do you?"

I walked over and set the summer stone right in the middle of the parchment.

She lifted her head. Her lips spread into a smile. "You got it."

I smirked. "I should have retrieved it earlier, but I was having too much fun. They don't even know it's missing yet." I leaned my hip against her desk.

"I was concerned when you first showed up here." She reached out and touched the stone.

"I didn't know you were here." I frowned. "It was unexpected. What I don't understand is why you didn't attempt to take the stone yourself when you had the opportunity."

Selina leaned back in her seat, which groaned at the movement. Her calculated gaze studied me with a look I knew all too well. She wasn't sure whether I was ready to know all the truth. She'd done that since I was a child—not knowing if I was smart enough for a particular spell, unsure if I was physically ready to learn the next step in a sword fight, or if I had practiced enough.

I was used to it, but it still made my skin crawl and anger flare in my belly.

"If you must know, I can't," she finally replied.

"Can't what?"

"Take the stones. Each stone was designed for each of the four kingdoms, gifted to them by your father. They were meant to be handed down from royal hand to royal hand." She scooted away from the desk. "As a sorceress myself, I am unable to lay a hand on them until they are in my possession. Which is why the winter stone remains on its pedestal." She walked around the desk and faced me but reached around and scooped up the glowing green stone. It threw an eerie light into her eyes.

"Because I brought this to you without incident, I would like to read my father's journals again."

She shifted her lusty attention away from the stone. "Oh?"

"It's been a decade," I added as if *that* would impact her decision.

"I suppose I can arrange that . . ." Selina straightened and carried the stone to the black box on the mantle. There were no mirrors in her room, and her bedroom door had a spell added to the lock. She set the green stone beside the lavender spring stone. "We have free access to the winter stone, so there is only one more to obtain." She turned, dusting her hands unnecessarily.

"Arington," I confirmed.

She smiled. "I am very proud of you, Gerard."

In spite of myself, I felt my chest swell. Her words of praise were too few and far between. However, I was holding onto a secret of my own.

Ever since Elisa's action of mercy, I'd been bothered. Showing up in Terricina to get the stone . . . there were multiple opportunities for me to have taken it. I should have grabbed it when Ulrich fell asleep the first night. I could have even slipped it away when they were in Zelig and handed it to Selina.

But these people . . . they were curious. Complete strangers willing to help one another just because it was the right thing to do. Of course, Odette pretended to be a hardened pirate, but all she wanted was the same thing I wanted—to belong somewhere. To have someone somewhere love her, and she sought that from an unstable mother.

As I watched Selina cross the room to the trunk at the foot of her bed, I knew I was just like Odette.

Mercy from Elisa and my own similarities with Odette had planted a seed of doubt.

I needed to stay focused on my intention of going to Arington or Selina wouldn't be pleased with me. But, unlike Odette, I knew Selina was manipulating me. In the end, however, it would be worth it.

Selina lifted the lid of the trunk, rummaged about, then lifted a stack of hand-written, leather-bound journals. "There you are."

I crouched and took them from her. "Thank you."

"Don't stay up all night reading them," she said in a mocking tone. Using an unspoken spell, she opened the door, making the protection spell pause while I crossed the threshold, then closed the door and returned the spell.

I walked the hallway to the room I'd been given at my previous appearance. However, when I rounded the corner, I nearly ran into Mathias.

His eyes narrowed at me. "How did you get here?"

"I walked," I replied flatly and tried not to look annoyed.

Mathias took a step nearer, and his chest was now pressing against my arms. We were the same height, so the movement wasn't threatening to me. "I know you've taken the summer stone. I know you and your grandmother have something planned, and I intend to find out exactly what it is."

I arched my brow with calculated calmness. "Shouldn't you be at the summer ball?"

He scoffed. "I flew back here as soon as I knew you'd taken the stone."

"Allegedly. Odette could have lost it." I shrugged and stepped past him.

Mathias grabbed my arm. "I remembered then how I knew you. You were in Griswil. The man engaged to Princess Elisa. I hear you attacked her with creatures of the underworld."

I tightened my lips, but didn't break eye contact. I knew, with Mathias's powers, he could see through me if I didn't keep my guard up. "And?" I asked, keeping my voice perfectly even.

"What are you doing in Zelig, Gerard?"

"I am visiting with my grandmother."

"Then what is all this?" He slammed his fist on the top of the books.

Because I only had my right hand beneath them, and my left hand steadying the pile, the unexpected movement caused me to drop all the books, which hit the ground and spread everywhere. One of them exploded, sending papers spiraling across the stone floor.

The anger in the pit of my belly stirred again, and my eyes narrowed. The darkness from the corners of the room elongated and towered over us. "You may be a phoenix, Mathias, but I am something far more powerful," I threatened, drawing the darkness in closer. "These are my dead father's journals, and you have just disrespected him and me. I recommend you mind your own business from now on or something might happen to your beloved twin sister."

Mathias swallowed uncomfortably and stepped back. "You and your grandmother should leave Zelig."

"We will. When we're ready."

Mathias sneered at me, then turned on his heel and deliberately stepped on the journal with the green cover, forcing it to slide further away. He paused a moment, then carried on back down the hallway.

I slowly exhaled, the dark magic swirling around my hands faded, and the shadows returned to their positions. I crouched and delicately put my father's journals back together, treating each piece of paper with tenderness.

Selina insisted my father was a horrible man for giving magic so freely. I wanted to read his journals and judge for myself. And I *would* stay up all night reading because I didn't want to wake and have Selina tell me my time was up.

I slammed the door closed behind me and set the journals on the bed. I crossed to the mirror, pulled it from the wall, then whispered a quick shrinking spell and tossed it out the window. I checked the room once more to ensure there were no other mirrors before I lit the candlesticks.

The familiar caw of a raven echoed from under the door before I heard it peck.

I frowned at the door. "Stupid bird." I tried to ignore it, but the crow pounded on the door. I rolled my eyes. All I wanted was some peace and quiet, to read my father's journals, and just . . . be alone for a while.

Instead, I had to open the door and allow in Selina's annoying bird.

Hazel the crow hopped into my room, then spread her wings and flew over to the pile of books.

"What are you doing?" I asked as if she could understand.

She landed lightly on top of the books, cocked her head, and started kicking the books off the piles one at a time.

"Hey, stop! Those are my father's!" I ran over and tried to shoo her.

She cawed at me, then nudged a particular journal with a red-brown cover.

"You want me to read this one?"

She ruffled her feathers and flew to sit on the footboard.

I studied her a silent moment. I'd always assumed she was on Selina's side. Now I wasn't so sure. I picked up the journal and opened the cover.

"Enchanting objects is difficult . . ."

THE FORGOTTEN KINGDOM SERIES

The Four Stones of Tern Tovan
(Prequel to The Forgotten Kingdom Series)

The Dragon Princess
(Sleeping Beauty Reimagined)

The Siren Princess
(Little Mermaid Reimagined)

The Beast Princess—coming 2020
(Beauty and the Beast Reimagined)

Receive the prequel to *The Four Kingdom Series* for FREE by signing up for my newsletter: https://mailchi.mp/78ba88ee86a2/lichelleslater

ALSO BY LICHELLE SLATER

Urban Fantasy
Curse of a Djinn

Science Fiction/Fantasy
Step Right Up
Come One Come All
Prepare to be Amazed

Christmas Romance Novels
Secret Santa
Accidental Secret Santa

ABOUT THE AUTHOR

Personal dragon trainer, lover of glitter, super nerd.

Lichelle Slater lives in Salt Lake City, Utah, with her adorable King Charles, Perseus. When she's not working full-time as a special education preschool teacher, she's living in the worlds she creates and shares with readers, painting, or doing any other assortment of crafting. One thing is for certain—you'll always find a dragon in her stories.

Sign up for my newsletter here: https://mailchi.mp/78ba88ee86a2/lichelleslater

To join my Facebook reader group, go to Lichelle's Book Wyrms: https://www.facebook.com/groups/753608364988213/

FOLLOW ME HERE

Made in the USA
Columbia, SC
20 November 2024

46639253R00193